It seemed no matter how hard they tried, they were unable to change the past…an innocent girl still died.

"Why don't we check online and see if anything has changed since we looked last time?" Elizabeth says.

The computer is turned on and, when the information comes up on the screen, the two are disappointed that the report of Alice's death is exactly the same as it has always been.

"I am starting to think that the past is written in stone and can't be changed by us," Elizabeth says, almost in tears.

"I can't believe this is true. Why would the clock come into our lives if we can't use it to do some good? It makes no sense to me," Matthew states very emphatically.

"I'm at a loss as to what to do next?"

"I've found out before, that if you stop thinking about something too hard the answer falls into place when you least expect it."

"I hope so," she says with a deep sigh.

Siblings Matthew and Elizabeth Janssen, eighteen and seventeen, together with their parents, take a long family vacation in Cape Cod, since Matthew leaves for college in the fall. Curious, the two teenagers start exploring and discover a secret room in the cottage they're renting for the summer. In this room, they find a dusty old grandfather clock with a letter hidden inside. This mysterious letter alleges that the clock is actually a time travel device. The letter writer, John, claims that, in 1927, he went back in time to save his cousin Alice, who was murdered in 1907, and whose ghost is doomed to forever flee down the beach, trying to escape her murderer—but to no avail. However, something happened, and John got stuck in 1907. He begs whoever finds the letter to figure out what went wrong with the clock and fix it, returning him to his own time of 1927. Is it all a hoax, or could it possibly be true? And once Matthew and Elizabeth figure out what went wrong, fix it, and return John to his own time, will they be able to resist temptation to try it on their own? After all, the clock's been fixed, so what could possibly go wrong?

KUDOS for *The Clock*

In *The Clock* by Leonardus G. Rougoor, Matthew and Elizabeth Janssen are two siblings on vacation with their parents in New England for the summer. In the cottage they are renting, the two discover a secret room containing a marvelous clock. It can take you back in time. The two also find a letter from the clock's previous owner, who got stuck back in his past and who needs their help to get back to his present. As the kids learn to work the clock, having some fascinating adventures in the process, they discover a murder mystery in the past that just begs to be solved, or stopped, but nothing they do seems to help. And time is running out as their vacation comes to a close, and they are forced to leave the cottage, and the clock, behind. While the plot isn't exactly new, the author gives it some unusual twists, charming characters, and an intriguing mystery— something YA readers should thoroughly enjoy. ~ *Taylor Jones, The Review Team of Taylor Jones & Regan Murphy*

The Clock by Leonardus G. Rougoor explores the premise of whether or not the past can be changed, and if we could go back in time, knowing what was going to happen, could we right the wrongs that were done? This is a question that Matthew and Elizabeth Janssen, two teenage siblings, grapple with when they find a time-travel clock in a secret room of a rental cottage while on vacation with their parents. The clock also contains a letter from John, the last one to use the device, detailing his attempt to go back in time and save his cousin from being murdered. He not only failed in his mission, he got stuck in the past and is hoping that whoever finds the clock next can figure out what went wrong, fix it, and send him back to his own time. Matthew and Elizabeth not only fix the clock and send John back to his present, they decide to help him save his cousin. But alas, it doesn't turn out to be as easy as they think, and they wind up putting their own lives in danger, right along with John and his cousin. *The Clock* is an intriguing murder mystery with a unique twist. The characters are charming, and the story is fast paced and packed with adventure. Just the thing a YA reader should love. ~ *Regan Murphy, The Review Team of Taylor Jones & Regan Murphy*

The

Clock

LEONARDUS G. ROUGOOR

A Black Opal Books Publication

GENRE: YA/SCI-FI TIME TRAVEL/MYSTERY-DETECTIVE

THE CLOCK
Copyright © 2017 by Leonardus G. Rougoor
Cover Design by Jackson Cover Designs
All cover art copyright © 2017
All Rights Reserved
Print ISBN: 978-1-626946-57-6

First Publication: APRIL 2017

Published by Black Opal Books **http://www.blackopalbooks.com**

Chapter 1

Coming from Des Moines the weather had been nice but that has since changed. It's been gray and cloudy all the way down from Boston. When they cross the bridge into Cape Cod, it starts to drizzle. By the time they reach Woods Hole the rain is coming down by the bucket.

"Not the greatest day for a sail," Mom says as she drives the black Mazda 6 into the line of cars waiting to board the ferry.

"It's a bad sign," Elizabeth mutters from the back seat. She has been quiet for most of the journey but those words will prove to be an understatement—an understatement indeed.

"I thought you were asleep," Mom says.

Elizabeth sighs letting out a long breath. "I wish I was."

"What's wrong, dear? You've been in a funny little mood since we left home," Mom says in a concerned voice.

"I wish this vacation was over and not just beginning," Elizabeth replies. "I have this really scary feeling, and I'm sure it's going to be dreadful. The closer we get, the more anxious I become."

"I'm sure everything will be just like every other vacation we have been on. When it's over, you'll see how wrong you were," Mom tells her.

Elizabeth lets out another sigh. "I'm sorry. I'm sure that you're right, but I can't shake this feeling I keep having. It's like a premonition or something."

"What do you mean a premonition?" Matthew asks. It's obvious that he has no idea what she is getting at.

"It's just an overactive imagination," Dad replies from the front passenger seat.

"It's more than that," Elizabeth protests.

"Never mind, dear, I was young once too," Mom says, trying to diffuse a situation she can see is coming.

"It has nothing to do with being seventeen, for goodness sake," Elizabeth snaps. "Nobody understands me anymore."

Buddy, the Janssen's Golden Retriever gives a sympathetic whimper and snuggles a little closer to Elizabeth.

"I can't wait to get on the boat," Matthew says excitedly, as the rain eases off.

His spirits haven't been dampened at all. Being eighteen and a year and a bit older makes him the big brother, a role he, at times, takes seriously. There, of course, are times when it is a burden he would sooner not have. He wanted to get a summer job and stay behind, but has been talked out of it. This might well be the last real family vacation they will ever have. His dad has told him that he will have the rest of his life to work. It will quickly lose its appeal, so Matthew feels that he made the right decision to put the job on hold.

The line of cars starts to move and, when they are parked and it's safe, everyone gets out. Matthew and his dad Leonard move to the railing as the ferry pulls away. The sky is beginning to clear a bit and the chill in the air is dissipating.

"It's too bad Buddy has to stay in the car," Mathew says to his dad.

Matthew turns to see a pair of sad eyes watching from the side window. The wind has died down and the waves are now small, making the ride to Martha's Vineyard pleasant. As Matthew watches the ocean, he sees what appears to be a dolphin jump out of the water. Unfortunately, it's gone so quickly that he can't be sure that's what it was. From a distance, the coastline of the island is a ghostly blur as a mist still hangs in the air.

It may well be an indication of what is soon to come, Elizabeth thinks as she approaches the railing.

Slowly the docks and the buildings begin to materialize as the ferry approaches the dock. The ferry churns up the water as it's maneuvred into position. Uniformed deckhands prepare things for the safe departure of its passengers and their vehicles.

"Let's go guys," Dad shouts as he gets into the driver's seat, letting Mom be the passenger for the remainder of the trip. Ten minutes later, they drive off the ferry and are on their way.

"I sure hope the rain is gone for a while," Matthew says as the car is turned onto the road along the coast.

"We have the whole summer ahead of us, so there will be plenty of sunshine and water time for us," Mom tells him.

Elizabeth is still quiet and a little withdrawn.

"Come on, sweetie, cheer up," Dad says, looking a little concerned.

"I can't help it, Dad, I just have this feeling something

is going to happen, and I don't know if it's good or bad. But I do know it will be big when it does happen."

"Please, dear, don't let this ruin your time. Your father's been gone to the oilfields in Canada for over five months. Now that the job is finished, we can spend almost two months on the vacation of a lifetime."

"I know, Mom." But under her breath she mutters, "If we survive it."

As they drive through the town of Oaks Bluff, with its ginger-bread houses and quaint little shops, they pass an ancient merry-go-round. The wooden horses appear almost phantom-like in the residual mist.

"Hey, guys, why don't we come back here when the weather really clears up and visit the arcade. We can all ride the merry-go-round," Dad says, trying to lift Elizabeth's mood.

They follow the road to Nantucket Sound and Sengekontacket Pond. Stopping at Edgartown to shop for groceries, they then drive to the Island Realty Company seeking out Christine Parker.

"Good to see you Mr. and Mrs. Janssen," Christine exclaims pleasantly.

"Please call us Kate and Leonard," Kate said, shaking hands then introducing the teenagers.

The keys are handed over and directions are printed out to make it easier to find *Lilac Cottage*, the rental home they have for the summer. The directions are not particularly easy to follow. Because of this, the agent has given them a map and traced out the route, putting little notes here and there.

After quite some time with only a few turn a rounds, Matthew spots a laneway with a sign *Lilac Cottage*. Driving a little distance down the driveway, they pull up to a good-sized house totally off by itself within a short walking distance of the ocean.

Near the cottage, along the driveway, is an old garage. Christine Parker told them of the building, warning that it's not safe to enter. Seeing it, they all understand why. Although the wood appears to be in fairly good shape, the whole structure leans to one side rather badly. A makeshift brace stops the garage from leaning any farther.

There are sand dunes between the house and the water. Being on the south side of the island means there will be more sunshine and warm breezes to be enjoyed making this a great spot.

The walkway to the house has flower beds on either side with only a smattering of plants. The porch though is inviting with several lilac bushes in front of the railing. Beside the house on the left is a solid barnlike building that looks like it might be a work shed of sorts. Just as all the luggage is placed on the porch the rain starts to come down. Any exploring has to be put on the backburner. Of course, a little water wouldn't stop Buddy from having fun but, unfortunately for him, this is not to be.

The house is a clapboard design that has seen better days, but still looks solid enough and has a lot of character. A fresh coat of paint would bring the home back to life. The house is furnished and the agent informed them that it has been prepared for them.

They see that everything is clean inside as they step into the foyer. The interior has an old charm to it and this must have been a beautiful home in its prime. To the right is a staircase with an old oak banister leading to the upstairs and directly in front of them a sprawling living room leads to the kitchen and dining room at the rear of the house.

It is time to explore, so Matthew and Elizabeth drop everything and run up the stairs. Their intention is to lay claim to the bedroom which appeals most to each. At the top of the landing there is an open area that appears to be a reading room with an ornate bookcase filled with hardcover books that look like no one has read them in quite some time. There are two comfortable old-style living room chairs on either side of it. Two paintings are on the walls. These depict interesting ocean scenes of a bygone era, judging by the way the people are dressed. These will require closer inspection later. At the moment, there are much more important things to be taken care of—dibs on the rooms.

Buddy of course beats both up the stairs and waits at the top, wagging his tail and giving a single happy bark. From the landing are three short stairways leading to four doors all facing the landing. Between two of them facing the back of the house is a rather large built out brick area going to the ceiling. Elizabeth yells down and asks why it is built so strangely.

"That is called a, *Good Morning staircase,*" her mom answers back, "and it is called that because when people got up at the same time years ago they greeted each other with a good morning. That large built out area houses the massive chimney that was required for all the fireplaces. Sometimes the old wood stoves that people had to use back then were vented into it too."

The choice of rooms, as it turns out, is easy as the first one Matthew runs into is obviously a grownup's room and the second is definitely too girly. That leaves only one room and this one is much more to his liking. The girl's and boy's room are at the front of the house and have a small walkway at the top of a single staircase with a railing overlooking the landing. The master is at the top of the stairs at the back of the house on the left hand side of the landing and the third stairway leads to a rather large bathroom on the right.

In Matthew's room, on the left facing the front of the

house, there is a painting. It is of an old two-wing airplane. On his right, hanging over the bed, is painting of an old time hockey player. The wall farthest away from the doorway has a window overlooking the driveway.

Elizabeth immediately walks into what, to her, has to undoubtedly be the best room of all. The bed has a canopy over it, and there are flowered vases on a pretty off-white dresser with decorative handles of silver.

On the wall over the bed is a painting of a girl running along a beach in the swirling mist. She's a pretty girl in her late teens, close to Elizabeth's age. There is a look of fear in her eyes as she glances over her shoulder. It would appear that she's running away from someone or something. *An odd painting*, Elizabeth thinks as she studies the scene. There is a fog of sorts, obscuring much of the background. At the edge of the picture there appears to be the beginnings of a hand. It's not very solid but translucent as if, maybe, not even a hand at all. The scene gives her an eerie feeling.

On the other wall on the right side of the room is a painting of a peculiar looking grandfather clock. The room that it is in is decorated with a quite fancy wallpaper and expensive furniture, and seems very similar to a room that would be in this house. There is the edge of a window the same style as the one in her room. It is funny how one can take possession of a room quickly. She already thinks of the room as hers.

There's something odd about the clock, but nothing that she can put her finger on. *Oh well something for later*, she thinks. The first order of business is to bring the luggage up and put things away. The way the rooms are arranged, the two bedrooms are at the front of the house. She would have preferred the large master bedroom and the rather large bathroom at the back of the cottage. This would have given her the view of the ocean.

The oversize bathroom, it appears, has at one time been much smaller. Another small bedroom must have been at the back of the house too. Going by the beam running across the ceiling, a wall must have been removed. The bathroom's expansion has given it two windows with a view of the ocean. The water is only about eighty yards behind the house. When the luggage is taken care of, Matthew and Elizabeth go downstairs and join their parents.

"Hey, Kate, look at this room," Leonard calls out.

Everyone comes into the large living room that has pegboard floors and a massive stone fireplace with a wide oak lintel. An ancient mantle clock sits on the shelf above. There is a pile of firewood off to the side, and Dad is just starting to place the kindling into the fireplace.

"This should take the chill out of the air. Have you ever seen anything as grand as this before?" he asks.

"It sure is something," Matthew says with Elizabeth agreeing.

"This house is absolutely gorgeous," Kate replies.

The sand dunes at the rear of the house block much of the ocean view. Fortunately, there's a low spot that is presumably used to walk to the beach. This looks like it has been widened somewhat to make the view better. The dunes must have been left there because they offer some protection from severe storms that hit this area now and then.

As the fire takes hold, Matthew picks up a few logs that have been split and carefully lays them over the burning kindling. He has learned his lessons at camp well. The damper has already been opened and the flue warmed up by a burning rolled up newspaper. This has to be done so as to start the air flowing up the chimney. Otherwise smoke will fill the house.

The logs, being nice and dry, catch fire quickly. The

warmth radiates into the room, giving the home an even cozier air about it. The feeling of foreboding that Elizabeth had earlier is pushed aside as the room loses the cool damp chill.

All the food is put away in the fridge and cupboards. The house had been modernized long ago so as to make living here far more pleasant. The old charm and special features have not been touched, though. It would have been a crime to destroy the aspects that make this home so unique.

"I think that we will be very happy here once the rain passes and the sunshine dries things up," Mom says.

Both kids nod their heads in agreement. Most kids in their late teens do not get along very well with each other or their parents. Both Matthew and Elizabeth have friends who can attest to this fact. A few years prior, this had been true with them too, but things for the last couple of years have gotten back on track, at least for the most part.

When she has warmed up, Elizabeth goes up to her room, saying that she wants to put things in order and check out the upstairs. Matthew helps his dad finish getting things in their proper place. When they are finished he decides that since the rain is finally stopping and the sun is starting to show, he'll take a walk outside.

"Elizabeth, do you want to go for a walk on the beach?" he calls out from the bottom of the stairs.

"Is it any warmer outside?"

Matthew walks out the front door and finds that it is, indeed, much more pleasant than it was earlier. "It's really nice now," he shouts from the bottom of the staircase. "Let's go while we can."

After getting their light jackets and runners on, they head for the beach. Buddy leads the way, sniffing at anything and everything he sees. He even marks the way here and there, lifting his leg to leave a scent.

No point in getting lost.

Walking through the sand is slower than on the grassy spots. When they are closer to it, they can see the entire beach with the waves rolling onto the shore. Elizabeth immediately recognizes the scene as the one in the painting in her room. This causes some of the feeling she had earlier to return. She tells Matthew this and says she will show him the painting when they get back to the house.

The breeze coming off the water is actually quite pleasant and as the clouds drift away, the sun grows warmer and warmer. They walk to the shore and touch the salty water.

"This is really nice and warm. We should be able to go swimming tomorrow. What do you think, Elizabeth?"

"Yeah that sounds like fun to me," she replies.

The walk along the beach takes the trio several hundred yards before they see other houses. They decide to go in the other direction to see if there are any closer ones that way. It ends up being about the same distance in that direction too.

"Well, so much for being bothered by anyone here. We seem to be somewhat isolated," Elizabeth declares.

Buddy is having the time of his life, running up and down the beach. It's great fun chasing the waves as they break on the shore.

This is all new to them, as none of the three have ever been to the ocean before. All of a sudden, Buddy stops when he finds a playmate.

A crab is making its way to the water. When it spots the dog, the crab freezes. Buddy starts to sniff at it a few times and makes the mistake of getting too close. There is a squeal as the claw nips the dog's nose. Buddy barks as the crab races for the water and safety.

"Buddy, come here before you get hurt. Leave the

little guy alone," Matthew says, loudly enough to get his attention. After one last attempt at friendship, Buddy comes running and wagging his wet tail then gives his body a good shake, spraying both kids with water that is flying everywhere.

"Oh, Buddy, you're getting us wet, you silly boy," Elizabeth shrieks.

"Come on, Buddy lets go back to the house, it's almost supper time," Matthew says.

With the sun shining, it has turned the day into a much better start for this vacation. As they approach the house, they take a detour to the barn/shed. It's constructed in a board-and-battens style and has weathered considerably over the years. Despite the weathering, the shed looks as sturdy as ever.

The two take a look through the dirty window. Inside there is a variety of stored items covered by canvas tarps that look like they have not been touched in years.

"It should be interesting to get in there and have a peek at some of the stuff," Matthew says.

The two walk over to the garage and carefully look through the window. The inside is empty, except for a small stack of lumber. They don't even consider entering it as it doesn't look safe at all. Even here, the sound of the waves crashing on the shore can be heard.

Heading back to the house, Elizabeth looks up and notices something a little queer.

"Hey, Matt, look up at the house."

"What am I supposed to be looking at?" he asks.

"There are only two bedrooms in the front of the house, yours and mine, right?" she asks, pointing up.

"Yeah," he replies.

"Then how come there are three windows up there? I only have one and, if I remember right, so do you," she exclaims.

He is puzzled as he realizes that she is right. "Then why is there a third window?"

"You know, now that I think about it, the wall that is supposed to be between your room and mine doesn't seem quite right. If I'm not mistaken I think there may well be a small space between your room and mine. That has to be the reason for the third window. But why that should be is beyond me," Elizabeth says.

"Well, we have the whole summer to get to the bottom of that little mystery," Matthew tells her.

Up the porch steps they go, with that unsettling feeling haunting Elizabeth once more. She is determined not to say anything to their parents, for fear of more ridicule, and asks Matthew to keep this between them, explaining why. He agrees that it will be best for now.

Chapter 2

As the sun starts going down, the meal is finished. Elizabeth excuses herself and goes to her room. She needs some time to herself so she can think things through. It has been a very unsettling day and this feeling of foreboding is ever present.

When she gets to her room, she closes the door and sits on the bed. Looking at the painting over the bed, she studies the scene.

"What is the girl running from? Who is the person that is just entering the scene if it is indeed a person and why was this painting done at all?" she says to nobody in particular.

What the reason for the painting being done the way it is troubles Elizabeth the most. Turning her attention to the other painting, she gets up and stands close to it, trying to take in as many of the details as possible. The room in which the strange grandfather clock stands is similar in design to this home. This might mean that the clock room was part of this house at one time. Looking closer at the timepiece itself, she notices that there are several peculiar things about the clock.

There are only two weights that can be seen. Of course, one could be hidden. She studies it intently, using a magnifying glass, and notices that the interior is not the same as normal clocks. She has a difficult time putting her finger on everything that is unusual. But she knows instinctively that this is no ordinary clock. A chill runs down her spine.

"What on earth is going on here?" she quietly asks herself.

This feeling of apprehension is starting to make her hands tremble. She walks to what should be the dividing wall between her and Matthew's rooms, examining it closely. The wall that forms the front of the closet runs all the way to the window. There's nothing that is obviously out of place as far as she can see. Her closet is in the portion of the wall near the door to her bedroom.

Opening the door to the closet, she walks in and examines the rather large interior. She knocks here and there to see if there is anything out of the ordinary. She inspects most of it, but at the back to the right side of the door there are a few items stored deep in the closet that prevent her from looking behind them. This closet is different than most she has been in. It's about three and a half feet deep, but there's about four or five feet of storage space to the right of the door.

She realizes that she will have to do a more thorough search during the daytime. Maybe she can enlist Matthew's help. She decides to see if he is in his room. If he is, would he want to look around in there?

Walking over across the upper landing, she hears his voice downstairs and so just goes in and looks around. She expects to find his closet at the end of the room closest to the outside wall at the front of the house. This should be the case because her closet is at the other end of the common wall. This way the closets would form a double wall between the two rooms, acting like a sound suppressor.

She is surprised to see that his closet is on the same end of the wall as hers is and the front of the closet forms a wall running the length of the room too. That means that there has to be a space between the two rooms. *An odd space at that*, she thinks.

"Why on earth would anyone build something like this?" she asks.

She decides to find a tape measure tomorrow. She and Matthew will take a few measurements inside each room. When that's done, they can do the same on the front of the house and see if her suspicions are right. Her curiosity has been piqued and now she just has to find the answer to this mystery.

It actually looks like there's a fairly large space unaccounted for between Matthew's room and hers. Could it be that there is actually another room between them? The feeling that has been haunting her all day is starting again and getting out of control. Her imagination is beginning to really run amok. What kind of place have they come to for a vacation?

Elizabeth has a difficult time getting to sleep. Every little sound worries her. There's an owl in the trees, making a hooting sound. When she finally falls asleep, it's not a restful sleep.

In her dreams, the girl in the painting runs past her. Elizabeth feels helpless as there is nothing she can do to help the girl.

When she wakes in the morning, it's much later than she is used to and she finds that the rest of the family has already been up for a while. Despite having a disturbing night, she still feels fairly well rested. She heads down the stairs and finds that only Matthew is now there.

"Where are Mom and Dad," she asks Matthew.

"They had to go see the agent about a payment or something," he says.

"Is there a tape measure around here?" she asks.

"There is one in Dad's tool box that he brought. He said he was asked to do a couple of minor jobs to the cottage. This way we got a reduction in the rent. Unfortunately, the tool box is in the car."

"Darn it, how can I take some measurements if there is no tape measure?" she replies in a rather dejected voice.

"Why do you need that?" he asks.

So she tells him about the rest of her discovery and a light goes on in his mind.

"I have an idea," he says proudly. "We can take that roll of string I saw in the barn and use it to take the measurements you need."

"That's a great idea. We can roll off enough to take a measurement of the front of the house. Then we'll cut off whatever the width of our two rooms is. What's left is the measurement of the space between the two rooms," she says excitedly.

They race outside, along the short path, and to the barn. The door is fastened but with a determined effort they get in without breaking anything. The roll of string is seized and a knife is extracted from Matthew's pocket. He holds the end of the string at the corner of the house while she unrolls enough to reach the other corner. Once the string is cut, they head upstairs and go to Matthew's room. The excitement is building as a story seems to be unfolding a little bit at a time.

The string is rolled off from the outside wall to the inside of the closet in his room. They cut that part of the string off and do the same in Elizabeth's room. There should be only a tiny piece of string left over, accounting for the thickness of the walls, but that is not the case at all. There is way too much left so they stretch it on the floor and pace off the distance.

"What the heck is going on here? There is about eight feet of string left over," Matthew says excitedly.

"There has to be another room behind those walls. I am sure of it, that's the only possible answer," she says excitedly.

"But how do we get in there?" Matthew asks, his eyebrow shooting into his hairline. "Is there a hidden entrance or did they just build the walls so no one can go in?"

"I guess we'll just have to use our imaginations and really look around. There has to be a way in, there just has to be," she asserts.

The feeling of dread is coming over her again as she thinks back on the painting with the grandfather clock in it. Could it be that the room behind the wall is that room? *No, that couldn't possibly be it,* she thinks, but her mind is racing.

Their plans are put on hold as their parents arrive home. Oh well, time for breakfast or should it be brunch?

"Do you have any plans for the day?" Elizabeth asks her dad.

"What would you guys like to do? Would you like to explore around here or hop in the car and drive around the island and check things out?" he asks.

"I've had enough driving for a day or two," Mom says with a tired sigh. "I'd prefer to relax and lounge on the beach, now that the sun has returned."

The decision is made and, after a bite to eat, they are off to the beach with swimming and sand castles on the agenda.

After several hours, Buddy has dug more holes than he knows what to do with. He is enticed into the water by throwing a stick. At least some of the sand is removed from his fur. Back at the house, he is rinsed off with fresh water to remove the salt so his skin doesn't become irritated. This is all a game to him, and he enjoys himself immensely.

It's still an hour or so before supper and both parents decide to catch up on reading in the living room. Matthew and Elizabeth have something else in mind, though. The two head upstairs to quietly investigate the mystery of the missing space.

They start in Matthew's room and search the entire length of the wall and then the inside of his closet. In order to check it thoroughly, it's necessary to remove some things stored in the back of it. After all this is done, searching very carefully, they are no further ahead than they were before they started. The two head for her room and are just walking through the door when Mom calls them down to set the table for supper. Darn it, they were on a roll and looking forward to getting closer to solving at least part of the puzzle.

When supper is all done and things are tidied up, the youngsters are asked to play a board game. This is something they used to do on a regular basis. Neither one really wants to right now because of more pressing business.

Both realize that their parents would not have asked if it wasn't important to them. After all, this kind of family time might soon be a thing of the past. It's entirely possible that Matthew may be heading out of state to go to college in the fall. He is just waiting to hear back from two colleges that he has applied to.

The rest of the evening is spent playing several different games and the time just flies by. Before anyone realizes, its bedtime and day number two of the summer vacation at the cottage is over.

Shortly after, everyone is in bed and sound asleep. All is going well, but Matthew, as usual, wakes up about two thirty in the morning and has to go to the bathroom. The sky is clear and there is a full moon. There's is enough light coming into the back side of the house to see where he's going, so he doesn't turn on the lights.

When he's finished washing his hands, he looks out the window toward the beach. Everything's illuminated by the glow from the moon. To his surprise, he spots someone on the shore. It appears to be a girl around his own age, but he can't be sure from this distance. Her head is turned around in his direction to look behind her. She must see something because she is running away from who or whatever is there.

There is a look of fear on her face, at least it seems that way, as he can't be certain from this far away. He's about to leave the bathroom and call to his dad so they can help her.

The strangest thing happens just then.

One moment she's running down the beach and the next she's gone, vanished like she was never there. *Impossible*, he thinks. *This cannot be happening, nobody is there one second and gone the next.* He would go out there and check for foot prints but the whole family and buddy have been running back and forth there today. It would be next to impossible to make sense of any tracks. He keeps looking to see if anyone else is out there, because something made her run. But, then again, was she actually even there? If she wasn't, would there be anyone else? *This is crazy.* He walks silently to Elizabeth's room, opens her door, and enters.

"Elizabeth," he whispers. No answer so he repeats the call. "Elizabeth?"

"Is that you, Matt?"

"Yeah, we need to talk, right now. You won't believe

what just happened." He goes on to tell her the story of what has just transpired.

"You must have been dreaming the whole thing," she tells him.

He shakes his head and runs his hands through his hair. "No, no, it really did happen and even stranger is that I could swear that she looked like the girl in the painting here on the wall."

"Come on, really, no kidding around, okay, Matt?" She has been at the wrong end of some of his practical jokes before and is not eager to be made to look like a fool again.

"I promise this is no joke. I swear it," he declares.

"What on earth is going on then? How can someone just vanish into thin air?" she asks.

"I don't have any idea how this can happen. I almost wish it was a dream so I could just wake up and laugh about it," he tells her.

"We'll have to figure it out in the morning. Try to go back to sleep."

He goes back to his room and, despite his doubts that this will happen, he falls asleep quite quickly.

Chapter 3

In the morning, Matthew studies Elizabeth at the breakfast table. He wonders if she really believes him. He would not blame her if she didn't. He can hardly believe it himself. As he looks at her, it's almost as if she knows what's going on in his head. She half smiles and nods at him.

"What's going on, guys?" Mom asks. "You seem preoccupied this morning."

Caught off guard, they both stumble over the words coming out of their mouths. Composing herself first Elizabeth shrugs. "Oh, just too much excitement, I guess."

Mom looks doubtful but doesn't pursue it any further. "What are you guys up to today? Your dad and I want to do a little shopping for a couple of hours, want to come?"

"No, I think we'll just hang around and go to the beach with Buddy, if that's okay," Elizabeth says.

"It's all right with me if it's okay with your father," Mom tells her.

Leonard just nods and smiles at his children, signifying he doesn't mind. In his mind are thoughts of how fast life has gone by. It was only yesterday when the pair was just toddlers. Wouldn't it be nice if they lived here instead of in the city of Des Moines?

The city is nice enough but the work has been so demanding and taken him away from home far too much. Is it too late? There's a college nearby and Matthew can commute. That at least will keep them all together for a while longer. *Oh well, we have the whole summer to think about it, hmmm.*

Breakfast done and the dishes put away, Mom and Dad drive into town. The two kids now have some time to explore.

"All right, we can look around your room and see if we can figure out how to get into the missing space," Matthew tells his sister.

She nods. "You know, I find these things a bit scary, but exciting at the same time. What you told me last night shook me up more than I let on, you know?"

"I could have sworn that you didn't believe me at all," he says to her.

Up the stairs they go and into her room. The wall between the two rooms is inspected first with nothing obvious as an entrance. Opening the closet door, they look inside. Before they can do a thorough investigation, it's necessary to remove the things in it. The closet proves to be much bigger than the one in his room.

"Can you get your flashlight, Matt?"

This he does, returning a moment later and turning it on inside the closet. The closet has been finished, the same as the bedroom.

"Boy, this is a funny type of closet. It's completely papered, plus it's deeper and longer than any I've ever seen. I bet it's at least four feet longer than average. I wonder why?" he asks.

"Let's check the back wall first. Maybe we'll see something out of the ordinary," Elizabeth says.

After a close look they find nothing out of place.

"Okay that only leaves the end to look at. If we don't find anything there, we may have to take a close look at the hallway between our two bedrooms."

They move to the end of the closet. Surprisingly, there is enough room to stand beside each other. Matt raps his knuckles on the back wall, hearing a hollow sound. Then he raps his knuckles on the end wall, hearing a far more solid noise.

Once again, he knocks on the end of the closet. "Hey, this sounds more like the sound you might get when you rap on a door. I'm going to try it on the bedroom door and see what it sounds like." Going to the door, he closes it and raps it. "Hey, guess what," he says. "It sounds fairly similar. I think that there might be another door in there. Only problem is that I don't see a door knob."

"You know, whoever built this may have made another way to get it open. It sure looks like they didn't want anybody accidentally finding this," she says.

"Turn off the light for a minute. Maybe there is some light coming in around the edges giving us a hint as to how to open it," Matt tells her as he steps closer to the end of the closet.

It takes a few moments for their eyes adjust to the darkness. Elizabeth then spots a tiny dull sliver of light a couple of inches long. The faint light is at waist height, along the edge of what might just be a door.

"There it is, Matt. See if you can figure it out, okay?"

Turning on the flashlight, Matthew runs his hands up and down the wall of what should be the door and finds nothing.

"Try the back wall Matt, maybe there is a special way to open it."

Matthew does this and finds a depression half way up the corner of the back wall. "There is a covering over what appears to be a cavity. He carefully pulls it out of the way, revealing a handle.

"All right, this is great, I think," Elizabeth shrieks excitedly.

First, Matthew tries to pull at the handle with no result and then gives it a push. The handle moves in and there's a click. Elizabeth gives the door a slight push and the end of the closet opens.

They are greeted with a very musty gust of air as the door swings into a room. The window in the room has been darkened somewhat but some light still finds its way in. They walk into a space that has a wide end near the window and narrows considerably at the end farthest away. It becomes obvious that the protrusions are the backs of the closets in the two bedrooms. The outside wall where the window is measures about eleven feet wide. This is even bigger than either suspected.

The distance from the window to the other end of the room, is the same as the bedrooms. The narrow portion between the two closets is only around six feet wide and that stretches the length of the closets, which is about four feet on one and about eight feet on the other. All this gives the room an odd shape but still leaves plenty of space.

"It's a wonder nobody ever noticed this missing room," Elizabeth mentions.

"It is surprising, yes. Of course, not many people are as smart or observant as you are," Matthew says with a faint smile on his face.

Elizabeth is unsure if he is serious or pulling her leg but decides to let it pass. Their eyes land on a dusty old clock in the narrow section against the wall. "The hallway must be on the other side, what do you think, Matt?"

There is other furniture in the room but what really draws their attention is the grandfather clock. It is immediately evident that this is the same clock as the one in the painting.

A chill runs down Elizabeth's back. It is the same feeling she has had throughout most of the trip. There are a multitude of questions going through her head. Too bad there are so few answers. They both slowly approach the clock to make a closer inspection.

At this point, there is the sound of a car pulling into the driveway.

"Darn it, they're back," she says, letting out a groan. We'll have to postpone this until later, Matt. Don't mention this to Mom and Dad okay," she pleads.

"No worry there. I want to find out a lot more before anyone else knows about this. Who knows? They may not let us in here and take over the investigation themselves. Maybe they might even bring in the actual owners of the house and the vacation will be over. Then we'll never know what is going on here," he exclaims.

They head out of the room, reluctantly close the door, and replace the things in the closet. They then do the same in Matthew's room.

"Hey kids, where are you?" Mom's voice echoes through the house.

"Up here, Mom," Matthew yells down.

They head down the stairs and into the kitchen. Dad walks in the door and gives Matt a pat on the back.

"Not bored yet, I hope," he says.

"No, no, Dad, we really like it here."

"Let's have lunch and then go to the beach," Mom suggests.

Everyone gives their approval, despite the fact that Elizabeth and Matthew would prefer to be in the newly discovered room.

The time on the beach is fun, and playing with Buddy takes their minds off their discovery, for the most part. Buddy is having the time of his life, running in and out of the water chasing after sticks and gulls. Elizabeth has a harder time not dwelling on the mystery before her. The feeling of dread is constantly in the back of her mind.

Later in the afternoon everyone heads back to the house and gets prepared for supper. Elizabeth wants to go up to her room but is asked to help make the meal. She looks for an excuse but can't come up with anything. Matt is already upstairs getting washed up, and she hopes he doesn't start looking without her. Finally supper is over and the dishes are done.

"I think I'll go to my room for a while if that's okay?" Elizabeth asks as she gets up.

Matthew stands up and pushes in his chair. "Yeah, I think I'll head up too. There are a few things I want to rearrange in my room."

"All right kids, but come down before it's bedtime, okay?" Mom asks.

Both kids agree and head up the stairs.

"I'll get my flashlight and meet you in your room in a minute," Matthew informs her.

"All right."

He gets the light and closes his door with the lights on. This way, his parents will think he's in there, in case they come upstairs. He enters his sister's room quietly and closes her door too. Elizabeth has already shifted things in the closet so they can just open the hidden door and slide into the room. Matthew turns on the flashlight and shines it around.

There is ancient floral wallpaper on the walls and a

pine plank floor. The ceiling is the same as the other two bedrooms. An old dresser stands against the far wall near the old grandfather clock, which is in front of the wall farthest from the window. Both head to the dresser first and pull open the dusty drawers. There are a few photo albums and some items that would have belonged to a girl. There is a hair brush, a hand-held mirror, and a rather-worn-looking music box. They decide not to open it at this time. Both are concerned it could make music that the parents might hear.

Next, they turn their attention to any wall switches that might turn on an overhead light but cannot locate anything as this part of the house has never been renovated. Making do with the light available and Matt's flashlight, they start looking a little more closely at the clock. The face seems to be made of molded metal with strange designs all over it. The numbers are not in the right order and the arms indicating the time are heavier than normal ones are.

"This clock looks just like the one that is in the painting in my room," Elizabeth states.

"Yeah, I see that."

Looking down toward the pendulum as the light shines inside, she notices there is a book at the bottom left side of the clock.

"Look, Matt, do you see that?"

"Let's see if we can open the glass door and get it out," he says.

Unfortunately, there's a lock on the side of the door, preventing it from being opened.

"There must be a key here somewhere," she tells him, as she starts to look at different parts of the timepiece.

Both look the clock over for a key but find nothing. Matthew runs his hand over the top of the clock. This would be an obvious place to hide a key, but finds nothing. Elizabeth feels behind the clock and comes up empty handed too.

Finally, he gets on his knees and feels around under the base putting his hand up underneath. Behind the front edge of the clock he feels something move. At first he can only wiggle a small section. Continuing his poking around, he feels a tiny hole. It's in a wooden compartment to the left side of the base. He pokes his finger into the hole. The compartment slides to the right and a metal key drops onto the floor. Reaching under, he picks it up.

"I wonder why someone would go to all this trouble to hide a key," he says.

Elizabeth takes the key, unlocks the door and opens it looking at the interior. This clock is like no other either of them has ever seen. There are strange looking parts inside which neither has a clue as to their function. She reaches in and lifts out the dusty book that when opened reveals itself to be a journal. There is, in bold capital letters on the first page a warning.

DO NOT START THE CLOCK UNTIL YOU HAVE READ THE DIRECTIONS.

Matthew looks at his sister. "I wonder what this warning means?"

"Maybe we should read this j—journal before we do anything that m—may hurt the clock," she stutters as her hands tremble. "L—let's go back into my room and read what the b—book tells us," she says as her hands tremble.

"Are you all right, sis?" he asks.

"I'm just a bit nervous about this whole thing," she says, obviously upset.

The door of the clock is closed and locked. As they leave the room, the door to the clock room is closed, and locked too. Sitting on the edge of the bed, Elizabeth wipes the dust off the book. She then opens it to the first page. They study the bold writing, wondering what it might mean. Turning the page, Elizabeth reads out loud what someone has written in ink a long time ago.

"'Please read this entire account before you touch the clock. You have no idea what you are dealing with. To work the clock, you need to know what will happen if you don't do it properly.

"'This is a very special clock. There is no other like it anywhere. The clock was made by accident and can do a marvelous thing, but this thing can turn into a disaster if you mishandle the mechanisms.'"

She looks at her brother and he can see the concern in her eyes. Turning back to the book, she continues.

"'If you are reading this book, please take it seriously because my welfare depends on it. I apparently have made a mistake and have gone back in time with no way back home. You see this clock allows one to travel backward in time and then home to the present, or at least back to where one left from. I am a relative of the girl that is in the painting. She passed away during the time she was trying to investigate the death of her father, Benjamin Berger.

"'She died years ago in a tragedy no one has been able to explain. Her body was found on the beach you see in the painting. There has never been a satisfactory explanation for her death. The only clue was the look of fear on her face when she was found. Everyone has always been sure that she was murdered and was running from someone at the time. Unfortunately, nobody knows who it could possibly have been.

"'That is why I have traveled back in time. I wanted not only to find out who did the deed, but to save Alice at the same time. I have no idea how my interference may affect things down the road, but I cannot stop myself from trying. What would life be like if my cousin was still alive? I am now thirty-nine years old and Alice has been dead for almost twenty years.

"'My uncle, Benjamin Berger, stumbled across this clock in a town in Eastern Europe during his travels. I believe it was in the Netherlands, as our ancestry is Dutch. These are a people that are well known for the intricate work they've done with timepieces. Uncle Benjamin was told that this clock could do amazing things. Although he was very skeptical, he bought it anyway. It cost him almost everything he had. It took a considerable effort on his part to figure things out. But he finally got it to the point that he could make it function the way he needed. He then knew it was worth every penny he paid for it and more.

"'The clock has been in our family's possession since nineteen hundred and three.

"'Shortly after Uncle Benjamin got the clock working, he died in an accident. My uncle Robert Berger inherited much of the estate and had for years attempted to use the clock but failed.

"'Uncle Robert was not an educated man and had a difficult time in life. He and Uncle Ben were often at odds. Many arguments happened between them. My uncle Robert, after years of trying, finally gave up attempting to make the clock work. He then allowed the clock to come into my possession. I only recently found out about the true abilities of this wonderful mechanism. I found the manual and my father's notes in a hidden compartment. My uncle Benjamin, I am sure had made use of the clock, but died some years after getting it to his home and working.

"'John Fielding Smith'

"There's an addition that looks like it was put in later," Elizabeth explains.

"'PS. I have hidden a letter in the clock. It is imperative that you read it. I am stuck in the past and need your help. PLEASE DO NOTHING UNTIL YOU HAVE READ IT.'"

Chapter 4

W ow, do you think this could possibly be true or is it some tale for kids?" Matthew asks his sister, more than a little incredulously.

"Let's see what the rest of the book shows us and then we can decide if any of this is actually a possibility. It looks like this part of the journal has been written at different a time and by a different person. I just did a quick scan of the writing describing how to operate the clock. Comparing the two, I think the part I just read was added later," Elizabeth says.

"So what you're saying is that this John person wrote the warning after he was trapped in his past."

"That's exactly what I think, at least going by what I see here," she confirms.

The rest of the book shows different parts of the clock. The most interesting part of it shows dials behind a panel. These dials according to the directions given can be adjusted. They can be turned to indicate a time that the operator wants to go back to. It can also be set to however long he or she wishes to stay there. There is one final dial that indicates how much time is left before the person is automatically returned to their own time. The earliest time in history that a person can travel back to is nineteen hundred AD.

Elizabeth's eyes widen and she blinks. "The journal shows a hidden panel just below the face of the clock. It also describes how to open the panel by pressing two disguised buttons. They are on the sides of the clock in line with the panel. That's where the dials that control the functions of this timepiece are."

Matthew shudders. "If the journal hadn't shown us this, we would never have even known there was a hidden panel. When we looked at the clock it just looked like a strangely built thing. Do you think this is all a joke or could there be some truth in it?" he asks, almost flabbergasted. "No, this is impossible, I can't believe this. It has to be a joke."

"I think the only way to make sure is to go to the room and check these features," she informs him.

"Yeah, I guess you're right. That will at least confirm some things in the journal," he agrees.

"We'll have to see what the date on the clock is. That will show us what year he went back to. Make sure that we write it down, Matt."

"I'll get a pen and paper from my room," he says, and heads for the door.

Just as he comes back, there is the sound of Mother's voice.

"Hey, guys, how about coming down for a while. You've been up there for almost two hours."

Elizabeth looks at Matthew. "Wow, has it been that long?"

"I guess time flies when you're having a good time. No pun intended, sis."

Both would much rather stay and investigate further. The two realize that their parents will get suspicious and interfere with their job if they don't go down. Elizabeth is still apprehensive about the clock, but now her curiosity has really been piqued. She loves a good mystery, and this one's already better than any ever before. Plus, it helps to have Matthew working with her. He's pretty good as far as brothers go.

"So what have you guys been up to for so long," Dad asks.

Elizabeth winces. "Oh, just checking the place out. Haven't found too much yet but some of the artwork is interesting. How about you and Mom? What have you been doing?" she asks, quickly changing the subject.

"We're wondering if you two would like to come to town in the morning and explore with us. There are a lot of charming shops and places to see," Mom says.

Elizabeth, being the quicker of the two, says that would be a great idea. Matthew looks at her and wonders why she would say that. He knows they both would much rather find out more about the clock. She gives him a look that indicates he should keep his mouth closed, which he does. He knows his sister must have a good reason for doing what she did. He tries not to let on that they are up to something.

When he goes to the kitchen to get a drink, Elizabeth follows.

"How come you were so eager to go tomorrow," he asks in a whisper.

"Because I don't want to raise any suspicions about what we are doing, okay?"

"All right, fine with me," he says.

In the morning after breakfast, everyone loads into the car, including Buddy, and off they go. After what seems like a relatively short ride, they arrive in West Tisbury.

There they locate a well-known open air farmers market. The fruit and vegetables are fresh. The meat is sold by the farmers who raise the animals. It's obviously superior to any they can get in the stores back home. Leonard suggests that it will be best to buy what they want on the way back to Lilac Cottage to keep things fresher.

After an hour of touring around walking, it's determined that lunch is in order. There is a pleasant little restaurant with a patio basking in the sunshine, and everyone agrees that this is the place to eat. Matthew heads for the washroom and asks to have fish and chips. Elizabeth seconds that decision and heads to the washroom too.

"I think the kids are having a really good time, don't you dear?" Kate asks her husband with a smile on her face.

"They sure seem to be. It looks like the scary feeling Elizabeth had earlier has been pushed aside by the fun she's having. It was really nice watching them on the beach yesterday. Isn't that right, Buddy?" he asks, patting the dog on the head. "So what do you want to eat, honey? Shall we make it four fish and chips or are you still on a diet?" Leonard asks grinning a little.

Maybe it is time for some changes in my life, he wonders. *I've been on a lot of work-related trips. They've kept me away from home far too much. The money has been good, and we have saved a lot. With the house paid for long ago, maybe it's time for life take a new turn. After all, one never knows how long one has. Matthew might go away to college out of state. The same may happen with Elizabeth in another year or so. If this all happens, things will get lonely for Kate if I'm off working somewhere. Maybe we'll go for a nice walk on the beach after supper and I'll talk to her about it.*

The lunch is nice and the family has a wonderful time.

The decision is made to walk around the town and explore awhile. To Matthew and Elizabeth's surprise, their dad pulls out his wallet and hands each of them twenty dollars.

"Wow, thanks, Dad, this is great," Elizabeth says.

"Yeah, thanks, Dad," Matthew seconds.

"We can meet back at the market in two hours, at three o'clock, so you two go have a little fun."

Both kids hug their dad and are off, looking for some places that cater to teenagers. Buddy stays with Leonard and Kate.

"Boy that sure was nice of Dad," Matthew says to Elizabeth. "By the look on Moms face it was a surprise to her too."

"Yeah, it was. I love them so much. Most of our friends' parents don't even seem to like their kids, so I guess we sure are lucky."

"Wow, this place is so nice. Don't you wish that we lived here?" he says wistfully.

"It would be nice, wouldn't it?"

In the back of her mind a little bit of the feeling comes back as she recalls the clock and the journal.

The rest of the afternoon is warm and pleasant. Both find what they are looking for. Elizabeth finds a book on the history of the island and decides to buy it when she sees a photo of the girl in the painting at the cottage. There is a long story about the house and its tragic history. She can hardly wait to get home and read the book.

Matthew decides to pick up a pair of binoculars. They're on clearance because of a scratch on the body. The salesperson assures him that this will in no way affect the performance. At more than half off, they're a steal and just what he has wanted for some time. He thinks that maybe he'll try to wake up at the same time he did when he saw the girl on the beach. The alarm will have to be set for two-fifteen tonight. He doubts this will happen again, but if he's lucky, he'll see her again. This time, he'll try to take a photo of her using his digital camera.

So everyone has some sort of plan for tonight, except Mom. But then again, the wheels of change are starting to turn in her head too. She's not exactly sure what changes she wants to make, but it will come to her. Everyone meets at the market and the choices of what to buy are made. They load the things in the car and head back to the cottage.

Supper is a little lighter for the parents, but still full size for Matthew and Elizabeth. After all they're still growing. Mom and Dad don't require two heavy meals in one day, which is why they have not packed on the pounds. When supper is finished, the dishes are washed and put away. Mom and Dad head out to the beach for a nice long walk. Arm-in-arm, they take in the early evening sun and watch the waves crashing on the shore.

"This is the life," he says warmly to his beautiful wife. In his mind he knows that he's a lucky man, a lucky man indeed. How to start this conversation is a question in his mind at the moment.

As soon as their parents are out of sight, Matthew and Elizabeth race upstairs. Elizabeth is eager to get to the book, but Matthew wants to see the clock and figure out exactly how it works. He is exceptionally mechanically inclined and Elizabeth is glad he's here for this part of the investigation. With flashlight in hand, he leads the way back into the newly discovered room. Elizabeth has the journal in her hand as Matthew shines the light on the elegantly carved clock. The light travels up and down the clock as he tries to study all the facets of its workings. He shines the light on the glass at an angle so the light is not reflected back at them or out the window.

He studies the inside, looking first at the pendulum then at the weights and control cables. One of the weights is at the bottom of the cabinet. There are only two of them.

"There don't seem to be any chimes on this clock, I wonder why," he says.

There are two small compartments at the back inside corners running from the bottom to the top. There are many small screws holding the two pieces on each side together.

"I wonder what is inside those two long boxes," he said.

"That'll have to wait. Let's look at the dials behind the panel, Matt. Do you know how to open it?"

Chapter 5

Leonard squeezes Kate's hand. "Say, dear, I've been thinking. I've been away from home quite a bit over the years, and we have done very well financially. You worked in banks for a long time and are eligible for a pension—not a big one, but at least something. I've got a pension too, and since we started this vacation, I've had an idea about maybe making a few changes."

Kate studies him. "Such as?"

"Well, Matthew will soon be going to college, and Elizabeth won't be far behind. He hasn't made up his mind a hundred percent yet about what to do, so if any changes are to be made, now would be the time to make them. I have missed too much of their growing up years and don't want to miss anymore. Do you have any ideas?"

Chapter 6

Matthew gently opens the panel, following the instructions in the journal. He presses the two buttons on the sides. The door is opened and swings down on old but functioning hinges. The dials from left to right are numbered from one to eight.

Six dials are close together on the left side of the opening. The other two are on the right hand side close to each other. At the end, past the last two dials, there is a simple metal switch. It is in the up position at the moment. Matthew wants to see what will happen if he moves it down. He decides against it when he remembers the warning in the journal.

"Okay, let's see what the journal says about them," Elizabeth tells her brother. She opens the book, finds her place, and reads aloud.

"'The six dials on the left control the function of setting a date that the operator wants to travel back to. The first has the months of the year one to twelve. The second has days of the month. This dial is larger than the rest because of all the numbers on it. They go from one to thirty-one. The third has only a one and a two on it. The fourth has from zero to nine, as do the last two.'"

Elizabeth looks up at Matthew. "The book states that dials can be positioned from a future time all the way back to nineteen hundred but no further. So if you want to go back to August fifth, nineteen twenty-four, the dials would be from left to right, eight, five, one, nine, two, and four."

"And what are the other two for?" Matthew asks.

"Those two indicate the number of hours that elapse before you are brought back to your own time. Each dial has numbers going from zero to nine. That means you can go back from one hour to ninety-nine hours. The longest you can go back in time is four days and three hours. These two dials work their way back to zero as time goes by, bringing the operator back when the allotted time is used up."

Matthew examines the dials. "It says here that you can turn the dials to a date in the future. John Smith says he never had the nerve to try it. You can turn these dials to read the year two thousand nine hundred and ninety-nine."

Elizabeth lets out a whistle. "Wow, I wonder what that would be like. No wonder he was reluctant to try it. If by chance this isn't all a big joke and turns out to be real, who knows? Maybe, just maybe."

He can almost see the wheels turning in her head.

Elizabeth reads from the instructions. "'Finally there is a switch that activates the time mechanism. This turns the time travel part of the clock on when in the up position and off in the down side. When the switch is in the on position, the time-travel mechanism functions at the top of the next hour.'"

Matthew nodded. "I guess there has to be a switch like

that or you wouldn't be able to control the time you're leaving," he says. "Didn't the book say that this John guy went back and didn't return? I wonder why he stayed there."

"Say, Matt, the journal mentioned a letter hidden in the bottom of the clock and that it must be read before touching the dials. Maybe you can study the clock a little closer and figure out why he didn't go back to his own time. In the meantime, don't touch anything, and I'll write down all the numbers on the dials."

He closely examines the clock, taking in every detail he can. Looking down, he notices an old envelope in the bottom, tucked off to the side, just barely visible. He would have missed it had he not stuck his head into the clock itself. He's about to reach for it, when there is the sound of a door banging downstairs.

"Oh, oh, I think Mom and Dad are back. We better get out of here," Elizabeth blurts out.

They hurry out and just make it back into her room as Mom comes up the stairs. Good thing Matthew turned off the flashlight and left it in the closet. He's sure that his mother would question him about it.

"What are you two doing? You seem slightly out of breath," Kate says, looking at Matthew.

Elizabeth jumps in and tells her mother a tiny untruth. "We were wrestling a bit just before you came into the house."

Matthew stifles a grin. *Boy she's quick.*

The rest of the evening is spent in discussions on various topics. The two siblings both have a feeling that something's up, and their parents aren't telling them everything. It's almost as if they're making some plans, but are unsure of exactly what direction they will be going in.

Matthew is asked what his thoughts are for college

and if they'll change, depending on where the family lives.

Elizabeth is asked pretty much the same thing but in a different way.

"What's up?" she asks her parents but receives a rather vague reply.

Kate shrugs. "We're not sure what we are going to do as far as the future is concerned. We're thinking of some changes but what they are is, at this point, totally undecided. Maybe by the end of this vacation we'll have an answer. Of course what we decide will depend somewhat on you two. We are so pleased with the way you have grown up, very proud indeed."

Matthew and Elizabeth look at each other and wonder what this is all about. They both want to ask for a little more information but know better. Their parents don't announce things without thoroughly thinking it through. Finally, it's bedtime and everyone goes to their rooms. Matthew sets his alarm for two-thirty and gets the binoculars and camera ready. He leaves his clothes on the chair. He wants to get dressed and leave the house as quietly as possible. There's a soft knock on his door and his sister walks in.

"What do you think is up with Mom and Dad?" she asks quietly.

"I don't have a clue."

He proceeds instead to tell her of his plans for this night, and she immediately tells him that she wants in. There's a trembling in her hands again.

"I feel that something crucial is about to happen," she says.

"I've been feeling the same way," he agrees. "Ever since we found the hidden room and the clock matching the one in the painting, I've been on edge."

Plans are made and each lies in their own bed, trying

to sleep, but having difficulty. Eventually, they both drift off but it is not a restful sleep they have. It seems that each knows subconsciously that there is an event coming but neither knows what it will be or how to handle it.

The alarm goes off, waking Matthew immediately. There's a small cushion covering the clock to deaden the sound so his parents won't be awakened. Quickly, he turns it off. Once dressed, he silently leaves his room with the camera and binoculars. As he enters his sister's room, he finds that she is already awake and dressed. She has gone into the closet and grabbed the flashlight. Silently, they make their way to the front door, thinking this will be the best way to leave not waking Mom and Dad.

The moon is still pretty bright, and they find that the flashlight is not required at this time. They round the house and head toward the beach. The night air is cool but not to the point where a jacket is needed. There is dew on the grasses that wets the bottom of their jeans. The sound of the waves crashing on the beach can be heard as they approach. Normally, it would be a pleasant sound but, at the moment, it lends an eerie feeling to an already tense adventure. A short distance from the beach there is a grassy knoll, and Elizabeth heads to this spot. This will give them cover and still allow them a clear view of the entire beach.

Looking out on the water, they see that there is a mist forming.

"That looks a bit unusual, doesn't it, sis?"

"I wonder why that should be happening at this particular time. It reminds me of the scene in the painting," she says.

The feeling of anticipation comes over both of them. The mist becomes a little heavier and starts to drift toward the shoreline. A real chill in the air comes in along with it. The mist works its way onto the beach and the coolness makes them wish they had brought jackets with them.

The entire beach is now covered in the light fog as a sound comes to them from a short distance to the right. Both Matthew and Elizabeth tense up. She grabs her brother's arm to help calm her nerves. The sound becomes more audible, and it's clear that what they are hearing is the sound of someone running. The person is almost within sight and would already be clearly visible if it weren't for the mist.

All of a sudden, there she is. The girl in the painting runs right in front of them. There's a look of fear in her eyes, as she glances over her shoulder behind her. Matthew, with the camera ready, takes a picture. Elizabeth jumps up and calls to the girl, but she keeps on running. Just as Matthew gets up too, the girl vanishes.

They are both on the beach at this point, looking all around, but the girl is gone. There is also no sign of a pursuer. They did not actually see the person chasing what must have been Alice. They did hear the sound of a second pair of footsteps. Matthew and Elizabeth look at each other quizzically.

"What just happened, Matt?"

Matthew just shakes his head. "I don't know. It's almost like a nightmare. Things like this don't happen in real life, do they?"

Elizabeth walks to where the girl was and notices footprints in the sand. These footprints, though, are unlike most that she has seen in the past. They are so light that it would appear the person making them just barely made contact with the sand. Just like she only weighed a few pounds.

"Hey, Matt, take a picture of this too all right?"

He does this and they both notice the mist slowly

leaving. The chill is still in the air, although it's lessening as they head back to the house.

Even though the incident is going through their minds, fatigue forces them to go back to bed. It doesn't take long and both are asleep.

Both also have dreams of the girl in her late teens running in a panic down the beach. She is a pretty girl with long blonde hair similar to Elizabeth's. She is about five feet seven inches tall and has a slim build, also similar to Elizabeth. The facial features are not the same as hers, though. Although both girls are very attractive, Alice has a more severe look about her. This, of course, might be greatly exaggerated by the fear she is experiencing.

In the morning, both wake up a little later than usual. As a result, they don't have a chance to talk about the previous night's adventure. Mom is on the upper landing and walks down with them. The two siblings look at each other but can't convey what is going through their heads at this time. Neither wishes to not let the cat out of the bag. Time at the breakfast table, drags by as brother and sister both want to discuss the event of the previous night. They desperately want to make some sense of what is happening to them.

"Do the two of you want to go for a walk on the beach?" Kate asks.

Elizabeth is the first to come up with an idea. "Mom, you should take Dad. This way, the two of you can spend some quality time together and enjoy the sunshine."

"Besides, you haven't seen much of Dad in a long time," Matthew agrees. "It will give you two a chance to catch up on things."

"Are you sure, dear?" Mom asks.

"Oh, we don't mind," Elizabeth says as her mother goes to collect their dad. The parents head for the beach a short time later, with Buddy bouncing around like a little kid. Matthew marvels at his sister's ability to think so quickly.

She grins at him. "Okay, bro, what say we check out the photos and the letter we found?"

Up the stairs they run. Matthew heads to his room to retrieve the camera and then walks to Elizabeth's room as she comes out of the closet carrying the letter. He sits on the edge of her bed and powers up the camera. The first photo they see is the one of the girl's footprints in the sand. The marks are so faint that it is difficult to see them. "You would think that she would have made much deeper impressions in the sand," he says.

"Yes, you would because she is at least as big as I am," she agrees.

"She sure is a pretty girl," he says with a smile on his face.

"Hey, don't go getting a crush on her. She probably isn't real, you know."

Matthew just sighs. He then flips to the photo he took of the girl, blinks then stares. All there is to see is a swirling mist. If you tried real hard you might convince yourself that some of the swirls were in the shape of a girl. But it would not be very convincing.

Elizabeth arches an eyebrow. "Did you move the camera as you took the photo, Matt?"

"No, not a chance. I saw her in the display screen when I took the picture," he blurts out rather defensively. "Get your laptop and I'll download it," he says.

When all is loaded, they sit in front of her computer and study the scenes. The tracks in the sand are there, but only faintly. The picture of Alice is so faint as to be almost nonexistent. They have to strain their eyes to make out the girl.

"How can this be?" she asks.

"I don't have a clue, sis. Let's read the letter and see if it sheds any light on this mystery," he says, reaching for the old envelope.

His sister beats him to it and opens the envelope, removing a letter. Unfolding the paper they see a handwritten letter with the signature of John Fielding Smith at the bottom. Elizabeth reads out loud what is written. The first line is again printed in large capital letters.

"'I BEG OF YOU NOT TO TOUCH THE DIALS OF THE CLOCK.'" Elizabeth looks at her brother, confused, then continues. "'I need you to follow my instructions to the letter, or I will be trapped in the past forever. I am talking about my past, not yours. Your time of existence is farther into the future than mine is. I don't know what year you are in, but I am from the year nineteen twenty seven.

"'I made my plans and have gone back in time to save Alice. The fact that you are reading this letter means that something has gone awry. Either I did something wrong and am stuck in the past or the clock has stopped working properly. It might be that I did not estimate the operating time of the clock properly. It is possible that it just wound down. It may have stopped before the mechanism at the back of the inside of the clock could be reactivated to bring me back. I don't know. Please read the directions and try to figure out what went wrong and help me to go back to my own time. At the very least you will have the adventure of your life, a stroke of the clock away.

"'I traveled back to the year nineteen hundred and seven in an effort to save Alice Berger, my cousin. We are or were very close in age and got along tremendously. I have missed her all these years. When this opportunity presented itself, I could not resist the temptation to go back and attempt to save her. I am now the one who needs help.

"'I also made another mistake by going back to the wrong time. I went back one day after her death and so, to make matters worse, what I set out to do I have failed at. Please, I beg of you. Help me and maybe we can save Alice together.

"'Signed, John Fielding Smith.'"

Chapter 7

That was nice of those two to think of us," Leonard tells his wife.

Kate chuckles. "Oh, I'm sure there's more to this than them just thinking of us."

She knows her kids better than her husband does. And they're up to something, but that doesn't matter. Kate also knows that if it were anything serious, they'd tell their parents. She decides to let them have their fun without any interference. They're in their late teens and need to be trusted. They have always made the right decisions and both she and her incredibly handsome husband are very proud of them. Her husband is handsome to her, at least, even though that's not everyone's opinion. *What the heck do they know anyways?* She feels blessed in life to have such a wonderful family. As mothers do, she is saddened at the prospect of her children leaving the nest in the near future. This, she knows, is also on her husband's mind.

"So have you given any more thought to what we will

be doing as far as our future is concerned?" she asks him as they walk.

"I've been thinking but haven't come to any potential decisions yet, how about you?" he asks.

"I know that they're really enjoying themselves, here but I doubt that this area could offer all of us a future. What would we do for a living here?" Kate asks in return.

"Yeah, you're right about that. Still, as I mentioned before, we do have our pensions. Maybe we could just relax and enjoy retirement."

Kate laughs. "Yeah, right."

They continue their walk along the beach, holding hands as they have always done. Some people have, at times, thought they were newlyweds because they seem so happy together. Who would believe that they have been married for almost twenty years?

Chapter 8

With the letter in hand, Elizabeth walks to the closet and into what they call the clock room, with Matthew close behind.

"Okay, Matt, take a close look at the clock and see if you can find out what went wrong."

She knows that if anyone can figure it out, it'll be him. He's so much like their father, who can fix almost anything. Matthew looks at the front of the clock and studies it from top to bottom. He looks at the two dials on the right hand side of the clock. These are used to indicate the amount of time left before the time traveler is to go back to his own time. The amount of time is just over the six hours. As his gaze works its way down the clock, he also sees that the weight on one of the chains is touching the bottom of the clock. The other weight is only halfway down.

"I think I know what happened. The amount of time on the dial is more than the weight was set for. In other words, the clock's weight was not raised high enough.

It's at the bottom of the clock, and it stopped working, just like John suspected. I believe that the other weight is used to operate the part of the clock that will bring him back to his own time. I should rewind the mechanism by raising the weight. If I start the pendulum swinging again, the clock will bring John back to where he started from. I don't think that I should reset the arms on the face of the clock to the right time now. It may create a problem and he will really be stuck in his past. What do you think?"

Elizabeth thinks for a minute and agrees with Matt's conclusion. "I wonder how long he has been stuck back there. When he returns to his proper time, will he be older than when he started out. This is something that would be a real conundrum, I think. I wonder if we'll ever find out."

Matthew raises the weight, rewinding the clock, and, holding his breath, starts the pendulum swinging. Nothing out of the ordinary happens as the almost silent tick tock sound emanates softly after the door is closed. Luckily, the timepiece is as quiet as it is. Otherwise, someone walking by in the hallway on the other side of the wall would hear it.

Elizabeth looks at her watch. "It's almost two o'clock now. At just before eight, tonight I want to be here to see if anything happens. I'm all jittery with excitement. I sure hope that John goes back to his own time and will be okay."

They head out of the room and close the door inside the closet, locking it.

"Hey, sis, we need to think of a way to be back up here, alone, before eight tonight without making Mom and Dad suspicious. Can you think of anything?"

"Let me work on it," she says. "I'm sure I can come up with something."

Matthew puts his hand on her arm. "Hey, you know

what? If we hang around them quite a bit for the rest of the day, we can go upstairs to our rooms without alerting them. What do you think?"

Elizabeth smiles. "You know that you're starting to think a lot like me lately?"

He wonders if this is a good thing or not. The two head out to the beach, looking to see if they can find their parents. Off in the distance, they hear Buddy barking as he spots the kids. The dog runs to them at full tilt. Their pet is barking happily as playtime has just ramped up to high gear. Matthew has had the foresight to bring a Frisbee with him and throws it in the dog's direction. Buddy changes course and, with the agility only an animal can muster, he jumps into the air and catches it. Wagging his tail excitedly, Buddy drops the Frisbee at Matt's feet and waits for him to throw it again.

This is the life, Kate thinks as she watches the scene. "You know, Leonard, this is going to be the best vacation we've ever had."

He nods. "Yes, I can see that. Wouldn't it be nice if it kept on going, and we just stayed here? I wonder what we could get for our house."

They keep walking and, as Matthew spots his father, he throws the Frisbee toward him. Leonard jumps and catches it. He throws it back at Matthew, deliberately aiming it away from him but angling it slightly. The disc curves in a graceful arc and ends up about two feet above the boy's head.

"Good one, Dad," Matthew says with a real smile on his face.

The two of them have always gotten along well together. There has been little competition between them, except when they wrestled together. That was the only time things got out of hand. There had been a few broken vases and a ruptured navel Leonard received when

Matthew got a little over enthusiastic. Another time, Matthew got carried away with his ninja antics. That time, he nailed his father in the eye with a broom handle, which caused a severe laceration. But all has long ago been forgiven and the two continue their close bond. Elizabeth and her father have a close bond too, but in a slightly less aggressive way. She has a real heart for the underdog like her parents and is always trying to help the less fortunate.

Buddy is finding out that seagulls make good playmates. At least, they would if they'd stay on the beach a little longer, instead of flying off continually. The Frisbee makes for a nice family entertainment time as everyone decides to get involved.

After almost an hour, Mom stops to catch her breath. "Is anyone thirsty? How about heading back to the cottage and having a drink?"

It is a unanimous decision and Buddy, after one final run into the surf, leads the way home.

Later on, as mother and daughter make supper, Matthew gets a fire started in the fireplace with his father relaxing in a chair.

"What's the matter, Dad, getting too old for the strenuous exercise?"

"It looks that way, doesn't it? I guess time waits for no man."

Matthew glances at his father. "You know that I' m only kidding, right?"

Leonard smiles. "I know, Matthew."

After a half hour, a voice comes from the kitchen.

"Supper is ready, boys," Kate calls from the kitchen.

Both jump up and, after washing their hands, sit down at the table.

"Whoa!" Matthew says excitedly. "Meatloaf and mashed potatoes with beets, this is great. It's one of my many favorites. Thanks, Mom."

Elizabeth says grace and everybody digs in. There is little of the dinner leftover and Kate is pleased that her family still enjoys her cooking.

The dishes are cleaned, this time done by Matthew and his father. This is a real nice surprise for both the females of the house. As they all sit in the living room, Elizabeth glances at her watch and is surprised that it's already just passed seven thirty. "Do you mind if I go up and read my new book for a while, Mom."

"No, not at all dear, it's good to spend a little time alone."

Matt gets up too. "I think I'll do the same, if you don't mind. Why don't you guys watch a little television together?"

They go up the stairs with Matthew heading to his room to get the flashlight. He retrieves it and quietly walks into his sister's room. Both head into the closet and into the clock room.

"I sure hope they don't come up and find us in here," he says.

"I'm not sure that I could talk us out of that one if they did," she says thoughtfully.

Matthew turns on the flashlight and stops. He turns around and walks to her bedroom door and locks it.

She gives him a quizzical look.

"It will be easier to explain a locked door than the clock room," he says.

She nods in agreement and the two enter the room. Elizabeth looks at her watch as Matthew illuminates the dials, revealing that there are only minutes left before the time runs out.

"Turn off the light, Matt. Maybe if something happens it might be easier to see it then."

The minutes tick down slowly. It is almost as if there

is a feeling of electricity in the air.

Elizabeth's fingers tingle as the feeling of an impending event draws closer and closer. Even Matthew senses that something is about to happen. But maybe this is just caused by the excitement of the moment.

"I can just feel that we're involved in something big here, sis," he whispers.

Elizabeth looks quickly at her watch pressing a built in light button. "Two minutes or less," she informs her brother.

The time drags by ever so slowly and then it happens. There is a click and a soft sound comes from within the clock. It is like a faint hum. Then the clock begins to glow ever so faintly. It grows slightly in brightness, for a moment, and both kids get ready to run. The glow lasts for a few seconds and is gone in a flash. The room is left in total darkness, and Matthew turns on the light, just to make sure they're still alone.

"I'm sure that we saw the glow only because it was totally dark in the room. If it had been daytime with the window clean, I doubt we would have been able to see it," Matthew says nervously.

Neither one speaks again for a long time. They are stunned by what has just happened.

Elizabeth is the first to recover. She tells Matthew to shine the light around the room and then at the clock. To their relief they are indeed alone. He gets up and moves close to the clock studying it to see if anything has changed. The clock itself is the same, except that there's another envelope in the bottom of the clock.

"Get it, Matt," his sister urges, not really willing to put her own hands into the timepiece.

Reluctantly, Matthew opens the door and pulls the envelope out quickly. Closing the door again, he backs up a few steps. His breath shudders as he exhales loudly.

Elizabeth is already by the door, hands trembling and eager to leave the room.

This is the strangest thing that has happened in either of their lives. How on earth did this fall into their laps? Elizabeth wonders why no one else ever stumbled onto this room and discovered the clock. Who in the world closed this room off in the first place and why? The mystery of it all is playing havoc on her emotions.

Chapter 9

Back in Elizabeth's room, the two sit on the bed looking at the envelope.

"Well, what do you think is in it?" Matthew asks.

"There's only one way to find out."

"Yeah, I guess you're right about that," he replies.

"Maybe you'd better unlock the door. I'll get some papers, just in case Mom or Dad comes in. That way we can hide the letter in with the rest of the papers. I doubt I'll be able to explain our way out of this if they see the letter and read it," Elizabeth says, just a little perplexed.

This done, the letter is extracted from the envelope and unfolded. Elizabeth softly reads what is written.

"'Thank you, thank you, thank you. I was at the point where I thought that I was trapped in the past and would never get back home. I had a difficult time blending in and think I may have inadvertently given Uncle Robert cause for suspecting me. I accidentally mentioned the year 1927 and I believe he may have overheard me.'"

"'I'm starting to think that Uncle Robert gave me the clock for the sole purpose of having me make it function. If this is true, then he will do what is necessary to make me show him how it works. I hope these are just fanciful thoughts with no real fact to them. I believe that I was being followed on occasion. But I could never identify who it was. Maybe it was only my imagination."

"'All is as it was when I left, even though I spent years in the past. I am now back where I started as if no time at all has gone by. I am the same age as when I left and am at a loss as to how this can be, but I am thankful.

"'I don't know if I can make another trip back in order to save Alice. Having run into my Uncle Robert when I went back, I still do not like the man. Even in later years his temperament hasn't gotten any better. Maybe I will change my mind about going back after I have a bit of time to collect myself again.

"'If, by chance, you decide to go back and attempt to help save Alice, be very careful who you trust. Although my uncle is not an educated man, he has inherited from my Uncle Benjamin a considerable estate. This allows him the means to get things done. I have always thought that he was somehow involved with Alice's death, but there has never been any proof. I could, of course, be wrong. I am thinking that I should talk to Uncle Robert, but I am unsure about the wisdom of this.

"'Good luck, maybe we will meet someday.

"'John Fielding Smith, August 23, 1927"

"So, what do you think of this, Matt?"

"All I can say is, wow. I wonder if that Uncle Robert is responsible for Alice's death," he says.

"Let's check our computer and see if we can find out anything about him," Elizabeth suggests.

The computer is fired up and a Google search is done.

To their surprise, a photo of John is on the screen. In actuality, it is an obituary. In it is written that the untimely demise of John Fielding Smith has prompted the local police to launch an investigation. The date is September 14, 1927. To the officer in charge of the investigation it appears as if the death is a case of murder. A number of people have been questioned, including Robert C. Berger, uncle of the deceased. Nothing conclusive has been found at this point but the investigation will continue.

"My goodness, do you think that Uncle Robert killed John," Elizabeth asks.

"That is the obvious conclusion as far as I can see. What I don't understand is why. If he was trying to get John to show him how to operate the clock, why kill him? Unless he got the information he needed and wanted John out of the way," he states.

"I don't even know John but I feel a loss just the same," Elizabeth tells her brother sadly.

"Yeah, me, too," he replies. "Let's type in the uncle's name and see what happens."

This done, another story comes to light.

October 13, 1927 a month after John's death is a story. The body of a man has been discovered in a wooded area one half mile from a popular hotel. *There is a photograph of the place the body is found.* To all appearances it looks like the death has been self-inflicted. The story goes on to say that a pistol has been found lying next to the body. One empty cartridge is in the revolver with five unfired ones left.

The death of Robert C. Berger has been labeled as suicide and no further investigation is to be done. There are theories being pondered. One theory being looked at is that the uncle may well have been involved with John Fielding Smith's death a short time earlier.

"It looks like John's Uncle Robert did himself in after he killed John and probably Alice," Matthew says in shock.

"Maybe John confronted his uncle or found some incriminating evidence about Alice's murder. I bet the uncle killed him before he could go to the police. What do you think, Matt?"

"It sure looks that way, doesn't it," he tells his sister.

Elizabeth sighs. "So what can we do about this whole mess we have here? If you or I go back, will the one that goes be in danger too?"

"Better yet, can two us go back at the same time? What happens if we go and end up in two different time periods? Should one of us go back while the other makes sure nothing goes wrong at this end? This is all so confusing," he says, agitated.

Only Matthew could come up with all these scenarios, Elizabeth thinks. She makes up her mind right then and there that if anyone goes back it will not be alone. She tells Matt her thoughts and they come to an agreement that, when the time comes, they will both go back in time. This makes Elizabeth feel much better. She knows her brother watches a lot of martial arts programs and is always practicing his moves. He is so fast in his techniques that she has an almost sisterly admiration for his skills. At least if there is a confrontation, she feels they will probably be able to handle it.

Time has slipped by very quickly this evening and, when they realize what time it is, they call an end to the discussions and head for bed.

More plans are made over the next few days, a bit at a time. The two have decided that it will be best if they wait until their parents have to go out for the day. When they do make their move Elizabeth thinks they should leave a note explaining what is going on and possible ways that their parents can help in case something goes wrong. When the plans are finalized, both think that a trial run is the best way to proceed. They will make a small jump back in time—maybe a day or two and only for an hour. This way they can control things and, if something doesn't work quite right, they may be able to correct it.

Together they figure out a time after the clock has been discovered and when the whole family has left for the day. The time is obvious because this way there won't be any chance of meeting themselves or their parents. Now the only thing to do is to wait for the right time to come.

It takes four long days for the proper situation to arrive. Mom and Dad have to go into town and run some errands, as well as check out a couple of ideas. They fail to mention what these ideas are but, even if they did, the kids are too preoccupied to pay attention.

Dad notices this. "What's wrong, Matt."

Caught off guard, Matthew's a little stunned and Elizabeth has to come to the rescue again.

"We're going down the beach to do a little exploring."

This brings Matthew back to reality. He smiles and nods his head. Leonard looks at his boy and instinctively knows that the two are up to something. "Come on, guys, I can see that you're not telling me everything. What's going on?"

"Oh, we heard there are some caves to explore about a mile and a half down along the beach. We thought you might not approve, so we didn't think we should mention it," Elizabeth says with a little smile on her face.

"Don't go in them if they aren't safe, promise?" Mom asks, rather concerned.

"We won't, we promise," Matthew says, finally getting back on track.

The parents get in the car, and Elizabeth runs to her dad's window. "How long do you think you'll be?"

"About six hours should about do it, I think," Leonard tells her.

Everyone waves goodbye and they are gone.

Elizabeth looks at Matt. "What happened back there?"

"Oh, my mind was so much on what we are about to do that I wasn't paying attention," he says. "Good thing you jumped in and saved the day, again," he adds, feeling slightly foolish.

They hurry up the stairs, through the closet, and into the bedroom. Elizabeth has already written the note and is about to put it on her pillow when there is a noise in the driveway.

Matt runs over to the window and sees the car driving back in front of the house. "They're back, hide the note and let's go to the kitchen so they don't suspect anything. Wonder what they want," he says as they race down the stairs and into the kitchen at the back of the house.

Dad walks in a few seconds after as the two greet him.

"Wow that was quick, Dad," Matt says.

"Just forgot these papers. We need them for the job at hand. See you later guys and stay out of trouble, all right?" Dad says over his shoulder as he heads for the door.

"Of course, Dad, you have nothing to worry about," Elizabeth says, smiling at her father.

He looks at his kids and, thinking what a lucky man he is, gets back in the car.

When all is clear, the two go back up. With a sigh of relief, they enter the clock room after replacing the note on the pillow. Matthew, at the direction of his sister, turns the dials one by one to the time and date they want to go back to, then he turns the dials for the return time to two hours later. The clock was stopped after the last time when John was brought back to his own time. This way there was no chance of the sound traveling through the wall. No use taking the chance of alerting Mom and Dad, despite the fact that it runs almost silently.

Matthew sets the time on the clock according to his wristwatch. Then he checks the manual to make sure everything has been done properly.

Elizabeth double checks all the dates and takes a deep breath. "I don't mind telling you, Matt, that I am really nervous about this."

Matthew looks at her. "What could possibly go wrong?"

He gives a little laugh but they both know that he is as worried as she is. He reaches into the clock, starts the pendulum swinging, and gently closes the door. They have about five minutes to wait and it's a long five minutes, very long indeed.

All kinds of thoughts are running through their heads and most are not pleasant ones. Several times, they are both at the point of stopping the clock, but curiosity prevents this.

The moment finally arrives. A sound emanates from the interior of the device, and everything clouds over.

Chapter 10

Leonard and Kate have a pleasant drive into town. They go to the bank and sign some papers. These will have any pay checks and any incoming funds transferred to a new account they have just opened. This is a small local financial institution they have chosen to do business with. After this is done, a trip to city hall is made. It proves to yield the desired information they are seeking. Before going anywhere else, the two decide to go for lunch at a delightful café with an outdoor patio.

Lunch is ordered and, as they are eating, Kate glances at her husband, "Are you sure that you want to try to do this?"

Leonard is thoughtful for a moment and finally nods. "I'm not positive but, at this point, I'm more curious to see if we can or can't do this. It will change our life completely. We'll have to discuss it with the kids to see what they think, as well as what all the other options are."

She smiles. Life with Leonard has been anything but boring. There has been a lot of work and a few moves to places she has sometimes wondered about. Overall, it has been a wonderful marriage. He's a kind and generous person and always does what was best for the family. No wonder the kids love their dad so much.

Kate, when she was young, had the option of many suitors. In the end, no one compared to the man she has chosen. The only thing she might change is his overactive sense of humor. But, then again, it also makes him that much more unique.

When the meal is done, the two go for a stroll along the main street, past all the shops. They look in some of the more interesting windows and study the wares for sale. When the time comes, he looks at his watch and sees that the last appointment of the day is at hand. They make their way to the person they have the meeting with. Many questions are asked and many answers received. The only problem is that some of the answers are not what they want to hear. Much headway has been made and possibilities are still available. When the meeting is done, the two decide to go to the beach for a talk and a stroll.

A new strategy must be worked out and presented to all involved.

The walk on the beach takes away any of the negative stresses that developed during the last meeting. Leonard, the eternal optimist, brings Kate back to seeing things in a better light. As far as he is concerned, most of life's problems have solutions. The answers are there, as long as you look in the right places for them.

By the time the walk is finished, a choice needs to be made. They can either go back to the cottage or back into town and have supper. There was that lovely restaurant with the fish nets and part of a small row boat hung up on a wall. They saw it during their walk through the streets. They decide that the teenagers would be happier if they had a little more time alone and the parents head off to the restaurant, calling home to inform their children.

Chapter 11

The cloud that surrounds the two dissipates. As things clear, it appears that nothing has changed. Both are a little disappointed and wonder if all this has been nothing but a farce. The room is the same and Matthew questions Elizabeth about it.

"To tell you the truth, we didn't do much in this room so maybe we should check out things we know should be different."

They head out of the room. The first thing they notice is the fact that the door going back into the closet should be open but it's locked. They look at each other and instinctively know that the clock is real. They unlock the door and the things in the closet need to be moved in order to get to Elizabeth's room. As they enter her bedroom, other things are different. The note that was on the pillow is not there. And things in the room are not as they were left. The pair feels an excitement building in them as the reality of the situation sinks in.

The two head downstairs and see that many things are

different. Both sit down and a discussion ensues.

"So now that we know the clock does indeed work, we can start making plans for our next trip. I think we should not go back to the room before the trip back happens today, just to clinch things," Matthew explains.

"Good idea, I think you're right, Matt."

The two get a drink from the fridge and Elizabeth makes the observation that it tastes just the same as always.

"Were you expecting something else," he asks.

"I was just wondering. I guess it would have to be okay, otherwise, John would never have survived his trip," she explains thoughtfully.

The time slips by before they know it. He tells his sister to get ready. They stay in the kitchen. The cloud reappears and, as it clears, they are back in the room, standing in front of the clock.

Elizabeth gasps. "Wow, who would ever believe us if we told them about this?"

"This sure is a crazy thing. We're really lucky to be the ones to come across this," he says happily as he thinks of what is about to come.

"I'm not as sure about that as you are. Remember that three people have died already, Alice, John, and Robert. This could be a lot more dangerous than you think," she tells him, more than a little worried.

Matthew thinks about this but is undaunted. To him, this is the adventure of a lifetime.

Back in her room, Elizabeth picks up the note that has reappeared on her pillow and puts it away for future use. Things in the closet are put back as they were and the door to the room is relocked.

Her hands are trembling again and her insides feel all jittery. Despite the fact that things have gone well so far, there is no guarantee that it will stay this way. Things went wrong for John in a very bad way. She is certain that he was murdered and the person responsible is certainly that miserable Uncle Robert. It seems to her that the person who killed Alice is probably that Robert man too. So this means he would think nothing of disposing of two snoopy teenagers as well.

The plans the two make will have to be thought through very carefully. Elizabeth is starting to think that maybe this is not such a good idea. Boys jump into things, throwing caution to the winds, figuring that they are invincible. Girls usually know better than that. Caution is what Elizabeth feels is necessary here.

"Hey, Matthew, I think we should go and see those caves, in case Mom and Dad ask about them."

He agrees and they head for the beach with Buddy leading the way.

Chapter 12

A lovely meal in an out-of-the-ordinary place and the excursion is complete. Much has been done today, and Leonard and Kate are on their way home. The sun is setting and the clouds in the sky are illuminated from the underside, giving the whole scene a golden hue. Kate has a slight smile on her face as she thinks of what the future may bring. Life is good and, if all goes well, it will be fairly predictable.

The two arrive home with both kids waiting in the living room. Matthew has started a fire and the cool evening air has been replaced by warmth only a fireplace can provide. The logs are crackling and the odd spark pops out, to be caught by the screen in front.

"Hi, kids, anything new and exciting happen today?" Mom asks.

Elizabeth, as usual, is the first to respond. "No, it has been an uneventful day here, how about you and Dad?"

"No, we just ran some errands and enjoyed the rest of the day traveling around. We found a wonderful restaurant we'll take you to sometime, though," Mom says.

"How was the cave experience?" Leonard says.

"It was interesting and completely safe," Elizabeth informs them, thinking it's a good thing they actually went for a quick trip there.

"Maybe you can take us there sometime," Kate mentions.

Matthew jumps in. "That's a good idea. I think you'd like it."

The rest of the evening is spent relaxing and, soon, it's time to retire for the night. Matthew lies in bed thinking about what he should take with them when the trip to the past is made. This is a real adventure, and he plans to make the most of it. He also comes to the conclusion that there could be some dangers.

A solid plan of action needs to be formulated. Ideas go through his head and, just before he falls asleep, he sets the alarm for two-fifteen. He wants to check and see if Alice will make another appearance. Maybe this time, he can find a clue as to who the second person is. He will try to see as many details about the other person as he can. This way he may be able to figure out who the person actually is when they go into the past at last. Matthew drifts off and doesn't wake till the alarm goes off softly.

Elizabeth on the other hand has great difficulty getting to sleep. She has the feeling of impending doom. To her, this is not an adventure at all. More likely a very dangerous time is ahead of them. She is so thankful that Matt will be with her.

At this point she senses that she is not alone and her door is pushed open without a sound.

It is difficult to keep from screaming as she lies there in bed. All of a sudden, there is a sound and she realizes that Buddy has entered her room. She must have left the door slightly ajar and her dog decided that meant he was invited in. The relief she feels almost brings her to the point of laughing.

"Come-on, boy," she whispers and the dog jumps up on the bed.

She is grateful for the company and, as she pets the dog, her fears drift away. She finally falls asleep.

Leonard and Kate talk in bed for a short time and discuss the day's events. Although some things are not working out as they would wish, some headway has been made. The future is their prime concern at the moment, and it will take some real effort to make the plans become a reality. It seems as if there are two obstacles jumping up every time one is worked out. They also drift off to sleep, wondering what is in their future.

The alarm is shut off. Matthew gets dressed and heads for the front door so he won't wake anyone. Just as he approaches the door, Buddy runs quietly down the stairs. There is little choice but to take the dog with him. If he doesn't take the dog, Buddy will surely wake someone in the house. Matthew makes a shushing sound, holding his finger in front of his mouth. Buddy seems to get the idea and follows him silently. Together they make their way near the shore where Matthew and Elizabeth first spotted Alice running down the beach. Matthew sits down and keeps hold of Buddy so he won't run if, and when, Alice makes an appearance. He waits anxiously for a time and nothing happens.

He begins to wonder if anything will happen tonight. He looks down the beach both ways and sees nothing. A slight feeling of disappointment comes over him. The mist that came last time starts to finally make an appearance off shore. It drifts across the water slowly, coming closer and closer to them.

Buddy starts to whine a bit as he senses something

isn't right. Matthew tightens his hold on Buddy, as the dog becomes more and more agitated. All of a sudden, there is movement off to the right.

Through the mist, the figure of a young girl can be seen running closer and closer to the boy and his dog. Buddy whines and lowers himself to the sand. The dog trembles as the figure comes closer and closer. Matthew stares at the girl, trying to pick out some detail and almost forgets that the reason he is here is not the girl but the pursuer.

He gets up and quickly walks closer to where the second figure was the last time Elizabeth and he hid in this spot. The girl runs past as Buddy backs up, whimpering. Matthew gets to the spot, just in time to see the hand materialize in the mist. The hand is there one moment and gone the next. Both the girl and the other person disappear at the same time.

Disappointment fills Matthew, as he was hoping to get an idea as to who the other person is. All he can determine at this point is that the hand belongs to a man. How old or anything else is still unknown. There are no distinctive features to help identify the man if, and when, he does see him, *darn it*. Matthew stands there, pondering the situation as Buddy comes back with his tail between his legs. He has been shook up and sniffs the sand the girl has run on. When he gets to the spot where the man was, he whimpers again and turns around, heading for the house.

Back in bed with Buddy by his side, Matthew goes over what has just happened and tries to work it into his plans. So far he really hasn't got any concrete plans, just a bunch of maybes and supposes. Besides, if they are careful they will be just fine, right?

Chapter 13

The next day brings sunshine and warm temperatures. It is a day for the family and everyone heads for the beach. Buddy runs ahead and as he gets to the beach area he starts sniffing the sand where the girl was. Mom is next in line and stops where Buddy is. She spots the tracks made by Alice.

"There must be some other people in the area going by these footprints," Mom says. "It looks like a young person was here, if the depth of the prints is any indicator."

"I haven't noticed anybody else around here." Matthew feels he may have jumped on that a little too quickly as his mother looks at him a bit strangely.

Off he runs with Buddy before she can ask him what he means. Sometimes the best way to avoid something is to run. Up to now there have not been many people anywhere in the area, so new footprints are noticeable. Buddy runs into the water and when he comes back, vigorously shakes himself, spraying everyone near him.

This is enough to get everyone on a different line of thought and the footprints are forgotten. This is a good thing because it might have been noticed that the tracks started and stopped rather abruptly. Elizabeth thinks of this and walks around messing up this evidence so no one will come to any conclusions.

The day ends up being quite entertaining and, by lunch, everyone is famished. The meal is finished and leaves Leonard and Kate in the mood for a rest. There is a nice little spot for a blanket behind the cottage. They decide now is the perfect time to lie down and maybe have a little nap. Matt and Elizabeth decide to go exploring and are off.

When they are well on their way down the sandy beach, Elizabeth turns to Matt.

"Do you have any ideas as to how to prepare for the trip back in time that's coming up?"

It dawns on him that he hasn't had a chance to tell her about last night. He does this and, when she finds out that he hasn't learned anything new, she asks him why he didn't wake her.

"I didn't think you would want to, to be honest," he replies. "You looked a little shook up yesterday and I thought it would be best if I went alone. Besides Buddy came along."

"Was he of any help?" she asks.

"I think he was more shook up than you were by the whole thing," he says with a little smile on his face.

"Okay, so when do you think we should make the attempt to go back to help Alice?"

"We need to have Mom and Dad away and who knows when that will happen again."

"You're right there. I wonder if there is any way of finding out so we can prepare ourselves. What do you think we should take with us?"

"Hey, I just thought of something. We need to make sure our clothes don't give us away. We can't wear wristwatches either because I don't think they had this type in those days," Matthew says, pointing to his quartz watch.

"Yeah, you're right. I never even thought about things like that. We better really think this over well or we'll be asked about these things."

The two stroll along the beach, each having their own thoughts running through their heads. Matthew still thinks of this as a problem to be solved and is looking forward to it excitedly. Elizabeth, on the other hand, is scared out of her wits. She knows that this whole thing could end in disaster, just as easily as not. By the time they get back to the cottage, they're not much further ahead with their plans than when they left. The only one that has really had a good time and is content with life is Buddy. He seems to have forgotten totally about the whole incident. Matthew, of course, feels far better about it than Elizabeth does.

As the next week slides slowly by, the two decide on exactly what date they will go back to. They want to go back ten days before the incident with Alice. This way they'll be able to familiarize themselves with the situation. They also figure it's best to go in several short one or two hour visits just to test the waters so to speak.

Elizabeth thinks that they may be able to see things that can help them plan a course of action that way. After a lot of discussion, the pair also agrees that it will be a good idea not to go back twice to the same time period. Neither thinks it's a good idea to attempt two trips like that. What would happen if they ran into themselves when they are already there?

The question comes up as to whether or not they can actually go to a time they have already visited. In actuality, they will already be there. Would that mean there would be two Matthew's and Elizabeth's there in the same spot? *Way too confusing to say the least.* They are both sure that there will be some kind of problem so Elizabeth starts a journal. In it she will keep track of every minute they are gone, where and when and for how long. This may just prevent a few problems for the two.

Time is spent on the computer, familiarizing themselves with the era. What really helps is the book Elizabeth bought describing a time long gone. It shows customs and how life is in a time when there are no computers or televisions. People have to deal with each other face to face or through letters. Very few people have telephones and the barter system allows goods and services to be exchanged.

The photos show styles in clothing changing as the years pass. Homes are beautifully built and decorated and prefabrication is unheard of. Men build homes by hand and mills make pieces to order as they were needed. The pace of life is such that things are enjoyed as long as your health is good. This, of course, is not always the case. There are outbreaks of influenza and many people die a horrible death. Infant mortality is high until such times as vaccines are discovered. When these advances are made, the health of the general population is greatly improved.

Flipping through the book, they find photos and a story that the homestead was much larger than it is now. There are several homes and buildings in Alice's time that are not here in the present. There is actually a hotel near the property that the cottage occupies. This must be the same hotel that was mentioned in Robert C. Berger's obituary.

After looking into it they find that there have been several fires later that consumed most of the buildings. Actually all the surrounding buildings are gone except for the cottage which is in several of the pictures. These fires happening over an extended period of time are deemed accidents as nothing suspicious is ever found. It appears that firefighting methods and equipment has yet to be developed very well. The two decide that they will make sure to eat before they go back in time. This way, it won't be necessary to find food while they are in the past.

Elizabeth tries to subtly question her mother about any upcoming plans. She finds little information that will help the two with their own plans. This first trip into the past is put on hold for the moment. Four days go by and finally Leonard and Kathleen get a call that requires them to go to town for a meeting.

"Why don't you make a day of it?" Matt suggests. "We're fine here by ourselves. We're going to go exploring and will be gone for several hours anyway."

He tries to be as offhand as he can about it, making it look like it doesn't matter one way or the other. Dad thinks it's a great idea and they get things ready. Another fifteen minutes and the parents are gone. Matthew is getting excited but Elizabeth is quite apprehensive about the upcoming event. Soon they are alone and ready to go.

Upstairs in the room, Matthew sets the dials on the clock. First the date that they want to go to is set and then the amount of time to stay there is dialed in. They will go to a time that is ten days before Alice's death. The day that is set is September 6, 1907. Matthew looks at his sister after checking the dials to make absolutely certain everything is as they want it.

"Well, sis, are you ready?"

With uncertainty filling her mind, she nods. "I guess so."

Matthew turns the arms on the clock to the proper time, winds up the clock to maximum and starts the pendulum swinging.

He turns to his sister with a smile on his face. "Okay, my watch is in my pocket and it will beep five minutes before we are to come back so we will be prepared. We're dressed reasonably close to the time period, and I think we're all set."

He trips the switch and they have an eight minute wait for the clock to reach Ten o'clock. The minutes drag by ever so slowly, at least for Matt. For Elizabeth, it just flies by. The moment comes and the clock starts to make a sound. The room becomes a cloudy glow and they know they are no longer in their own time.

Chapter 14

When the air clears, things have changed considerably. The room is no longer small. Both Matthew and Elizabeth realize that they are in a room that is totally different from the one in the cottage. There is beautiful flowered wallpaper with wainscoting along the walls. As they are looking out the window it is obvious that they are not even in the same house. On the wall there hangs a calendar. The date that is shown is the month of September, 1907.

"No doubt about it, we are now where we wanted to be," Matthew says, just a little shocked by it all.

"We'd better get out of here quickly before someone sees us," Elizabeth whispers.

"Study the room and memorize where everything is," Matthew suggests. "This way we can position ourselves properly back home for the next trip. We don't want to be in the open when we come back."

Quietly they go to the door and, seeing the way is clear, they slip out of the house. Looking around they see several clapboard homes nearby and a few outbuildings.

Off to the right, maybe two hundred yards away is the hotel. They saw it in the photos on the computer and in the book. The beach and the ocean are only a hundred feet away. Both feel this is the best place for them to go and assess the situation.

As they are walking, they see a few people scattered here and there. One in particular draws their attention. Matthew nudges Elizabeth and she follows his gaze. There is Alice, talking with a boy at the water's edge. Alice is wearing a white floral patterned dress and the boy is in a shirt and long pants. She and the lad are deep in conversation and oblivious to their surroundings. There is a look of frustration on both their faces. It is certain that something is wrong. Elizabeth starts to slowly wander closer to the pair.

"Are you sure this is a good idea?" Matthew asks quietly.

"No, but I can't think of anything better so please come with me," she whispers back. Maybe we can find out something that might help us figure out this whole mess."

"I guess you're right, we only have a little bit of time here."

The two approach the teenagers on the beach. As they get close, Alice and the boy who they now realize is John, stop talking.

"Is there something I can help you with?" Alice asks.

"My brother and I are new here and don't know the area," Elizabeth explains. "We were wondering if you could be of some help."

There is no real age difference between the four teenagers. The conversation soon takes on a friendly tone and everyone relaxes fairly quickly.

It is obvious to Elizabeth that Matthew is quite taken by Alice.

The two find out that Alice has a middle name they didn't know about. Alice Victoria Berger, the name Berger is, of course, of Dutch background. This strikes a chord with Matthew as it sounds so regal and his family background is also Dutch.

The time flies by and Elizabeth gets some information that she is looking for. She finds out that there has been a lot of trouble between Alice's father, Benjamin Berger and her uncle Robert, her father's brother. It all started years ago when Benjamin inherited most of the property the family owned. Uncle Robert thinks that he is entitled to the majority of the holdings being the older of the two.

Benjamin came across a peculiar grandfather clock in his travels. Uncle Robert thinks he should have it as partial compensation for being short-changed in the will. The two men are constantly at odds and uncle Robert has been becoming more and more unreasonable. Earlier this year, Alice's father, Benjamin, met with an untimely accident and died. The estate has since fallen into Robert's hands.

There is a little beep and John asks Matthew what it is. Matthew looks at Elizabeth and both realize that it is time to move.

"I'm sorry but we have to go," Elizabeth says. "but we will be back later, okay? Meet us here in an hour all right?"

Alice looks at her. "I'll try to be here." She takes a quick look at Matthew with a smile on her face.

The two head away as quickly as they can.

"We need to be out of sight in two minutes," Matthew says, looking at his watch.

They head to a stand of trees and, when no one is watching, they duck into the middle. They sit down so they won't be seen. Shortly, cloudiness in the air appears around them and when it clears, they are sitting in front of the clock again.

"Holy smokes, that was amazing," Matthew says excitedly.

"It sure was. I think more than ever that Uncle Robert is the one we need to stop. How we are going to do it is still up in the air, though," she exclaims.

"We'll come up with something, don't worry."

Chapter 15

atthew looks at the clock in Elizabeth's room. "You know, we spent two hours in the past but we were only gone from here about two minutes. The clock has only changed by that much but, according to my watch, two hours have passed. Do you know what this means Elizabeth?"

She shakes her head, puzzled, and then it comes to her. "That means we can leave almost any time we want. No matter how long we stay in the past, we will only be gone from here for a minute or two."

Matthew smiles. "Right on, sis, we won't have to wait until Mom and Dad are gone. We can make the trips whenever we feel we won't be disturbed or needed."

"This makes things a lot easier as we won't have to wait all the time for opportunities to come," she says with a smile on her face. "You seem to like Alice a lot, don't you?"

Matt just blushes a little. Much of the nervousness Elizabeth felt earlier has dissipated.

The two would like to go back right now but need to make some serious plans first. Both are now certain that Uncle Robert is the perpetrator of the crime. They desperately want to find a way to foil his plans. Something else they want to find out is why he has done this. Maybe then they can do something to change the past and save Alice.

Chapter 16

Leonard drives the car along the country roads with the warm scented air coming in the lowered windows. There is the aroma of the vegetation growing along the winding road as well as the unmistakable smell of the ocean air.

As they are driving, an unwanted passenger flies into the car. Leonard quickly pulls over and the two exit the vehicle hastily. With the windows down a rather large bumble bee slowly flies around the interior. After a few moments, it exits the car, flying toward the flowering plants at the side of the road. The two have a laugh about the incident and the trip to town is resumed.

"This is the life," he says to his wife.

She has her hand out the window feeling the warm air rush between her fingers. "I wish we could make this last forever," she replies wistfully.

Leonard decides to make a little side trip to visit Christine Parker this morning while they are in town anyway.

The drive takes them to city hall for a meeting about zoning restrictions. This meeting goes fairly well but there are still many hoops to jump and questions to answer. Next a lunch is in order which is had at a small café with a shaded patio. The sun is shining brightly with few clouds in the sky.

Afterward, Leonard heads to the office of Island Realty, dropping in to see Christine. He has an idea and wants to run it by her. It would be nice if she was there, but she has a meeting elsewhere. He finds out that she will be gone the rest of the day.

"So what is it you wanted to see her about, dear," Kate asks.

"I have an idea but I'm not sure it's feasible. There is something else I would like to check into which you are probably better at doing than I am," he tells his wife as he looks thoughtfully at her.

"What's that?" she asks.

"I've been thinking that there is a college nearby that has a program to train auto technicians. Matthew is an absolute wiz with mechanical things. I think we should fill out an application for him. Who knows? He might like this as a career. I doubt anything will come of this but you never can tell. There do seem to be an awful lot of roadblocks jumping in our way."

"You know I have always found that if something is meant to be, it will happen when the time is right." Kate tells her husband.

She has noticed in the past that once an idea enters Leonard's head, he is like a dog with a bone. Sometimes it is like he is a little too focused on it.

Chapter 17

Leonard and Kate drive back to the cottage and walk in the front door, calling out to the kids. "We're in the back yard," Elizabeth calls back.

"Did you have a hard day so far," Dad asks.

"We've been to the beach and played with Buddy for a while, then did some exploring."

Buddy's ears perk up at the sound of his name as if thinking it might be play time.

Mom looks at her two children. "Do you two like being here? I mean, what would you think if we could make this a more permanent life?"

They look at each other and wonder what's going on. Matthew, for a change, is the first to recover. "What about college in the fall? I'm looking forward to starting training for a career," he says. "But I am open to new things, just not sure what they are, though. Do you have plans that you're thinking of?"

Elizabeth jumps in at this point. "I, for one, would love to stay right here. I think this house and being by the beach is the best thing that could happen. Please, tell me that you're considering doing this."

This time, Dad throws in his two cents. "We've been checking with the city and real estate office about just that. So far there are several obstacles in the way and we aren't sure that we can make this happen. We were thinking of starting a bed and breakfast, but I'm not sure it's going to happen, but that's okay. I might start a consulting business online which I think will be better and a lot easier. Your mother and I have been talking and think a change is in order. It may take more time than we have right now. It may not happen, so don't get your hopes up too high."

Matthew is thinking that he really did want to go away to college. But he wanted it only because his father was away on jobs for considerable periods of time. If his dad's going to be around more, Matthew might be interested in staying here.

The clock does make things a lot more interesting, but only if they live here. If they have to live in some other house, how can they maintain access to the clock? It's not as if they would be able to take the clock to the new home, would they? There are way too many ifs in the equation. Plus, what school would he go to? It isn't as if he can just walk in and say here I am where do I start?

Elizabeth, on the other hand, is already trying to think of ways to influence her parents into buying this house. No other home will do because this is the one with the clock, and they won't be able to take it with them, will they? Hmmm, that's something else to think about.

The rest of the day is spent with the wheels turning in everyone's head. Supper is done and the fireplace has a fire burning brightly in it.

"Say, Dad, do you really think that we could end up moving here?" Matthew asks.

"To tell you the truth, I'm not sure. Some of the things we checked at city hall give me the indication that things here don't change easily. I've been trying to get answers and nobody seems to be able to give me a direct reply. But that part may not matter. Plus on top of that the real estate agent is hard to get a hold of when I want her. So I really don't know Matt."

Elizabeth has already gone upstairs and is reading the book she bought earlier.

"I wonder what caused the fire at the hotel. It was never found out just what happened to it or if anyone has ever been suspected of arson. Could Uncle Robert be responsible for that too?" Elizabeth mutters. "Gosh, I also wonder what Matthew and I can do to prevent John's and Alice's death. I really like them and I know Matthew sure likes Alice."

Just then footsteps sound on the stairs. They keep on coming right to her door and there is a gentle knock.

"Yes," she calls out.

The door opens and there's Matthew. "Were you talking to someone a second ago?" he asks.

She laughs a little self-consciously. "Actually, I was just running things through in my head and didn't realize that I was talking out loud."

"Really, ha, ha, I never do things like that," he says to her in a light-hearted manner.

"Yeah, right, you're the one that mows the lawn with your mouth moving half the time talking to yourself," she replies laughingly.

"Oh, I didn't think you knew about that. So what are you thinking about?" he asks, just a little embarrassed.

Elizabeth fills him in and relays her concerns about being able to help Alice and John. Now that they have met the two, there is an even stronger desire to assist them.

"I think we should sleep on it and see what we can come up with in the morning," Matthew says as he leaves the room to get ready for bed.

He's tempted to set the alarm for two-thirty in the morning again but decides against it. It's doubtful that there's anything new to be learned on the beach.

This has been quite a vacation so far and he wonders what's to come.

Elizabeth reads a while longer, gathering information. Something nags her thoughts—something that she has read—and it points her mind in a certain direction, but it isn't clear what it is. She drifts off to sleep with the answer to something vital eluding her.

The morning brings a new day and, after breakfast, Leonard talks on the phone. He makes an appointment with Christine, through her helper. Elizabeth helps her mother to clean up after breakfast. Together, they tidy up the rest of the cottage while they're on a roll.

Matthew goes outside and into the small barn to see what interesting things he can find. Once inside, he finds a lot of discarded junk that has been saved over the years. A layer of dust covers everything inside. Making his way past all the junk, he starts to find things under old tarps that actually look like they are well worth saving. As his search progresses, he discovers that the tarps toward the rear of the building have the appearance of being far older and dirtier than the ones near the front.

At the back of the shed, against the rear wall, is a tarp covering an old dresser. This looks as if it has not been disturbed in many, many years. After he clears a few things out of the way, he takes a closer look at the antique. The dresser looks like it would be used in a bedroom, as it is about four feet high and around two and a half feet wide with drawers top to bottom.

This is a piece of furniture that has obviously been

handmade. A very skilled craftsman has taken great care to build this beautiful piece. What attracts his attention even more is the fact that the top drawer is six inches lower than in most dressers he has seen. Matthew, being who he is, knows instinctively that things always have a reason for being made the way they are, especially in this case.

He studies the dresser front to back and top to bottom without finding anything of consequence. Taking hold of the handle on the top drawer, he pulls it open and then, when he sees nothing inside, is just about to pull it all the way out when there is a voice at the door to the barn/shed.

"Hey, Matt you in here," his father asks.

Matthew covers the dresser quickly and turns toward the door.

"Oh hi, Dad, I was just looking around, seeing all the junk that's stored in here."

"Do you really think you should be going through other people's things? The owners may not like it you know."

"To tell you the truth, Dad, I think that if it was important to them they would have moved the stuff to a better place than this."

"I see your point, son. Just be careful not to make a mess or damage anything, all right."

"I will, Dad, don't worry."

With this, Leonard walks back to the cottage, leaving Matthew to his investigations.

Pulling the tarp off the dresser, Matthew opens the top drawer again and feels around inside. After finding the hidden compartment in the clock, he thinks that this dresser might have some hidden qualities to it too.

Not being able to get his hand in all the way, he decides to pull the drawer out completely. When it's out, he lowers himself to look into the opening and notices that just above the drawer opening is a wood panel.

"It has to either be a panel or the top of the dresser is made of a piece of wood almost six inches thick," he mutters to himself.

"Oh, now you're talking to yourself too or should I say, again?" Elizabeth says as she walks up behind him.

Stunned, Matthew jumps up, spinning around gasping.

"Geez, you scared the crap out of me. What the heck do you think you're doing?"

"Oh, sorry, Matty, I thought you heard me come in," she says with a smile on her face.

"You're real funny, aren't you, you little brat," he replies, knowing that he has done this type of thing to her many times in the past.

"So what *are* you up to, Matt?"

"I found this old dresser here. From what I can see, it's unique compared to all the other things in here. This thing is handmade, really old, and has a top that looks odd. I was just about to inspect it when you surprised me."

"So what's odd about it, bro?"

"If you look inside, you can see that there's what looks like a compartment in the top. Either that or the top is made of one big chunk of wood, which doesn't make sense." He reaches inside and raps the upper part of the opening. There is a hollow sound and his suspicions are confirmed. "Just as I thought, it's a false bottom. I don't see an obvious way to open it, so let's turn this thing around and see if there is something at the back that allows entry."

When the dresser is turned around, they study it for anything that will give them an idea as to how the hidden compartment is opened.

Finding nothing to indicate a solution, she sighs.

"What the heck, Matt? There must be a way to get into it."

"You know, now that I think about it, this dresser has a similar look to it as the clock does. Do you think that it was made by the same man in the Netherlands? I doubt that many people have the skill to make something this intricate."

"So what are you getting at?" she asks, puzzled.

"The clock has a hidden part in the bottom. Maybe this thing does too."

Getting down to his knees, he is about to inspect the underside of the dresser.

"Hey, guys, are you still in here?" Kate shouts.

"Yeah, Mom, we were just coming out, wait there," Elizabeth yells back.

This is not what they want at the moment but have no choice. Matthew quickly covers the dresser after he puts the drawer back in. Elizabeth walks to the front door to draw her mother's attention away from what her brother is doing. A moment later, he joins them having a difficult time hiding his disappointment.

"So what are you guys doing in there?"

"Oh, just investigating. There's a bunch of neat old stuff in here. Dad said it was okay," Matt tells her quickly, wondering if he jumped on that one a little fast again too.

"That's okay, Matthew. We were thinking that it might be nice to go into town and visit the arcade we saw when we first arrived. I know you two love these kinds of things. Your dad and I have a meeting with the real estate agent just before lunch."

"That would be great," Elizabeth says enthusiastically.

Matthew closes the door, taking one last wistful look at the tarp-covered dresser at the back of the shed.

Chapter 18

Everyone is loaded into the car. Buddy hangs his head out the window as they drive down the winding road back to town. He just loves the wind blowing in his face. Occasionally drool is caught by the breeze and hits the side of the car. Now and then some spit lands on a car that happens to be following too close. This, however, makes them back off rather quickly when they realize what just happened.

When they reach the arcade, Leonard looks at his watch and sees that it is almost time for the meeting. He hands each of the kids a twenty.

"We'll be back in an hour or so. You two have some fun and we'll go for lunch then, okay, guys?" he says with a smile on his face.

"Thanks, Dad, this is great," they say at almost the same time.

When they're on their way, Kate looks at her husband. "Feeling kind of generous, are we?"

"I figure that this could still be the last real vacation

that we have as a family, and I want the kids to enjoy it and remember this time.”

“I guess you’re right, after all we can well afford it,” she agrees.

Pulling up to the agent’s office, they get out of the car and take a look around them. The scene they view is one of a town set back in time. The shops in the area seem to be the same as one would think they were seventy or eighty years ago. There are some signs of modern advancements, but overall the feeling is like stepping into the past.

Inside, they are escorted to an office with Christine walking in a moment later, greeting them.

“So how are you enjoying your stay here so far?”

“To tell you the truth, we absolutely love it,” Kate tells her.

“As a matter of fact, this is why we have asked to see you,” Leonard tells her as they seat themselves.

“Oh, what do you have in mind?”

“We would like to know if the owners of Lilac Cottage would be interested in selling the property,” he tells the agent expectantly.

“Oh, my, I’m so sorry to have to tell you this, but it has already been sold. This is the last summer that the cottage will be available. Some folks two months ago from North Dakota had the same idea as you and put in an offer six weeks ago. The owners have accepted the offer and the deal closes right after you leave.”

Leonard struggles not to show the disappointment he feels. Kate rests her hand on his shoulder, trying to comfort him.

“There are a few other places for sale if you would like to see them,” Christine says sympathetically.

“Are any of them on the water? By the way, what did the cottage sell for,” he asks.

"One is across the road from the water, but, unfortunately, there are no places for sale that are as nice as the one you're in. The price it sold for is actually quite reasonable."

When they find out what the final price is, they let Christine know that they would have had no problem paying that for the cottage. After asking the agent to keep them informed of any new places that may come up, the two walk out onto the street. Kate looks at her husband and, for the first time in quite a while, sees a look of defeat on his face.

"I know that you're very disappointed right now, but who knows what will come to pass? Maybe another place will come up. I know you have your heart set on Lilac Cottage because of the kids. But it's gone, and we can't do anything about it. Christine said the deal is solid and will go through soon. It won't make the kids happy, but there is nothing we can do to change that either," she tells her disappointed husband as they walk slowly along.

"I know you're right. We never had a chance, as it was sold before we even got here. I don't want Matthew and Elizabeth to feel bad but, like you said, there's nothing we can do about that. I guess there is no point in sending in the application to the local college for Matthew now."

"Oh, that has already been done. I did that when you were in one of the stores, on our last trip to town. We may as well see what happens there. We'll have an answer to that in about three weeks. Who knows? Another place may just come along. Then we'll still be able to stay here."

"I think that we missed our chance. It's doubtful anything else will come up. There just aren't that many suitable places here. The likelihood of one being put up for sale between now and then is really slim." Leonard tells her dejectedly.

The two get into the car, and it is so evident the mood has changed from optimistic to one of bitter defeat. Matthew and Elizabeth are aware of it as soon as they see them drive up.

"What's wrong, Dad," Elizabeth asks.

"We went to see the agent and have been informed that Lilac Cottage has been sold. We are the last vacation renters the place will have."

The feeling Leonard has is soon evident in both children. Kate sees that the happiness everyone had up to this point will be hard to bring back. Everyone agrees that lunch out will be a waste of time, so the drive home is started. Even Buddy senses the disappointment and just lies down on the seat. He's no longer interested in hanging his head out the window. The ride home is a long quiet one.

After a subdued lunch, Elizabeth asks Matthew to go for a walk on the beach. He wants to turn her down no longer having an interest in it. He sees the look on her face that means she wants to discuss something important. So off they go, leaving two unhappy parents behind.

"Matt, we have less than six weeks left here so we better make the best of it. I know we're all sad about the situation but there is nothing to be done about it. We have to help Alice and John and that has to be our main concern for the time being. This other thing will just have to be."

"I know you're right, but it's hard to put it aside. What do you suggest?" he asks sadly.

"I think that we should get back to the dresser. I can't think of any reason someone would go to that much trouble to build such a piece with a hidden compartment and not use it."

This starts Matthew thinking again, and it doesn't take

long before he's raring to go. On their way back to the cottage, they meet Mom and Dad with Buddy tagging along.

"Hey, Mom, where are you two going?" Elizabeth asks.

"We thought we would go for a walk on the beach. There is no use having our vacation ruined just because some plans fell through."

"I think you're right. Matthew and I feel the same way so we've decided to make the best of it while we can, right, big brother?"

"Right you are, as usual."

They head for the cottage. At least this is what it looks like to the parents. When they get near the home, the two kids detour to the storage shed. This is missed by Mom and Dad, as they are already walking down the beach arm in arm.

The dresser is uncovered and Matthew pulls out the drawer again. He feels around inside again, just in case he missed something the first time. Satisfied that there is nothing to be found in that area, he kneels down and lies on the floor.

"Hey, sis, can you tilt the dresser back so I can get a better look at the bottom. Be careful not to tip it too far, though."

"I'm going to move it a little closer to the wall then I can just tip it till it's leaning against it, all right?"

"Good idea," he says.

After this is done, both are happy with the results.

Matthew slides close to the dresser and looks underneath. "Darn it, there isn't enough light to see clearly. I wish I had my flashlight."

"I'll go get it. Be careful it doesn't fall on you, okay?" she tells him as she runs to the house.

She's back quickly and hands him the light. Shining

the light on the bottom side, he studies as much as he can see there.

"I don't see anything here."

"Hey, Matt, where was the hole on the clock that opened the hidden box?"

"It was at the front of the clock. I see what you're saying." He feels all around the front of the dresser and finally feels a slight depression about an inch and a half long with a very small lever in it. "Found something, I think it's a tiny handle to pull or maybe push. Here let me try to push."

He does this with nothing happening. He then tries a light pull and finds he needs to use a little more effort. The metal lever pulls out and there is a noise inside the top of the dresser. The panel drops and Elizabeth reaches inside to retrieve another journal.

"Holy cow, I wonder who's this is?" she says as she starts to open it after blowing the dust off.

Matthew puts the panel back in position and replaces the drawer. The two recover the dresser with the tarp before going to the cottage with the journal.

Chapter 19

Arm in arm, Kate and her husband walk down the beach. Buddy is running in and out of the water, trying to catch the waves. Unfortunately, he only gets a mouth full of salt water for his efforts.

"Boy, those two kids sure are tight lately. I wonder what keeps them so occupied," Leonard says to his adoring wife.

"I'm not sure but it is nice to see. I hope another property like this one comes up before we have to head for home. Of course, we can keep an eye on things here through the internet and have Christine look for us too."

"I think this is the best vacation we have ever had, aside from the letdown, that is. You know, I think something will come up for us, despite this turn of events. We always seem to land on our feet," he tells her, much more optimistically.

This is the man I married, Kate thinks, *the eternal optimist right to the end. No matter what comes along, he always comes back, looking at the positive side of life.*

The walk continues for more than an hour. Both their moods are greatly elevated during that time.

Chapter 20

The two close up the shed so Mom and Dad won't know this is where they have been. At this point neither wants to have to explain what's going on. In the kitchen, the two get a drink and go upstairs to read the journal. Sitting on the bed, Elizabeth starts to read aloud while Matthew closes his eyes, sitting in a chair. There are a number of entries that are just personal things that Alice has written and are meaningless to Matthew and Elizabeth. Finally, she gets to a point that is pertinent to the case at hand.

"'Diary of Alice Victoria Berger:

"'I believe that the unrest between my father Benjamin Berger and Uncle Robert is escalating. They seem to be at odds constantly. Uncle Robert really feels that he has been cheated out of his birthright. My father has tried to set things right, but nothing less than full turnover of all the inheritance will satisfy Uncle Robert. I have tried to listen to their arguments as discretely as I can but I fear I have been found out by my uncle. He quite suddenly walked out in the middle of one of his tirades and caught me by the door. I tried my best to make it look as if I just got there but I think my reaction gave me away. The look that crossed his face frightens me to no end.

"'My father has been especially nice to John and me all our lives and has always done his best to make sure we want for little. This fact also irritates Uncle Robert as he believes what we are given belongs to him.

"'Uncle Robert sometimes disappears for days on end and no one knows where he goes. Father, however, is working for hours in his work shop. He keeps the door locked with several padlocks and clasps. He only allows us in there on rare occasions. He seems to be working on a strange looking grandfather clock. I do not know what his fascination is with it. Uncle Robert once burst into the workshop and demanded he be given the clock as part payment of the inheritance. Father absolutely refused and threw him out of the room. Since then the room is always locked, even when Father is in there.

"'I asked Uncle Robert what is so special about the clock, but he won't discuss it with me. He just glares at me and walks away in a huff. I believe Uncle Robert is up to something. The way he looks at his brother out of the corner of his eye is frightening me more and more. I have mentioned my concerns to Father but he does not take me seriously. I also see my uncle staring at me.'"

~~~~

"'I can't believe it, my father has died. How am I to deal with this? I love my father so much and now he is gone. It has to be Uncle Robert but the police have yet to find any evidence. I told them of my suspicions, and they have done nothing. It is determined so far that the
~~~~

incident is an accident. Now that he has what he wants, he has stopped staring at me. He knows I can do nothing to harm him.

"'Time keeps going on and the police have stopped looking into my father's death. I get no help from Uncle Robert, despite the fact that his brother was my father. He is not nice like my father was. Dad's sister Willemina Smith, who is John's mother, has taken me in. She has always treated me like I was her child. Maybe this is because she never had a daughter of her own. She married an Englishman who died in a shipwreck several years ago leaving Aunt Willemina fairly well off.

"'Uncle Robert seems to be obsessed with the clock. I asked him about it, and he actually screamed at me. He told me to mind my own business if I know what's good for me. He frightens me. I see two men come to visit him from time to time and when they do meet, Uncle Robert is even angrier than before. Has he hired these men for something? I think these men came to see Father once but I can't be sure.'"

Elizabeth stops reading at this point and looks at her brother. "So what do you think about this?" she asks.

"It certainly looks like Uncle Robert has to be the culprit, that's for sure. There don't seem to be any other people that are suspect."

"Yes, that's what I'm thinking too. It's too bad the police can't—or should I say, didn't—do something about this Robert character. If they had, John wouldn't have died the way he did," she says quite sorrowfully. "It reinforces the fact that he is responsible for John and Alice's deaths when he killed himself."

"Hey, kids, we're back. Why don't you come down and we can get things ready for supper?" Mom calls from downstairs.

The journal is put away, and Matthew asks that she not read any more unless he is there to hear it.

"No problem, Matt, I know you're just as interested in this as I am," she tells him as the two head downstairs.

Chapter 21

I hope you two aren't too disappointed the way things have turned out, Kate says, attempting to comfort her children. "There is always the chance that something will come up for sale. We know that it won't be this cottage but at least it might be in this general area."

"Oh, I think we will survive this," Elizabeth says. "Like you just said, something may come up. If it is meant to be, so it shall."

Matthew has a faraway look in his eyes and is thinking of possible scenarios. He's wondering what their chances would be of making off with the clock and bringing it to another home. That is, if they find one somewhere nearby. He also wonders if it is really stealing, if the new owners never know or find out that the clock is in the cottage. He could always close up the room again and maybe even make it harder to get back into it, thereby safeguarding the treasure.

If by chance, they don't move here on the island, would it be possible to come back at some later date with

Elizabeth and a truck. They could bide their time and when things are right, gain entry and take the clock back home with them. Too bad that, anyway he looks at it, he feels it's still stealing.

There is a pain in his shin and he realizes that Elizabeth has kicked him under the table a couple of times.

"Welcome back," she says to him, "where were you just now? I bet you were daydreaming about living here and being able to swim in the ocean any time you want, right?"

He quickly understands that she has just given him an out. "Yeah, how did you know?"

"It's the same thing I have been thinking since I heard the news."

Kate and Leonard look at the kids and wonder if the conversation they just heard is actually what's going on. The looks that crossed their son's face seemed more like he was thinking of something else entirely. Oh, well, everyone is entitled to their own thoughts.

The supper goes by with the dishes washed and put away. The rest of the evening is spent playing board games. At eight-thirty Matt says that he wants to go upstairs and do some reading. This brings Elizabeth's thoughts back to the journal.

"I think I'll do the same thing."

She gets up and gives both parents a hug before climbing the stairs.

Chapter 22

So what were you thinking about when I had to kick you in the shins?" Elizabeth asks.

Matthew fills her in on his thoughts. "I don't like the idea of having to steal the clock but I don't see any other options at the moment, do you?"

"I can't at this time, but I guess we'll have to do what we think is best when the time comes. Let's read the rest of the journal," she says. This she does softly so as not to be overheard.

"'I don't know what's going on anymore. My uncle has pretty much shut himself up in my father's old workshop and is seldom seen. What is it about the clock that has him so obsessed? I talk with John whenever possible. We are going to wait for him to leave the room one day and see if we can get in to discover what is going on.'"

"'It has been two months since John and I came to the decision and we have just found out that Uncle Robert has to leave town for a few days. We've tried our best to stay out of his way, having no contact with him at all. In two days he will be gone, and John and I may possibly have our chance.'"

~ ~ ~ ~

"'The day has come and gone. My uncle left to go out of town and so, at first opportunity, we went to the workshop door and tried to gain access. We were about to gain entry and who comes out of hiding but Uncle Robert? He screamed and yelled at us for the better part of ten minutes.

"'When we had the chance, we told him we were only trying to help him. He looked at us incredulously and called us liars. In his mind, we are nothing but thieves who are trying to take what belongs to him. Just the way my father did. He said that he would kill the both of us before he would let us do this. I have never been so frightened before.

"'These two men who keep visiting my uncle every number of months seem to be after something. Neither John nor I can figure out what it is. If they wanted the clock, I am sure they would just take it, but they don't, so they must be after something else.

"'I think I will keep a closer eye on things. John is hesitant to get involved and I can't honestly say I blame him. We shall see what happens. September 16, 1907.'

"This is the last entry in the journal. There are no other dates in it to show when each of the entries are made so we are left here hanging," Elizabeth says to her brother.

"I wonder if we should pick a different time to go back to and maybe find out what is going on with the uncle and the two men."

"Do you remember when exactly Uncle Robert gave

the clock to John?" she asks him as she puts the journal on the bed.

"It was a long time after Benjamin Berger died and that was in early 1907. Oh, yes, I remember now, it was in 1924 that John was given the clock."

"Looking back at the records, I see that Benjamin's mother was born in the Netherland's too. That would possibly explain his ties to the man who made the clock. Otherwise, I doubt very much that the clock would have been sold to him. It would have to be kept in the family," Elizabeth explains.

"Alice was murdered later in the year after Robert got hold of the clock. Do you think Alice found something out about Benjamin's death and that's why she died?" Matthew asks, thinking of Alice.

"I was wondering the same thing. What other reason would there be for killing a young girl like her?"

Matthew heads to his room, wondering just how they will be able to set things right. The thought about whether or not they should doesn't even enter into his thoughts at all. Elizabeth, on the other hand, is wondering if this is the right choice they are making. These things have already happened long, long ago. Is it wise to tamper with the past? It has the potential to change many things if they are successful. Some of the things that change may not be good, not good at all.

Chapter 23

In the morning when everyone is finished breakfast, Leonard announces that Christine has called and would like to see them.

"Do you guys want to come along with your mother and me?"

"What is it she wants you for, Dad, do you know?" Elizabeth asks.

"She didn't actually come out and say, but I think it has to do with the search for another property."

"What do you think, Matt?" Elizabeth asks. "Want to tag along? It might be interesting to see if there is a chance to move here."

Leonard thinks that these two children of theirs have really bonded since this vacation started. He's really starting to hope that this potential move becomes a reality. Too bad this cottage is already sold. It would have been perfect. *Oh, well, you can't have everything.*

Matthew nods. "Sure, let's go. Who knows? It could be nice, and we might really like it." In his head are plans for the possible abduction of the clock sometime in the future. He knows this is wrong but feels he will be able to justify it somehow, down the road. What is important is the fact that Alice needs saving and John too, of course. *Is she on my mind a little too much? She sure is pretty.*

When they are on their way to town, Buddy's head is hanging out the window again. There is an air of hope in the car. The family arrives in town, parks the car, and enters the office of the realtor.

"Good morning. What attractive kids you two have, but then again what would you expect from parents like this?" Christine says, shaking the youngster's hands.

She must have forgotten meeting them when they came to pick up the keys for Lilac Cottage. Leonard and Kate know this is probably done to make the kids feel at home, but like it anyway.

"So the reason I asked you to come is that a potential home has come on the market. I'm not sure this is exactly what you want, but I thought I'd show it to you, anyway," Christine tells them.

"Do you have any photos or other information about the place?" Kate asks.

"No, I don't at this point. It only came to my attention this morning and isn't actually on the market yet. The papers are all signed and it will be listed on the sites later today or tomorrow. I thought I would try to give you a chance ahead of everyone else. I felt really bad that you missed out on the one you really wanted. Maybe this one will be suitable for you."

"Well, we have nothing to lose by looking. All right let go see the home," Leonard announces.

The ride to the home is pleasant enough but goes in a direction away from Lilac Cottage. This makes Matthew think that it will be harder to get the clock to the new home, complicating things.

After a fifteen-minute ride, they enter an area with homes in closer proximity to each other than where Lilac Cottage is. They pull in front of an older home, considerably smaller than where they are staying at the moment. It looks like it could use a lot of TLC. The paint is peeling and the roof will need to be replaced in the near future. This is not a good first impression. Christine however urges them to look inside before discounting it.

Inside, the story takes on a much more pleasant note. They walk into a small foyer that opens to a kitchen area. Off to the right, there is an entrance to the living room. In the center at the back of the home, is a doorway to a sunroom that spans the entire width of the house. The view shows the ocean a short distance away. Unfortunately, there are also other houses between them and the water, giving it a slightly closed in feeling. There is a staircase from the sunroom to an upstairs area that has three bedrooms and a small bathroom. It seems to Leonard that the stairway is in an odd place. It's functional but not where he would have put it. The upstairs is not on par with the downstairs and will need extensive renovations to make it appealing to the family.

When they drove up, Leonard and Matthew both noticed that there's no garage, only a carport. This is not what these two men need. A garage is of prime importance to men who like to work on projects. The rest of the tour is completed and Christine asks what they think.

"So what is the price of the property?" Kate asks, getting right to the point.

"It is actually ten thousand more than what Lilac Cottage sold for. But the thing you need to remember is that Lilac Cottage sold for less than it's worth. The main reason for this is that it was a private sale and the owners were very motivated," she says as she looks through her notes.

"We'll talk it over and get back to you this afternoon, all right?" Leonard tells her with his keys in his hand.

Christine nods, unable to hide her disappointment. "All right, but if you want it I wouldn't wait too long."

The ride home is less fun than it was driving out here today.

Kate is the one to finally break the silence. "Does anyone have any opinions on the property?"

"Disappointing to say the least, there is no garage or workshop," Matthew responds. "I know Lilac Cottage doesn't have a garage that's in good shape but we could have fixed that, right, Dad? The outside of the home is rather neglected and the upstairs looks like it needs a lot of work."

"I think so too," Elizabeth says, having a hard time hiding her disappointment. "The sunroom is nice but it's so far from the water. The kitchen is in the front of the house, which is okay, I guess, but I'm not real fond of the layout."

"What do you think, dear?" Kate asks, turning to her husband.

"I think it's absolutely perfect. I love all the work that needs to be done. I think Matt and I will have a great time replacing the roof and rebuilding the upstairs. And just think, we only have to pay ten thousand more for all this fun."

Everyone looks at him in disbelief.

This changes as soon as he starts to laugh. "Ha, ha, I'm only kidding, you guys. We needed to laugh at something so we'd see the better side of this situation. I'll let Christine know that she needs to keep looking, and that we're looking for something more like Lilac Cottage. Of course, you may have to prepare yourselves for a bit of a wait. There is bound to be a place for us somewhere."

A feeling of relief comes over everyone as they all laugh. Kate looks at her husband and wonders what she would do without him. He really is a large part of what bonds this family together.

Back at home—funny how a person considers wherever they are to be home—lunch is made and all is back to normal. But, then again, two of the family are about to embark on a new adventure, only this one is possibly fraught with danger.

Matthew and Elizabeth go for a walk on the beach with Buddy. Both realize that they need to make some kind of plan. They know they'll be going back on another exploratory mission. It's important to get the information necessary to bring about a satisfactory resolution to the dilemma at hand.

"How do you think we should approach this next trip back into the past?" Elizabeth asks a little concerned as the feeling of apprehension takes hold of her once more.

Matthew shrugs. "I really think that we need to find out what Alice was up to in the days before she died. I think this will take several trips. We have to get her and possibly John to confide in us. I doubt that it will happen very quickly, though. She knows nothing about us and won't trust us with any of her deepest thoughts. What do you think?"

"As usual, you're right. How do you propose to win her trust? How long will we have to stay there this next trip? Should we take some food with us?"

"I don't know how to win her trust at the moment," he says with a faraway look in his eye. "I do think we should stay at least three or four hours, this time. Yes we do need to bring food and water with us just in case. We can always hide it."

"What happens if we are spotted by their Uncle Robert? How do we explain our presence there?"

"We'll tell him we're visiting an aunt there. Maybe we can look up some names of people who live in the area on the computer today. I think we have to go soon, though. There isn't going to be a lot of time. We don't know how many trips it will take to fix this. That is, if we can fix it. We'll be dealing with more than just Robert, remember those men he sees every so often. We still don't know who they are. Hey, I just had an idea. Do you suppose it is possible to take a video recorder and leave it there in a suitable spot? It could help us to get more information on Robert and his visitors? What do you think, sis?"

"It sounds like an idea, but I doubt that it will work because the men don't come around at any predicable times," she tells him. "Another big reason is that the only really good place to hide the camera is in the workshop after he moves the clock to it. Although we have a way of getting in there, I think we won't be able to hide it well enough. Once he moves the clock, he'll keep the room locked and will also spend a lot of time in there. If we were to appear in that room while he is there, he'll have his proof that the clock works. If he isn't there and the locks can't be opened from the inside, what do we do? Each time we go we have to leave through the window, as it is. The problem with this is that we have no way to relock it, so he will know someone has been in the room. Have you thought about what would happen if you got caught with the recorder? What would happen if it got stolen and fell into the wrong hands? The entire future might be changed. I really think you should forget anything like that."

"I see what you mean, yes, it could have disastrous consequences."

"I think that we have to make sure that we dress just

like we did on our first trip back. We can only go back while the clock is still in the living room of his house. Once he moves it to his workshop we may have some real problems," she informs him.

"You're right, so when do you want to go, sis? Do you think we should time our arrival to bring us back an hour after we left them?"

"That's a good idea. We did say we would see them in a short while," she says, "Let's try for tomorrow an hour later than we came back. Yes, let's do it."

"Okay, let's head back to the cottage and spend a little time with Mom and Dad, so when we go upstairs later, they won't question us."

All the time the two have been making plans, Buddy has been digging holes and running in the surf. It's time to get him washed off and then rinsed down back home.

The rest of the afternoon is spent hanging out with their parents. Dad, for all his joviality, seems a little forlorn. It's obvious that he is more bothered by the morning's outing than he likes to let on.

"Hey, Dad, you okay," Matthew asks.

"Just thinking things through, I'm not sure of how to handle this problem of ours. I wonder if we should buy something now even if it's not what we really want. We can always sell it again when the right one comes up. Or should we just wait and see what comes on the market."

"To tell you the truth, Dad, I think we should wait. If you buy right now, you may not be able to sell in time to buy the right one."

"Yeah, I think you're right. We could get ourselves into a bit of a bind. We still have almost five weeks here, so a decision doesn't have to be made right now," Leonard tells his boy, amazed at how much common sense his son already has.

"Supper's ready," Mom shouts from the kitchen. "Why don't you two go get washed up? Matthew, can you feed Buddy at the same time so he won't be trying to beg for food from the table?"

"Okay, Mom, I'll get right on it," he says back.

He doesn't mind giving part of his supper to Buddy but knows it's not good for him.

With the evening meal behind them and a bit of family time under their belt, Matthew and Elizabeth head upstairs. Once they're in her room, Elizabeth suggests that they get their provisions together after Mom and Dad have gone to bed. "We need a glass bottle for our water and wax paper for any sandwiches or just put them in a brown paper bag. These are things that are common enough back then."

When the plans are finalized the two try to get ready to sleep. Matthew has his alarm set for one o'clock and, although he's anticipating tomorrow, he's soon sound asleep. Elizabeth, on the other hand, is feeling the edginess. This has the potential to become quite a precarious situation tomorrow. She knows full well that they are dealing with a very dangerous man who has already killed twice and will undoubtedly have no hesitation in killing them too. Elizabeth knows this feeling she has is perfectly justified.

∽∾∽

The alarm goes off softly, and Matthew is up and on his way, quietly waking his sister. The two are sneaking downstairs when Buddy comes up to meet them. His tail is wagging so hard it hits the wall with a thump, thump, thump. Matthew grabs his pet, stopping the tail's motion just in time to receive a lick on his cheek. Elizabeth listens for any signs of Mom or Dad getting up.

Fortunately, there's no one getting out of bed. Matthew shushes Buddy so he'll stay quiet, which thankfully he does. It might be difficult to explain why both of them are downstairs at this time of night.

They make the sandwiches and hide them in the back part of the fridge. The drinks are in the glass bottles, and soon both are back in bed. Matthew again falls asleep quickly, looking forward to another adventure. Elizabeth has Buddy with her and wonders if it might not be a good idea to take the dog with them. After all he might offer protection in an emergency. She decides to ask Matthew in the morning.

Matthew and Elizabeth hang around with their Mom and Dad all morning. They keep them occupied doing minor things around the house. The plan is to keep them busy so that when afternoon arrives, Leonard and Kathleen will want some alone time. The suggestion will be made to have them go for a nice long walk on the beach. Maybe they'll want to go for a ride to town and maybe go out for supper too. The parents might even be convinced to do a little exploring, looking at potential homes. The two are quite proud of themselves for thinking of this plan.

One o'clock arrives and the subtle hints that have been delicately put forth during the last hour or two finally pay off. Leonard suggests that he and Kate go for a ride and maybe look around at homes that may work for their future plans. Another fifteen minutes, and they are on their way. They both have a little chuckle at this time.

"Do you think that their suggestions were low profile enough?" Leonard asks. "They were really trying hard to get us out of the way for a while, don't you think?"

"It really is quite funny how you kind of dragged it out. I thought they would try to forcibly remove us if we had dallied any longer. They really are quite hilarious.

What do you think those two are up to this time?"

"I haven't got a clue, but I haven't seen them this excited for a long time. I'm sure we'll find out before this vacation is over, though."

The two drive off toward an area they have yet to see. Who knows? Maybe there will be a piece of property for sale by the owner that will meet their needs.

"How long do you think it will be before we hear from the college about Matt's application that we put in for him?" Leonard asks.

"I think they said we would hear sometime next week. Why do you ask?"

"If he is accepted and wants to go, we need to have something lined up here. Otherwise, he will have to board somewhere near the college. At least until we have the opportunity to buy something and move ourselves. So far we haven't had much luck. Do you think this might only be a pipe-dream for us?" he says, just a little concerned.

Chapter 24

Everything that Matthew and Elizabeth need is in the clock room with them. The lunch is in a brown paper bag and the rest they are wearing. The clock has been set and the return time ready at four hours. Matthew has his watch in his pocket with the tiny alarm set to go off in three hours and forty-five minutes after they get there. The clocks hands now show ten minutes before two o'clock, just like his watch is. The pendulum swings back and forth and the weights are set to the maximum. The note explaining all is on Elizabeth's pillow, just in case. With hands slightly trembling, she watches the minutes tick by. They go by much faster for her than they do for Matt. He's eager to see Alice again.

The clock comes up to the top of the hour and the room clouds over once again. When the mist clears, it is quite evident that the trip has been made successfully once more. A quick look around and Elizabeth suggests that they get out of the house as quickly as possible. Just as they are about to run, there's the sound of a man's voice as he walks down the hallway outside the room. Matthew looks quickly around for a hiding place. There's a closet at the side of the room and both kids quickly hide inside, just before the person enters the room.

The man mutters to himself. He is clearly upset about something. As the one-sided conversation continues, it becomes evident the he is greatly upset with Alice. This must be Uncle Robert. He rambles on about the nosey teenager meddling into his business. How dare she question him? He is the adult, not her. Besides, she's a female and should know her place.

"So she wants to know about the clock, does she? What would a mere girl know of such things? It must be young John who put her up to questioning me about it, I'm sure. As if I don't have enough troubles of my own. How am I to get that infernal clock to work? Benjamin, I'm sure, made the blasted machine work, so why can't I? I've been at it for months and still nothing. I'm sure Benjamin sabotaged the clock so no one else can use it. I'm going to have to move it to the workshop again if this interfering persists."

There is a curse followed by a crash as an object is smashed on the floor. Heavy stomping echoes throughout the closet, as he leaves the room and goes down the hall.

Matthew slowly opens the closet door and peers around the room, seeing a broken vase on the floor by the table. They are alone and take this opportunity to make good their escape.

Elizabeth feels a little bewildered. "Geez, what an angry man Robert is, I wonder what makes him that way?"

"Darned if I know, to tell you the truth, I don't care. I just want nothing to do with him. We'll have to give him a wide berth if possible."

"Let's see if we can locate John and Alice. They were

over by the water last time so let's go look over there," she says.

After walking for a while, Elizabeth and Matthew look back in the general direction of the house. Off to the right a fair distance away they see two men walk up to and into the entrance of the hotel. They are dressed differently than the people they have seen here and in the photos they have seen of this time period.

"Who are those men, Matt?"

"I don't know for sure but they are dressed in European clothes. I think that's the way they dress in the Netherlands. I could be wrong but I don't think so. Maybe we can ask Alice if we can find her."

"Don't you mean Alice and John, Matthew?" she says, smiling at her brother as he blushes again. She enjoys bringing out this part of Matthew because it happens so seldom.

"Yeah, yeah, that's what I meant, geez."

After about ten minutes, they find Alice in a flower garden. She tries to make it look like she is working in the bed of roses. It becomes obvious, soon enough, that she is watching the entrance to the hotel.

"Hello, Alice," Elizabeth says

Alice spins around slightly startled. It's apparent that she has been caught totally unaware of the two of them.

"Oh, hello, I see that you've come back," Alice says as she smiles at them.

"Yes, we like it here and wonder if you and John can show us around," Elizabeth asks.

"Oh, yes, certainly, it will be my pleasure," Alice says, glancing at Matthew, who now has a huge grin on his face.

"I was wondering who those two men that just walked into the hotel are," Elizabeth inquires offhandedly. "You know, the ones who are dressed differently from everyone else. They seem a little out of place."

The look on Alice's face changes immediately. She looks toward the hotel and then asks Elizabeth a question herself. "What do you know about them?"

"Actually nothing. We only saw them for the first time a few minutes ago. They look a little sinister to Matthew and me, so we thought you might know who they are."

"Those men are from Holland and have been coming here for quite some time. The first time I saw them was when they came to see my father. I think it was early 1904. No, now that you ask, I believe it was shortly after my father came back from a trip overseas in 1903. He brought back a strange grandfather clock with him," Alice tells them. "My Aunt Willemina says they are bad men. She remembers hearing about when she lived in the Netherlands. My aunt came to live here shortly after her brother, my father, moved us to this country. My father died in an accident here when he was traveling to Edgartown. The bar that goes between the two horses came undone from the carriage, and it went down a ravine, killing my father.

"My mother passed away when she was very young in Holland. I was five years old. Aunt Willemina is my father's sister and she has helped raise me. She moved here from the Netherlands in order to be close to us. We were very happy until my father died suddenly last spring. We still don't know exactly why the carriage came undone. They say it was an accident, that a connecting pin bounced out, causing the carriage to veer off. But I think there is another reason rather than just bad luck. I have talked to Uncle Robert about it, but he gets angry and refuses to discuss it with me."

To Elizabeth, this explains Alice's slight accent. Learning all these new details gives her some food for thought. She and Matthew will have to try and figure out their next move when they get back home.

"Do you think these men are friends of your Uncle Robert or maybe they work for him?" Matthew inquires of Alice.

"They arrive here every three or four months. No smiles are exchanged and neither offers to shake hands. I do not believe that they are friends. As for whether or not they work for my uncle, that I don't know either but I don't think so. You see, as soon as they arrive, they all go into the entertaining room where the clock is kept and the doors are closed. I have heard raised voices coming from inside on several occasions. On more than one occasion I have seen Uncle shaking his fist at the men. But the housekeeper has recently been given instructions to keep all people out of the house when the men are here. I think that Uncle Robert believes that I suspect him of being involved in my father's death. You see, he inherited everything when my father died. He and Father did not get along. Since the men started coming here, things have gotten worse," she says with a sad expression on her face. "My uncle has pointed to me on at least one occasion when he has been with these men, and I am becoming very frightened. I think they are up to something bad," Alice finishes, a look of terror etched on her face.

"I wish we could help you, but I don't know what to do," Matthew tells Alice.

Elizabeth gives him a stern look that lets Matthew know not to say anymore. The two are here to gather information and need to stay emotionally uninvolved. If they can't keep their feelings under control, it will surely jeopardize the task they have chosen to undertake.

As Alice has been revealing the facts, it has become clear to Elizabeth that this is indeed a very dangerous situation. She feels more than ever that she and Matthew can easily become casualties here too. The feeling of dread becomes more predominant, over-riding her common sense somewhat. She knows that they have to step back from the situation. It's imperative to think things through from the safety of their own time. Elizabeth decides to ask her own questions in order to get as many facts as possible.

"Do you know anything about the clock? Is it special and, if so, why? I think you need to be careful, going by what you have told us," Elizabeth tells her, trying to stay detached but having a difficult time doing so.

"The clock *is* special. My father said it is, but he never indicated why. It's the men who scare me, though. My uncle doesn't like me or John, but I doubt he would hurt me. Do you?"

Elizabeth shakes her head. "I'm am not so sure about that. But I do believe something is afoot, and it makes sense to be careful. You never know what others are capable of, so promise me you'll be careful, all right?"

"I will. Maybe we should find John to let him know too."

With Alice leading the way, they hurry to find John. Their route takes them near a home she tells them is called Lilac Cottage. It looks considerably different than it does in their time. The basic structure is the same but over the years there must be some changes that are made. Seeing the cottage, reminds both Matthew and Elizabeth just how far they have come. It gives them both a queasy feeling in the pit of their stomachs.

"There he is, over by the hotel's dock, he must be cleaning the boats," Alice says, bringing the two back to their present reality.

Matthew looks at Elizabeth in surprise. It's strange seeing a rather large dock in a spot where there is nothing in the future. He wonders what will happen to it. They both know that the hotel burns down in about thirty years.

So it's possible that the dock is removed or sold at some point.

"John, come with us, we need to talk to you," Alice calls out.

John runs over, smiling at Elizabeth and Matthew. Alice explains what the three of them have been discussing. "Do you know anything about the clock or why those men are here?" she asks him.

"To tell you the truth, I don't know anything more about the clock than you do, or about the men from Holland. I have noticed Uncle Robert look at Alice with an angry expression on his face, though. I too believe that Alice should be careful. Some of the questions that she has asked, I'm sure have aggravated the man. This is because they suggest an accusation of guilt in his direction concerning the death of her father."

"What do you think we should do next?" Alice asks.

"I think we need to get more information on both the clock and the visitors," Elizabeth volunteers. "We need to find out what is so special about the clock and why these two men are here. They can be either working for Robert or they could be partners in some endeavor. Alice said that her uncle yelled at the men, which leads me to believe that they may work for him. What do you think, Matthew?"

"I think you're right and we need to find this stuff out. Is there any way we can overhear what the three are saying to each other?" Matthew asks the others, glancing at Alice.

Elizabeth catches this, of course, and thinks that Matthew is too attracted to Alice. She knows this is not a good thing. How on earth could something like this work? He would have to stay in the past or keep visiting her. No, not a good idea at all, she will have to talk to him about it.

"The three are probably with the clock right now," John says. "Maybe we can go near the window at the rear of the house. It's not far from the hotel. We can listen to what they are saying."

The four take a long route around and approach the house from the rear. Sneaking close to the corner of the home, they work their way over to the window of the room where the clock is. As they near the closed window, they can hear voices coming from the room.

At this point a man in the employ of Uncle Robert comes around the corner of the house carrying garden tools. The four immediately get up and walk away. The man has seen them but only after they were already standing. Alice turns around and walks back to the man, talking in a low voice. The conversation goes back and forth and concludes with the man nodding to Alice. She rejoins the rest of the group as they walk away.

"What did you say to the gardener?" John asks.

"I asked him not to say anything to my uncle about us being by the house. He was my father's employee before he started working for Uncle Robert. His loyalties lie toward me instead of our uncle, whom he does not like. We should be safe, from him at least," Alice says for the benefit of Matthew and Elizabeth.

"So, now what do we do?" Matthew inquires. "We can't find out anything about the three of them if we can't hear what they're saying. Does your uncle have any notes or records of his dealings with the clock or the men? Better yet, are there any notes or papers that your father kept about the clock?"

"I saw my father writing in a journal on occasion when he was working with the clock, but I have yet to find it. I don't think my uncle knows where it is either. Otherwise he wouldn't be so upset about the clock and its uses. I have never seen any papers with notes concerning his dealings with those men either," Alice declares.

"Just what is it about the clock that makes it so important?" John demands. "It's just a time piece, how can it be anything else. I don't understand why they are in such a state over it. As far the journal is concerned he must have hidden it somewhere. I think he was worried that someone else may have been interested in the clock too. Exactly where he would put it, I have no idea."

"I guess we're right back where we started. I doubt it would do us any good following the two men when they leave," Elizabeth says and immediately regrets voicing this opinion.

She realizes that she and Matthew won't be here much longer as their time will run out in the next hour or so. If Alice or John starts to raise suspicions with any of the three men, they could be in real danger. She wonders if their interference here could change when Alice is murdered. The feeling of uneasiness comes back with a vengeance. *What have I done?*

"They are staying for a few days at least, if their past visits are any indication," John says to them breaking Elizabeth's train of thought.

"On second thought, I think it may be a good idea to stay away from those men," Elizabeth confesses. "I don't have a good feeling about following them. They look like they are capable of doing some very bad things." "Then how will we find out what is going on?" Alice asks.

"I don't know but we'll try to think of something soon," Matthew tells her.

"I sure hope so," John says. "We have been trying to get some answers ever since Alice's father died suddenly. We both suspect Uncle Robert is responsible because he and Uncle Ben were always at odds. The only one who benefited from his death is Uncle Robert, what do you think?"

"We think the same as you," Elizabeth says. "It would clear things up if we knew more about those men from Holland. Could it be that they are relatives and here to make some business investments? Have you asked your uncle about this? They were here before your father died, weren't they?"

"Yes," Alice admits. "They came here after my father brought the clock back from Holland. They were very friendly with my father when they first came. I don't know that my father trusted them, though."

A tiny beep is heard.

John looks at Matthew. "What's that noise?"

Matthew shrugs. "I don't know. Maybe a bird chirped nearby."

"Oh, I just remembered we have to go to a friend's house for a little while," Elizabeth says. "We will be back as soon as we can, all right? Come on, Matthew."

But Matthew would rather stay, judging by the way he's looking at Alice.

"Come on, Matt, we have to go."

Finally, Matthew is able to pull himself away and follow Elizabeth. Finding a place that is out of sight, they wait for ten minutes. Suddenly everything goes cloudy and when things clear up, they are back in the clock room.

"Matthew, I think we need to talk. You seem to be getting way too attached to Alice, and it has to stop," she says rather sternly. "You can't get involved with someone from another time period. You know this, don't you?"

"Why not? I could always go back to her time four days at a time. I don't think it would hurt much."

"Matthew, you're not thinking this through properly. A situation like this can't last, something will go wrong and you might get stuck in the past. It seems nice right now because of Alice but we don't belong there."

"I guess so. It's just that I've never met anyone like her before."

"I know she's very pretty, but it's not meant to be. So you have to control yourself, all right? Please," she pleads.

"Okay, you win," he says, looking at his watch. "The amount of time that has passed on my watch is four hours. Let's see what it is on the alarm clock in your room."

Entering her bedroom, the two see that only a few minutes have passed since they left.

"We just made this day four hours longer. I bet by this evening we're going to be pretty tired," she says, thinking a nap may be in order.

"We have some time to ourselves before Mom and Dad come back home. Why don't we try to figure out how to stop Alice's murder? Right now, I still think that the uncle is the prime suspect. When we first got there, we overheard him talking about her like he is real angry with her. He is the only person so far that could have killed Benjamin Berger that we know of. It's likely that he is the one who is going to kill Alice. So how do we stop him?"

"I think that the only way to do it is to catch him red-handed in the act. We've got to stop him while he is attempting to murder her. We know when and where it takes place, so all we have to do is be there to prevent it. He won't use a gun or a knife, because there aren't any wounds on her when they find her on the beach. That means he does it with his bare hands, what do you think?"

"So far as I can see, I don't think that we have any choice. We haven't found out anything other than the fact this man is the murderer. There is no one else, the visitors could be in his employ but I get the feeling that they aren't. They wouldn't have arguments with him if they worked for him. Robert isn't nice at all to Alice and obviously doesn't like her in the least. The frustration he has with her must get worse. I know she wants to ask him about the clock and about those men. Maybe that's what finally drives him to kill her. Let's go back on the computer and see what the time of her death is and wait ahead of time for him. Do you have any ideas how we can stop him," he asks.

"We could get a baseball bat and hit him in the shins as he chases Alice. You have your slingshot don't you? You're a real good shot with it and, if all else fails, we can always start yelling. I doubt he will proceed if he knows there are witnesses. Of course, he could then just postpone things. If he's seen by us we could threaten to expose him, thereby preventing him from doing harm to Alice later," Elizabeth says almost out of breath.

"All right let's check the computer."

After a few minutes, they have an answer. The time of death is estimated at eleven o'clock in the evening of September 16, 1907, which turns out to be a Monday.

"I wonder what she is doing out so late at night," Elizabeth asks.

"I have no idea. As a precaution, I think we should get there about two hours ahead of time. That way, we can set the time there for three hours just to be safe," he tells her as his mind continues to look for more ideas.

"Sounds like a good plan to me," she agrees, lying on her bed and closing her eyes.

Matt decides to go to the back of the cottage and relax in one of the loungers so he can think things through. This he does for a while then falls asleep dreaming of saving Alice.

Chapter 25

"Hey, sleepy head, have you had a hard day?" Mom calls out through the kitchen window.

Matthew wakes with a start, slightly disorientated. It takes a minute to get his bearings and when he does, he smiles at his mom.

"I guess I must have zoned out for a bit."

Buddy, he finds, is just lying on the sand beside him. He has no idea of how long he's been there.

"So what did you and Dad do today?"

"We drove around for a while, looking at various areas. Your father and I wanted to see if there is anything of interest for sale, but we came up empty handed," she informs her son.

Elizabeth walks into the kitchen, and it's clear from her face that she too has just had a nap.

Kate wonders why both of her kids are tired enough to require naps at the same time. Maybe all the fresh air and activity on the beach just wore both of them out. Truth be known, she wouldn't mind one herself. The day so far has been a little disappointing, as have all the ones since they found out the cottage has been sold. Oh, well, maybe something will come up, although she has a feeling nothing will.

Matthew and Elizabeth go for a walk after supper to discuss their options. They are about to go when Leonard asks if they would mind the parents tagging along.

"We would love to have you with us. I'm sure Buddy wants to play," Elizabeth says in return.

The situation won't change any in the short time they'll be on the beach. The time to return to the past is quite adjustable because they can pick whatever time works best for what they have in mind.

Matthew, on the other hand, wants to get back and help Alice. She's on his mind a lot, even though he knows this isn't the best thing for his peace of mind. Maybe he should stick to playing the hero and leave it at that.

For the next little while, everyone's mind is on other things. Buddy, as usual, has a great time chasing the gulls and the occasional crab. He doesn't try too hard with the crabs because he remembers what happened last time he caught one. The family is happy being here together. This kind of vacation is what memories are made from. As evening comes, it's time to go back to the cottage. Washed off and dried, the dog lies in front of the fireplace, enjoying the warmth. With Dad and Mom both reading a book, the pair excuse themselves and go upstairs.

"So tell me, have you come up with any plans to help Alice yet?" Elizabeth asks her brother.

"I think that I have a pretty good plan of action. We know approximately what time the murder takes place, so we get there two hours early. We also know where it takes place, so we will hide and wait for Alice to run by.

While she is running past us we jump out and confront the murderer, Uncle Robert. We'll tell him that we will go to the police if any further attempts are made on Alice's life."

"Why don't we just go to the police and tell them what is about to happen? If we stop him, why don't we tell the police about it and have him arrested right away?"

"What happens if they first check out who we are? We have no records of birth or residence there. What happens if they hold us for questioning and we disappear from the cell they have us in?"

"Oh, yeah, I see what you mean. We could get hold of something there to fight him off if we have to, right?" she suggests to her brother.

"I guess we could do that as long as it doesn't get too out of hand. I have no desire to accidentally kill the man. He is a criminal or is about to be, but I still couldn't do that."

"So when do you want to go?

"Soon, very soon, we need to wait for Mom and Dad to go out again, though. I want to prepare things ahead of time because we don't know what we'll run into," he tells her, rather emphatically.

☙☙☙

The next few days are spent planning and waiting for the right time to come. Even though they will only be gone for a few minutes real time, they have no idea if they will need more time here or in the past to work things out properly.

Much of the time is spent doing things with their parents so that, when the opportunity comes, Mom and Dad won't think anything is out of the ordinary.

Buddy is happy because he gets to go to the beach and play even more than normal.

Matthew, during a lull, goes into the shed and explores a little more. He finds a few interesting items hidden at the back. There is a free standing full length ornate mirror made from a beautiful dark wood. He finds another dresser that seems to be a match to the one they found earlier. This one however does not have any hidden compartments. There are several other things of interest that would look great in the cottage.

"I wonder why these things are stored away when they could be used? They must be very valuable pieces, so why waste them?" Having seen pretty much all there is to see, he leaves the shed, relocking it.

"Where have you been, Matt?" Elizabeth asks.

"In the storage shed. I found a few more nice things in there. There is a beautiful mirror and a matching dresser to the one we found, but no hidden compartment. There are a couple of other things there too. They'd look great in your room."

"Oh, nice. By the way, I found out Mom and Dad are going out tomorrow morning. I think that will be a good time for us to go see Alice." She sees Matthew's face break into a smile at the thought. "Hey, don't get too excited about her. You know this can't be what you might want it to be."

"I know, I know."

"Okay, what do you plan to do? Are we still going to wait for Alice to run by and then jump out, confronting Uncle Robert, or have you come up with something else?" Elizabeth asks.

"That's the only thing I've been able to come up with, short of violence, which I'm not eager to get involved in."

"I think you're right. Violence can get out of hand so

easily and then you have to live with the consequences. If something goes wrong, I doubt that we can correct it very easily," she realizes as she thinks back on John being trapped in the past.

So with the plans made, the two prepare for the upcoming event. Matthew looks forward to it as usual. Elizabeth again sees it with that same foreboding that has plagued her since coming on this vacation. The rest of the day goes by fairly quickly and, as Mom and Dad pull away the next morning, the two are eager to get underway. Packing a little lunch and grabbing the slingshot, the team heads up to the clock room.

Standing in front of the clock, Matthew adjusts all the dials to send the two back to September 16, 1907. The two dials that display the amount of time they will spend there are set to three hours. The hour hands on the clock are moved back to eight fifty. When the clock moves to the top of the hour it will send them back to nine o'clock of the day they want. Matthew raises the weights to the top and sets the pendulum swinging.

The two sit and wait for the clock to count out the ten minutes. Finally the room begins to cloud over and, when it clears, they are in the room where the clock sits in 1907.

Chapter 26

Something is not right. That's obvious immediately. Looking out the window, it is bright and it should be dark. Where they are seated is far enough away from the clock to place them in the corner of the room. This is a good thing because the housemaid walks right by the door looking into the room. Luckily, with the two sitting down they are out of the line of sight and the housemaid doesn't see them.

As soon as possible the two slip out of the house with Matthew glancing at a clock on the wall on the way out. The clock shows nine o'clock but it is in the morning not the evening.

"So what do you think went wrong, Matt?"

"I think that I moved the hands of the clock from the afternoon backward to just before nine in the morning. I should have moved them ahead to a little before nine in the evening instead. Now we're stuck here for three hours until twelve noon. I guess we should do something constructive with our time. There's nothing we can do about it now so let's see if we can find Alice or John," he says, feeling just a bit dumb at having made such an obvious mistake.

"What would happen if we warned Alice about what is going to happen tonight? Do you think that we could avert the murder?" Elizabeth wonders.

"To tell you the truth, I think it would just postpone things, and it would just happen on another day."

"Yeah, I think you're right, let's go see where they are," Elizabeth tells him as she scans the area around the hotel. She starts walking toward the water and then nearer to the dock. The two continue to search for about ten minutes with no success.

"I wonder where they are?" Matthew asks.

He sees a group of people next to a number of boats that are tied up near the shoreline about a hundred yards from the dock. The two walk over near the group trying to see if they can spot Alice or John. On the far side of the gathering, they see John talking animatedly with an older man. The man it turns out is the uncle, and he does not look very happy. The two try to maneuver themselves closer so they can hear what John and his uncle are arguing about.

"You tell me where she is, young man, or my sister will be hearing from me," Uncle Robert yells at John.

"I tell you, I don't know where Alice is. She said she had to go somewhere but didn't tell me where that was, I swear," John shouts back, quite exasperated.

At this point, the uncle storms off, heading toward the hotel. When the way is clear, Elizabeth and Matthew signal John. He walks away from the others, heading over to them.

"What did your uncle want with Alice?" Elizabeth asks.

"I think it has something to do with the death of her father and the clock Uncle Robert has."

Elizabeth blinks. "Does she actually accuse Uncle Bob of being involved in her father's death?"

"Yes, she has always thought that he knew much more about his brother's death than he let on. Alice has asked him what is so important about the clock too and why she didn't inherit it rather than him."

"Where is Alice, do you know? We would like to talk with her. We actually think that she might be in danger. Uncle Robert we feel may have it in for her," Matthew says, with a great deal of concern in his voice.

His sister gives him a sharp look, conveying her displeasure, a look he misses completely.

"Alice had to go somewhere, but she didn't say where. She was upset when she left, though, and was gone at nine this morning. I'm sorry, but I need to see my mother and warn her about Uncle Robert," John tells the two as he starts to walk away to his home.

"I wonder where Alice went," Matthew says to his sister.

"I have no idea. I sure hope everything is okay. Matthew, I thought we agreed not to warn Alice about our suspicions."

"I'm sorry it just slipped out before I had a chance to even think about it."

"Oh, well, I guess it's too late now. I think we need to concentrate on finding Alice and keep an eye on the uncle. Do you have any ideas about where we should look, Matt?"

"I think we should listen by the window again. Maybe we'll hear something that will give us a clue."

They head for the house and work their way around the back. Sitting on the grass on either side of the window, they hear the voice of the uncle on the telephone. Not many people in this time period have telephones, only people with money.

He is obviously upset with whoever he is talking to.

"I know, I know. What is it you want from me?" A short pause. "I'm trying my best and can't figure it out," he yells. There is silence for a moment and then he starts again. "No, you can't take it. It's mine, and if you want to use it after I figure it out, fine. Who knows if it actually works anyway? It might have been something else that my brother did and have nothing to do with the clock itself. Quit bothering me for a while and I will see what needs to be done. I have to find my niece and have a word with her," he yells, hanging up the phone's ear piece with a crash and stomping out of the room.

"Let's get out of here before we're discovered," Matthew whispers as he gets up.

When they find a spot where they won't be overheard, a conversation begins, discussing the things they have just found out.

"What do you think he was talking about to the person on the other end of the line?"

"I'm sure they were talking about the clock. He hasn't figured out how to make it work yet and has a suspicion that maybe it doesn't do what they think at all. He refuses to give the clock to the other person. He told them that if it does do what they think it does, they can use it for their own purpose too. But he doesn't sound very sure of this being the case," Matthew states.

"What do you think they want to use the clock for?"

"I have no idea, but he is looking for Alice and it doesn't sound good. He is very frustrated, that's one thing for sure," Matt tells her.

"Who do you think he was talking to? Do you think it might be those men from Holland?"

"It could be, but there is no way of knowing for sure. It has to be someone who knows something about the clock. I wonder if they suspect what the clock really can do or are they guessing at things," Elizabeth speculates.

With this, the two take a walk around the general area.

"This place here is quite a distance from town. If Alice went to see someone there, she would have to get a ride. Are there any other houses nearby?" he asks. "Gosh, I wish I hadn't made the mistake with setting the time on the clock. We wouldn't have to spend all this time here for nothing."

"That's okay, Matt, it hasn't been a total waste. We found out a few things about the uncle. We know he is involved with someone and that it has to do with the clock. The uncle is trying to figure out how to make it work and must have some idea as to what it does. They have plans to use it for a specific purpose that's for sure. The person wants him to give it to them because he hasn't had any luck with it."

"You're right and the uncle wants to talk to Alice quite badly. Maybe he finds her tonight and kills her. I so wish I had gotten things right," he repeats with a sigh.

"We can make the trip back here whenever we want so it really doesn't matter that much. So don't go beating yourself up over it," Elizabeth says, trying to console him.

The two walk around as many homes as they can in the area but see no sign of Alice anywhere. With only an hour left before they will be taken back to their own time they still have no idea where Alice is. John has not been seen either, which concerns them considerably.

"Do you suppose that because we have been coming back in time more than once already, we may have disrupted history? Do you think Alice is already dead," she asks.

"Oh, I hope not, what would we do then? I suppose we could always check the internet to see if things have changed, at least we'll know what to do then."

After a bit more exploring, they see John off in the distance. Matthew looks at his watch and notices that they only have fifteen minutes left. "There's John but we don't have much time left. What do you want to do?"

"Let's hurry over and find out if he's seen Alice. We'll tell him we have to get home and see him later if possible," Elizabeth tells him.

They start out at a run, only slowing down when they are close to him.

"Hi, John have you seen Alice yet," Matthew asks.

"No not yet, I wonder where she is. I'm starting to get worried about her," he tells the two.

The three of them talk for a few more minutes and then the beep sounds again.

"What's that sound I keep hearing from your pocket, Matthew?" John demands.

"Oh, that! It's just a reminder that we have to get home quickly. We'll see you later if we can get back here."

Away they walk, rather briskly, because they need to be out of sight very quickly, or there will be many more questions to answer.

☙❧

The cloud clears and they are back in the clock room. No one is in the cottage. The two of them check the internet to see if the death of Alice has changed in any way. When they find out that all is as it was, there is a relief that floods over them.

It isn't long before the two hear a car pulling into the driveway.

Chapter 27

"We're home, where are you?" Mom calls out. The voices of Matt and Elizabeth come from the back of the cottage where the loungers are.

"We're back here, Mom. What did you two do today?" Elizabeth asks.

Both kids have sunglasses on to hide the fact that they both had a nap. It has been a long day for them, what with the extra three hours added on.

Mom grins. "We did a little exploring on other parts of the island. We drove to Chilmark along the ocean and saw some spectacular homes at spectacular prices too. It was really nice to see and I think you two would like to come with us next time we go out."

"That sound like a good idea. Where's Dad? Did you leave him there?" Matthew asks.

"No, no, he's outside, cleaning some of the sand out of the car. What do you want for supper?"

"Why don't you pick something for us? We love surprises," Matthew says, smiling at his mother.

The supper being finished, everyone heads out to the beach for a bit of family fun. Buddy gets to chase the Frisbee and a few gulls, now and then, as an added bonus. The sun sends its glow across the water as it sets in the western sky.

The waves gently roll onto the shore and the air has a pleasant fragrance. It seems to clear the breathing passages of all the pollutants that have accumulated over the course of time. Stresses seem to be released from both parents but not the kids who have important things on their minds.

"Hey, guys, what's up?" Leonard asks. You seem distracted. Is there something bothering you?"

"Hah, what, ahh, no, sorry…well, maybe a little bit," Matthew says, not knowing exactly what to tell his dad.

"I think what Matt means is that we're kind of wondering if we will be able to move here or not. We have just fallen in love with this place. We know that this cottage is out of the question, but hope something else will come up," Elizabeth tells her father, saving the day.

"Yeah, that's what I'm thinking about," Matt says quickly.

At this moment, Buddy comes over and decides that it's a good time to shake the sea water from his fur. Everyone turns their back and runs away as the spray flies through the air. They all laugh and the tension is gone, momentarily.

Dad puts a hand on Matthew's shoulder. "Don't worry about moving here for the time being. Something is certain to turn up sooner or later. We can always come back if we have to when a home comes on the market. I'm sure Christine will send us the listings when they do, and we can check online ourselves too."

ഡഽഡ

The next morning brings a new day. Matthew and Elizabeth go back to the beach with Buddy so plans can be made to save Alice. By the time lunch rolls around, they have figured out what they will do. Now they need the opportunity to present itself. The rest of the day is spent doing family activities. The following morning Leonard asks Matthew and Elizabeth if they want to go into town with them.

"We need to do a little shopping for groceries."

"Actually, Matt and I were going exploring along the beach, if you don't mind," Elizabeth says.

"That's just fine. You may as well enjoy yourself as much as you can," Mom tells her.

The parents drive away, and Elizabeth starts to pack a quick snack to bring with them as they prepare to return to nineteen hundred and seven.

Upstairs in the clock room, Matthew takes a good look at the timepiece. There is the little door that swings down to reveal the dials that set the date and length of time to stay in the past. He takes a good look at the two little pins projecting from the top two corners of the opening the swinging panel sits in when it is closed. There are two buttons, one on each side of the clock. He presses them in while looking at the front face of the panel. The two pins retract as the two little bumps that are part of the ornate carvings push in. The journal explains this and that is why Matthew knew how to open it the first time.

All of a sudden, it comes to him why the man can't make the clock work. The panel is closed in the past, and Robert does not know that there are dials behind the panel at all.

When it is closed the fit is very tight so it's next to impossible to see the panel. The hinges are also hidden, making it even more difficult to detect. This is a major clue about what has happened in the past. This he explains to Elizabeth when she comes into the room with the provisions.

"That's great detective work, Sherlock. I doubt that I could have figured that one out," she tells him with a bit of admiration in her voice.

Matthew sets the clock to the proper time, making sure that they will get there at the right time of day.

Elizabeth and Matthew place themselves in the room so that they will be out of sight when they appear in the room in the past.

"I wonder if the room clouds over for the people that are in the room already when we make the trip," Elizabeth asks.

"I think it might show a little because when we managed to get John back to his time the clock glowed just a little. You would have to be looking at the clock when it happens or you would miss it. It did that when it was sending him back to his own time, do you remember that?" Matthew asks as he thinks about this.

"Now that you mention it, I do remember," she says.

"There is only one thing that might be wrong with this assumption."

"And what would that be?" she asks.

"We saw the glow because it was this clock that was being activated. The clock in the past is sitting idle and so I don't think it would glow too," he explains.

"You're probably right. So far we've been lucky that no one is in the room when we show up, hopefully it stays this way."

The time approaches and the room clouds over.

Chapter 28

The air clears and Matthew and Elizabeth are in the back corner of the room in Robert Berger's home. It becomes evident quickly that they are alone, which suits the two just fine. How on earth could they explain their presence there, except for the clock, if the man was here? He would know immediately what was going on and demand that they show him how to operate the clock.

The two manage to make their way out the window and then close it again. There is still enough light to make the walk easy. They head to the area of the beach where the murder happens. There is quite a lot of brush and tall grass in a spot near where Alice will run past. This place looks like the right spot but who can know for sure, as things may change through time. The photograph online didn't show the scene very well. At this point, they are approximately an hour and a half early.

"Should we wait here the whole time together or should we split up to cover more area?" Matthew asks.

"I think it would better if we stick together. I would at least feel safer," she says, while her eyes continually scan the beach.

At the moment, there is no one anywhere around, and it is already dark.

"Did you bring the flashlight with you," he inquires.

"Oh, darn, I forgot all about it. I was so busy getting the other things together that I forgot it. I'm sorry."

"That's all right, don't worry about it. I brought the tiny LED one I have. It doesn't shine very brightly but will do in a pinch. I'm sure we'll be okay," he assures her gently.

The time draws nearer and the two decide that it will be best if they keep quiet. Matthew keeps an eye out on the time by shining the light on his watch periodically. There is the occasional rustle in the bushes nearby, but there is nothing to see when they look around.

Matthew is afraid of using the light to scan the area for fear of alerting the uncle if he is somewhere nearby.

The time drags by and, as it nears the moment of the incident, nothing immediately happens. The two sit in the bushes as they wait for another twenty-five minutes, wondering what is going on.

"Shhh, I think I hear something," he whispers quietly while surveying the area.

Looking toward the dock area, they see a figure running down the beach. There is a mist coming from the ocean which is partially obscuring their view. Looking closely, it becomes apparent that the running figure is Alice. There is a voice calling after her.

"Wait, wait, I need to talk to you."

The voice belongs to her uncle Robert. Both now know that their suspicions were right all along. He repeats his call urgently. "Wait, I tell you, wait! I have to explain something to you," he pleads.

Alice runs past their hiding place and, as the two begin to get up, there's a sharp pain in the back of their heads, and they both lose consciousness.

It is sometime later before the two begin to stir. Each has a massive headache forming as they regain consciousness.

"Ohhh, my head hurts, what happened?" Matthew asks Elizabeth but she is not fully conscious yet.

Matthew turns her over and checks her breathing. He feels breath coming from her mouth and puts his fingers on her wrist, feeling for a pulse. It takes a second, and then he finds the strong beat of her heart pushing blood through her veins. Shortly after, she also starts regaining her senses and moans.

"Matthew, what happened to me?"

"The same thing that happened to me. We were hit from behind. The noise in the bushes must have been someone sneaking up on us," he tells her.

"How long were we out?"

"I don't know but it must have been quite a while because I just noticed that we are back in the clock room. When we saw Alice running past us on the beach we had less than half an hour left before the clock brought us back. Maybe only twenty five minutes. How long we have been out is anyone's guess. Is it normal to be out that long when you're knocked unconscious?"

"All I know is that I have this great big headache. Do you think that I could have a concussion, Matt?"

"Let's go online and see what the symptoms are."

After doing this, they find that they don't have any of the symptoms described. They check each other's heads and only find a bruise with no cuts.

"I think that we're lucky it wasn't worse for us," he tells her as he gently rubs his head.

"Who do you think did this to us? As far as I can

figure it out it has to be those bloody Dutchmen. They're the only other people involved in this that we know of. I bet that they're partners with that horrible Uncle Robert character. You know, it's always possible that he's working with someone else too. We really don't know who the man associates with. Check and see online if the death of Alice is still the same as it was," Elizabeth says with a furious look on her face.

Matthew scans the information displayed on the screen and learns that the whole story is still the same. There is no mention of anyone else at the scene, which means they were left unconscious in the bushes and just disappeared when their time was up. Hopefully, the perpetrators weren't around when they made the trip back home.

"So nothing we have done in the past so far has changed anything at all," he says. "I just hope we haven't given any of the baddies a clue as to whether or not the clock works. I hope whoever hit us wasn't nearby when we disappeared. Of course it would have been pretty late by that time."

"I guess we should feel lucky that we only got knocked unconscious and not killed too," Elizabeth exclaims. "So now what should we do, I don't think that we can go back to the same time. There would be two pair of us on the beach at the same moment. I'm sure there have to be some kind of rules governing this type of travel."

"I think you may be right about that. Let's see if John is still murdered later on and try to make sure that his Uncle Robert is the only one involved in his death. He certainly is or was involved in Alice's death, but I'm not sure he is the only one now."

"I think we need to heal from these wounds first," Elizabeth suggests. "At least somewhat. Next trip we are going to have to take better precautions, that's for sure."

"Let's go downstairs. I need to get something for this aching head of mine," Matthew says, grimacing in pain.

Chapter 29

Hey, guys, we're home. Can you help bring the groceries in from the car?" Mom calls out from the inside of the cottage.

"Sure thing, Mom, I'll go around the side of the house to the front and carry them in," Matthew shouts from the back of the house. Thankfully his headache has dissipated considerably. "Hey, Dad, how's it going? Did you get everything you were looking for?"

"We did. I hope you're in the mood for corn tonight. We picked up a dozen cobs of peaches and cream. The farmer we got it from claims this is one of his best tasting crops in years."

"Great, I love corn on the cob. Can we have hotdogs with it?"

"You're in luck. We bought some of those too. I'll mention it to your mother, but I don't see any problem," Leonard says with a smile on his face.

They head inside, carrying the bags of groceries.

The meal is prepared with Matthew and Elizabeth

peeling the leaves off the cobs, exposing the brightly colored kernels. Buddy wants to help but no one wants dog spittle on the corn so his offer is turned down.

Both Matthew and Elizabeth still have mild headaches but that's getting better as the day wears on. Both are painfully aware that their attempt to save Alice has been a dismal failure. They also know that a second trip to the same time is probably not a good idea and are at a loss as what to do about it.

There seems to be no solution to this dilemma. Poor Alice, being chased down the beach by that awful man. The look of fear on her face haunts both of them. It is one thing seeing a painting of the scene but another entirely witnessing it firsthand.

"Is the corn ready, you two seem to be off in a daze?" Mom asks.

"Oh, yes it is, just thinking about things. Here, sorry," Elizabeth tells her mother as she gets up to bring the corn to a pot of boiling water. "Do you want me to put all of them in or just half of them?"

"Why don't you put in half? I don't think they will all fit in anyways," Dad pipes in.

"Matthew, your dad and I have been talking and were wondering about something."

"What's that, Mom?"

"We were wondering if you have ever given any thought about becoming an auto technician. You are so good at figuring things like that out and cars nowadays are so computerized that it's no longer just a job. It's considered a highly skilled trade which you might like."

"As a matter of fact, I have been thinking about doing something along that line. Why do you ask?"

"Your father and I filled in an application at the local college for you and we should hear back from them in about a week or so."

"If you applied for me at the local college, that means we will move here for sure, is that what you are saying?" Matthew asks them excitedly.

"That would be great," Elizabeth replies filled with enthusiasm. "Matthew and I would love it if you were able to pull this off. This has been on our mind ever since you first looked into buying Lilac Cottage."

"I get the impression that you would consider going to this college, Matthew, is that right?" Leonard asks.

"Yes, I have been thinking of this already but wasn't sure if you would think it was a good idea or not."

"All right, now all we have to do is wait and see if you are accepted or not. It would help a lot if we can find a suitable home for the right price too," Leonard says wistfully to the family.

This supper, all of a sudden, seems to taste even better than normal. The hotdogs are cooked over an open flame in the fire pit and the corn lives up to the claims of the farmer. When the meal is finished and the few dishes are cleaned up and put away, Leonard and Kate go for a walk on the beach. Elizabeth and Matthew head up the stairs to her room with plans of their own.

Chapter 30

Well I'm glad to hear Matthew is eager to go to a local college," Leonard says. "How about you, Kate?"

"I had a suspicion that he would like the idea. The two of them seem to absolutely love this place. I think we have our work cut out for us if we want to find a property before the holiday ends, though."

"I'll call Christine tomorrow and ask if there is anything new coming up. Who knows? Maybe our luck will change as far as this is concerned."

"Do you think we should take something even if it isn't what we really want, just to get us here?" she asks.

"To tell you the truth I think that might be a mistake. Matthew and I talked about this already. If we buy something, we might end up being stuck with something we don't want. If the ideal place were to come up later, we'd have to either try to buy it too or pass on it. I really feel we should wait. We may have to go home and then come back here if the right place comes up."

"What about Matthew? What would he do?" she asks, being concerned for her son.

"Matthew would come to the college here if he is accepted and board somewhere until we find the right home. He would have been doing that if he went to another college anyway," Leonard says somewhat subdued.

The rest of the walk takes on a more somber tone as each withdraws into their own thoughts.

Chapter 31

"Do you have any idea as to what our next step should be, Matt?" Elizabeth asks, becoming very concerned.

"I have been thinking about it. Do you think it would be a mistake to go back to the same time again? I have no idea what will happen if we run into ourselves there. I'm not even sure that it is possible to be in the same place we already are."

"So far nothing we have done has affected the past in any way, except for the knock on the head we got. I wonder what would happen if we went back but stayed in the background to see who it is that hits us. What do you think about that?" she asks

"That's an idea, but do you think that we could stand by and let it happen without doing anything at all? What would happen if I nailed the person with my slingshot and that stopped them from hurting us? Then we would have no reason to go back the second time. Wow, is this ever confusing. Can you imagine trying to explain this situation to someone if they didn't know about the clock being real?"

"I see what you mean," she says thoughtfully. "It would be weird. I'm not sure we have many other choices, though. What can we do to stop the murder?"

"You know we could go back and take the uncle out of the picture by knocking him out and tying him up with a gag in his mouth. That way he wouldn't be able to do anything to Alice. That might be enough to make him think twice about doing anything later," he tells his sister.

"Oh, you mean that he would know he is being watched and would then be afraid of being caught. We could leave him a note too."

"Hey, that gives me a better idea. Rather than knocking him out, why don't we leave him the note? It could say that we know what he is up to and that he will be arrested if he continues. That should be enough to make him stop. What do you think of that, sis?"

"I think that's a great idea. There would be less chance of something going seriously wrong if we do that. Way to go, Matt, I knew you could do it."

"It was you that got me to thinking of it, so I can't take all the credit. I think we make a great team together," he says, smiling at his sister.

"I'll go and write up the note. I think that I'll use a pencil though. That is what they have back then, right?"

"You're right. I doubt they had ballpoint pens back then," he says.

Elizabeth takes out a blank sheet of paper and begins writing. She stops crossing out a word then continues with a rough draft. When she is satisfied with the letter, she writes the whole thing out in a new sheet. Matthew reads it over and gives his approval. The letter is short and sweet. It states that they know he is planning to kill Alice and if he does he will be reported to the police.

"I think we should leave the note in an envelope addressed to Robert Berger. We can travel back to a time a day before the murder and arrive there at two or three in the morning and leave the note on the desk where the clock is."

"There is only one problem that I see with doing it that way," he says.

"What is wrong with it?"

"If we leave it in the clock room, I think it might confirm that the clock does indeed work the way he suspects. It will make it that much harder for him to give it to John later on. I think we should arrive in the daytime and deliver the note to the housekeeper at the front door. I'll wear a hat to somewhat obscure my face. This way he won't be able to identify me from when we are knocked out, in case he answers the door. What do you think of this plan?" he asks.

"Yeah, you're right. When do you want to go, Matt?"

"Let's go right now while Mom and Dad are out on the beach. We'll stay there only one hour and then come back, that should be plenty of time. Besides, that's the shortest time we can stay there anyways."

With that, the two head for the clock room and Matthew makes the adjustments to the dials under Elizabeth's watchful eye. When they are ready to go, they get into position just as the room clouds over and they are in the past once more.

Chapter 32

They appear in the corner of the room behind a table which they found on their first trip back. This gives them at least some safety against detection.

The two climb out the window, when they see it's clear, and make their way around to a spot near the front of the house. Matthew wears a rather large brimmed hat that covers much of his face as he goes to the front of the house alone. This hat has been borrowed from one of the locals here and will be returned shortly. Hopefully, the owner of the hat won't see Matthew with it before he's finished his little errand.

He knocks on the door and, after a minute, the housekeeper opens it. He hands her the envelope turning around and walking away before she can ask anything or get a good look at him. He and Elizabeth meet up a fair distance from the house. After taking back the hat, they quickly walk toward an area where Elizabeth thinks they might run into John or Alice.

A breeze is blowing gently off the ocean, cooling off the effect of the warm, end-of-summer sun. Looking around, it is obvious why the hotel has been built here. The scene inland shows a wooded area extending a considerable way in every direction. There are a number of dwellings in close proximity to the hotel. Plenty of things are here for the guests to do, keeping them entertained. A little town is not too far away, in case they need something the resort can't supply. The ocean views are magnificent and there is even a tour boat for hire. There are many private boats tied up at the dock as well.

Guests staying at the hotel wander along the water's edge. The bathing suits cover the ladies almost completely and the men have sleeveless tops with knee length bottoms. The ladies closer to the hotel wear full-length dresses and beautiful hats and most of the men wear either suits or shirts with ties and a sleeveless sweater. No one dresses in anything like they do in present times. There are, of course, youngsters who are more casually dressed but they are, more than likely, locals.

The ocean is calm and seems to go on forever. The hotel is white clapboard with black shutters on either side of the windows, giving the whole scene a feeling of peace. Only problem is that for these two there is little peace to be had at the moment. They are on a mission and know that they cannot be distracted from it. There is an anxiety that keeps the two moving, constantly looking for either John or Alice.

Matthew wishes that he had allowed more time here so he could see more of Alice. Elizabeth notices this unrest in her brother and wishes she knew how to make him see the futility of it. She is sure he will see this on his own eventually, though.

There seems to be no sign of either of them. The two

men from Holland are coming out of the hotel and heading toward the uncle's home. The men look around carefully, as if trying to see if anyone is watching them, at least this is what it looks like to Elizabeth.

"Hey, Matt, did you notice the Dutchmen are heading to Robert's house?"

"Yes, I did. I wonder what they are up to. Do you think that Robert will show them the note we wrote?"

"Let's get to the window in the clock room, maybe we can overhear something," she suggests.

The two run as quickly as they can without attracting too much attention to themselves. Once they are by the window they sit down, trying to listen to voices inside. There is a heated conversation going on. It is hard to make out exactly what they are saying because the window is closed. They do, however, catch parts of the argument.

It is obvious that the Dutchmen are upset with Robert and his lack of progress with the operation of the clock.

"We have paid you money as an incentive to work harder on this project and we expect results," one of the men says with a strong accent to his speech.

"I am doing my best. I really don't think this clock can do any of the things that you claim it can," Robert yells back.

"Why will you not let us take it back to Holland? We know clock makers who can disassemble the clock and see what makes it unique."

"Over my dead body. If I let you take it, I would never see it again and it is my clock, not yours. I don't care what you say about rightful ownership. It was sold to my brother, and now it's mine," Robert retorts.

"We shall see about that. Have you talked to that nosey niece of yours yet? She is poking her nose into our business and needs to stop immediately. She is asking questions that we don't want her to know the answers to. The death of her father was an accident, wasn't it?" the Dutchman asks.

"Of course, it was. Why would you think anything different?" Robert demands.

"Because the girl thinks else wise. She thinks that there was foul play involved. The police found nothing suspicious, correct?" the other Dutch voice asks.

Robert sighs, clearly tired of the argument. "They found nothing, nothing at all. It's time for tea and we have nothing further to discuss, so leave me alone."

"One final thing, if you find out how the clock works, we will pay you a lot of money for it. You will be a very wealthy man. That is what you want, is it not? We suspect that the authorities have been watching us, which limits our involvement here, so the job is mostly yours. We do not care how you get the information you need, just get it," the first man says.

With that, they leave the room and, once the men are outside the door, Matthew and Elizabeth hear the door being locked. Matthew looks at his watch and notices that they only have another ten minutes before they will be taken back to their own time. It is a good thing the men left the room because they might then have noticed the clock if it was glowing slightly as the two traveled back to the present.

At this point a thought strikes Matthew. "I wonder, if the men are in the room when we go back to our time, would this clock glow too? Or is it just ours that is affected?"

"I've been thinking about that, and I'm sure that it is only ours because this one isn't running, is it?" Elizabeth says thoughtfully.

"I think that you're right, ours is the only one running. I was a little afraid that it might be possible that all of us near the clock would be sent to our time. If I was holding on to someone at the time we are transported back, would they come with me?" he asks with a little smile on his face.

"Don't even joke about trying something like that. Alice can't come with us back to our time. I doubt very much that she could cope with all the things that will change between her time and ours. You do understand that don't you, Matt?" Elizabeth says, almost pleading with her brother.

"I guess you're right. We better get to a secluded spot we're leaving in two minutes."

They barely make it to the cover of some trees are just getting out of sight the air starts to cloud over and they are back in the cottage again.

Okay, do you think that the Dutchmen have anything to do with Alice's murder," Elizabeth asks.

"Going by the way they were talking to Robert, I would say not."

"I don't think they do either. I think that Robert is the killer. What about Benjamin Berger, do you think he was murdered or was it an accident like Robert is trying to intimate?" Elizabeth asks.

"Alice and John, I am sure, believed that Robert killed him in order to get the inheritance he thought was rightfully his. I am inclined to go along with their line of thinking. He probably was behind his brother's death just like he was or is behind Alice's death, I'm sure of it."

"I don't think Robert showed those two men the letter we wrote. I wonder if he will take it seriously enough to stop his attack on Alice," she asks.

"Why don't we check online and see if anything has changed since we looked last time?"

The computer is turned on and, when the information comes up on the screen, the two are disappointed that the report of Alice's death is exactly the same as it has always been.

"I am starting to think that the past is written in stone and can't be changed by us," Elizabeth says, almost in tears.

"I can't believe this is true. Why would the clock come into our lives if we can't use it to do some good? It makes no sense to me," he states very emphatically.

"I'm at a loss as to what to do next?"

"I've found out before, that if you stop thinking about something too hard the answer falls into place when you least expect it."

"I hope so," she says with a deep sigh.

Chapter 33

The walk is over and Leonard and Kate head back to the cottage. Buddy has had a wonderful time and is ready for his meal. As the dog approaches the family's temporary home, Matthew, in anticipation, grabs the water hose and starts rinsing off Buddy. As he finishes, Buddy starts to shake himself dry with water flying everywhere. Luckily, everyone is prepared for this and is already out of the way.

"So how was your walk on the beach, Mom," he asks.

"It was nice and relaxing. This sure is a nice place for a vacation."

"We just love it here, thanks for bringing us. It will be a vacation to remember that's for sure."

"You're not upset over the cottage already being sold?" Dad asks.

"Elizabeth and I are disappointed with that part but we realize that this is the way things are and nothing can be done about it. If we are meant to be here, something else will turn up."

"That's quite a mature way of looking at things, son," Leonard says, quite proud of his boy.

With this, everyone goes inside and starts preparations for supper.

"Do you guys want to have hamburgers and fries for supper tonight?" Mom asks.

It is unanimous and Matthew goes outside to start a campfire. There is a special taste when an open flame is used to cook the patties on a grill. Kate starts the fries in the oven and, as things are cooking, drinks and table settings are brought out to the patio table in the sand.

The sight of the ocean calms everyone as they watch the waves roll in. There is a gentle breeze bending the tall grasses back and forth and gulls squawk in the distance. The few clouds in the sky drift slowly past on the way north along the coastline. This is a serene scene indeed. Every now and then a little smoke from the fire pit is blown in their direction, but no one seems to mind.

For a time no one speaks, as each is lost in their own thoughts. Buddy has a snooze, lying on the sand near a clump of grass.

Leonard wonders if a suitable property will come up for sale before the end of the vacation. It will make things more pleasant if it happens soon.

Kate looks at her children and wonders where the time has gone. It was just yesterday that they first started going to kindergarten and look at them now.

Matthew looks at the ocean and wonders what causes the waves to roll into shore all the time. At least they are whenever he's looking at it.

Elizabeth wonders if there is a solution to the horrible crime of Alice's murder. How can anyone kill such nice young girl? Plus weighing on Elizabeth heavily is the later murder of John. Did she and Matthew rescue him from being trapped in the past, just to have him die at the hands of someone like that horrible man, Uncle Robert? How can she and her brother come up with an idea to save even one of them, let alone both?

After a time, Mom breaks the silence, by asking if anyone would like an ice cream cone. This is met with a resounding yes. Who wouldn't want an ice cream cone on a day like this?

Elizabeth helps her mother make the cones and Matthew challenges his father to an arm wrestle for the biggest one. As the two get themselves into position for the match, Elizabeth comes over, picking up the one they are fighting over. She walks away, eating it before either can do anything about it. Everyone bursts out laughing as they realize who the winner is now.

The time here has just flown by and there is now less than two weeks left on this vacation. Elizabeth frets about their dilemma.

Matthew, having let his mind drift off into other things, comes up with an idea. Going for a walk with Elizabeth, he tells her what has come up.

"Hey, sis, what do you say we go back to when John is murdered and see who the killer is? I'm sure it's that Uncle Robert, but I think we should make absolutely certain by catching him in the act. Then we can go back and stop Alice's death by coming up with a plan to prevent Robert from committing that crime. I don't know exactly how to stop it yet but I am sure we'll come up with something. We just have to."

"Do you think we can actually do this? So far, we haven't changed a thing and we've been back there many times. We even got knocked on the head. What's to stop the one who hit us from remembering us and killing us, this time? I'm really getting scared, Matt. The feeling I had coming here is back. I think we may be in big trouble. We don't even know who hit us. It wasn't that

Uncle Robert because he was chasing Alice. We think it was those damn Dutchmen but we can't even be certain of this. We didn't see them. Maybe he has someone else working for him. It's entirely possible because those men from Holland are not always in the country," Elizabeth says, almost in tears again.

"I know this is really confusing, but I am sure we will get to the bottom of this without getting hurt again," Matthew says sounding far more sure of himself than he really is. "I'll try to come up with some safeguards to prevent our getting hurt or worse."

"It's a nice thought but it isn't making me feel any better."

Back at the cottage, Matthew goes to his room to think things over. Because he has some thoughts about Alice, he decides to set his alarm again. He is going to go to the beach again tonight to see her. Maybe he can pick up some details he and Elizabeth missed before.

As he lies on the bed, his mind drifts over the events of the past number of weeks. He plans to take another look at both the clock and the dresser in the storage barn. It's always possible that the two of them missed something that may give them further clues. After changing and going to the washroom, he lies in bed, slipping off into a troubled sleep. This whole episode is affecting him far more than he has let on to Elizabeth.

Chapter 33

Leonard looks at his wife and sees that she has something on her mind. "What are you thinking about dear?"

"The application we sent in to the college will be at the post office in a few days. We aren't any closer to finding a home here than we were when we started the search. I think we need to start looking for accommodations for Matthew soon."

"I see what you mean. I'll call Christine in the morning and talk to her about finding room and board for Matt. Maybe something else has come on the market in the past few days too."

"Do you think this will work out for us? I'm not so sure anymore, it seems like there is always something getting in the way for us lately," Kate tells her husband a little dejectedly.

"I'm sure it will work out. If not while we're here on vacation, then it will when we get back home. There have to be other people who are thinking of selling. It's just a matter of time."

He knows that things always seem to work out in the end for them. It is just a matter of not giving up. The search needs to keep going on.

Chapter 34

Elizabeth lies on her bed, desperately trying to lose the feeling of impending doom that is plaguing her. She has felt this way on and off since the holiday started. The two could quite easily have been murdered when the person or persons knocked her and Matthew unconscious. She wonders why they didn't kill them when they had the chance. Is it possible that the culprits thought that maybe the authorities would blame her and Matthew for Alice's death?

Is it possible too that the two were brought back by the clock in time to prevent that very thing from happening? If and when they turn up at the scene of John's murder, will they run into the suspects again? Will the two be remembered despite the amount of time that has passed? Will the fact that they are no older than the first time they were seen be confirmation that the clock does indeed work as a time machine? Will it turn out far worse this time? Should she leave all this in the note on her pillow? Will her parents believe what she has written? Too many questions with no answers. It's starting to drive her crazy. At this point, there seems to be no way out.

This isn't helping her to fall asleep at all. It is almost midnight before Elizabeth finally drifts off, but the sleep is not a restful one. In her dreams, she is pursued by different men with no faces. She barely escapes their clutches and her legs seem to be running in slow motion, just like when you are waist deep in water.

Chapter 35

The alarm sounds softly, and Matthew is up and dressed in a flash. As he heads out the back door, Buddy comes alongside him, rubbing himself against his friend's leg. The two pals make their way to the beach and take up their position. Normally, Buddy would be bounding up and down the beach but memories of the previous night time excursion seem to keep him beside the lad.

"Hey, Buddy, are you here to protect me? Maybe next trip back we should take you with us. At the very least, you could warn us of something that might hurt us," Matthew says gently to his dog.

This idea is starting to make more and more sense to Matthew. Buddy will, of course, have to be kept on a leash, otherwise, he might run off somewhere. A memory of the time that a jerk tried to hurt Elizabeth comes to mind. Buddy had intervened immediately and almost taken a bite out of the jackass. Yes, Buddy will be coming with the two on the next trip into the past.

The air starts to cool and the mist gently glides across the water toward the shore. Buddy becomes uneasy, and Matthew grabs hold of the dog's collar. He is determined to take in all he can from the scene unfolding before him. When it begins, it is all he can do not to focus on Alice.

There she is, running down the beach with that look of fear on her face. Matthew forces himself to take his eyes off her and concentrate on the pursuer. There is that misty hand coming onto the scene but little else so he quickly scans the area to the side and then behind him. There he sees the ghostly figure of either one or two men not more than thirty feet away.

Desperately, he tries to study their features, trying to find something to help to identify them. The men are so misty that he can't see a single thing to give him a clue as to who they might be. He is even unable to determine their sizes as they are crouched down waiting for what is undoubtedly the opportunity to help the uncle. He can't even be certain if there are two people or only one. The mist swirls around making it difficult to see anything for certain.

Surely, he, or they, are in the uncle's pay and are here to help dispose of the young girl. Matthew is agitated almost to the point of jumping up and attacking her Uncle Robert. *How can a man kill his own niece?* he wonders as the whole scene disappears once more?

All the time this is happening, Buddy gets more and more frightened. He lies close to the sand, whimpering and trembling. When the scene disappears, he is on his feet turning his head this way and that, as if looking to see where everyone went.

The boy and his dog head back to the cottage. Once there, each goes back to their respective bed. As Matthew lies there, he realizes that this has been a good idea getting up and studying the event one more time. He would never have known there are one or two other people involved in Alice's murder. He and Elizabeth will definitely be taking Buddy with them.

He wonders if they should make one more attempt to save Alice. Knowing that there are others there may allow them to take up another position in order to thwart the crime. The only thing that frightens him is the fact that they are already on the scene. He is concerned that there may be some sort of problem created by four of them being in the same place at the same time. If something were to go wrong because of this situation there would be no way to correct it. Who knows? All four could be in a terrible predicament. As he falls asleep, he decides that it's not worth, it as the effects may be irreversible. They will have to go back to find out who kills John and attempt do something about it then.

Chapter 36

"Hey, sleepy heads, are you going to stay in bed all day?" Mom calls from downstairs.

Matthew and Elizabeth are roused from their sleep by her calling. They are both a little groggy but manage to answer back, saying that they are now awake.

Elizabeth makes it to the bathroom before her brother, for which she is glad. Sometimes Matthew leaves an unpleasant aroma behind for others to deal with.

Breakfast is made and the day's events are planned.

"I just got in touch with Christine, and we have a meeting with her this morning. I guess we should let Matthew know what is going on. What do you think, dear?" Leonard asks.

"I think now is as good a time as any. Matthew, your dad and I, as you know, sent in an application for you to attend college here this fall. We just received word that you have been accepted, and so your father talked with our agent, Christine this morning. He asked her about finding you a temporary residence in the area near the college. She has found a few places that are available and we are going to see them today."

Leonard clears his throat. "We'll be leaving in about half an hour, so you need to get ready. Christine has also found two new properties for us to look at tomorrow too. We won't actually take any place for you to stay at, until we see if one of these homes works out for us. Is that all right with you, Matt?"

"That's great. The main thing is that we have a chance of moving here. I looked online at the college, and it looks like a really nice school. It would be nicer if we find a home to our liking but that can always come later. By the way, if we move here, do I get a car to drive back and forth to school?"

"We'll look into that once we're here," his father tells him with a chuckle.

With the plans made the group drives into town to see the agent. The drive is a pleasant one but Matthew is eager to relay the previous night's revelations to his sister. This, of course is out of the question with Mom and Dad in the car with them.

Elizabeth notices this and, despite that fact that the feeling of dread is still with her, she is interested in finding out what he knows.

The family walks into the agent's office and are given the directions to three possible places for Matthew to stay while going to school.

Christine pats him on the back. "If you need any help while you're here alone, you can call on me. I don't mind helping you with things that may come up. I know this is your first time away from home, and it may be difficult at times."

This brings a smile to everyone's face, as it is always a stressful time when someone leaves the nest.

With the directions fed into the GPS unit, they drive to

the first address. The room is in a private home, and they are met by a motherly woman in her fifties. Mrs. Robinson is very friendly and puts Kate's mind at ease almost immediately.

"We're pleased that Matthew will be fed as well as housed here. You know kids don't always eat properly when they have to make things themselves," Kate tells the lady, somewhat relieved.

"I have grown children and know that this is a worry for mothers. I'll make sure he is fed very well," she tells Kate with a warm smile on her face.

"We do have two other people that are expecting us so we should see them too out of courtesy. Just to let you know, we are looking to buy a home somewhere in the area. We love it here so much that it will be difficult to leave for even a short time," Leonard informs the lady.

"I understand. There is no rush to make up your mind. If you do want Matthew to stay here, a deposit will be needed. If by chance you later find your home, we can come to a mutual agreement as to a full or partial refund, if I find another tenant."

"All right, we will let you know in a couple of days," Kate informs her.

They continue on to the next place which turns out to be totally unsuitable. The room is in poor condition and the landlord has alcohol on his breath at ten-thirty in the morning. Finally, the third place is nice enough, but not on par with the first home owned by Mrs. Robinson. There are a few shortcomings so it becomes obvious where Matthew will be staying, if they don't find a home soon.

Leonard makes a phone call and lets Mrs. Robinson know that her home is their choice. He asks for two days before making a deposit which is granted. She is a pleasant lady in surprisingly good shape, all things considered and the Janssen's all feeling good about their decision.

"Are you okay with this, Matthew?" Mom asks. "I doubt it will be for that long a time. I'm sure that a suitable house will come up sooner or later."

"I think it will be just fine, Mom. Mrs. Robinson seems like a nice lady, and I can always help around the house if she needs it."

In town, they eat a nice lunch at a place that sells delicious wraps with seafood in them. When this is done, they go shopping for a few groceries and head home. After the groceries are put away, Elizabeth and Matthew go for a walk on the beach with Buddy. The air is warm, blowing off the water, and the sky has only a smattering of light fluffy clouds. The sun shines brightly, causing little glistening spots as the waves gently roll onto the beach with a little foam at the crest. The smell of the ocean wafts into their nostrils, completing the scene.

"It seemed like you wanted to tell me something when we were in the car on the way to the agent's office," Elizabeth tells Matthew.

"Oh, yeah, I wanted to tell you what happened last night. I got up and went to the beach again. I took Buddy with me and waited for the visitation to happen again. I wanted to see if I could find anything new that we might have missed the other times. This time I made sure not to focus on Alice and her uncle."

"Did you find out anything new," she asks.

"As a matter of fact, I did. While Alice was running passed me and the hand was coming into view. I looked around quickly and noticed behind me one or two people crouching. I couldn't make out any features at all, except that they were probably male. They were very vague shapes that had no substance to them at all."

"Matt, do you think it was those two Dutchmen or could it have been someone else?"

"To tell you the truth, it could have been almost anyone."

"I think one, or possibly both, of those two are the people who hurt us when we went to save Alice," Elizabeth tells him.

"Yeah, you might be right, but I'm not sure it's them. I suspect it just might be someone else."

"Have you come up with any ideas on how to handle things yet?" she asks.

Matthew nods. "I actually have. I think that we should go to the day John dies or maybe a day before. We can assess the situation and maybe warn him about the danger he's in. If we have to, we will stop the attack and find the culprit or culprits. Then we'll know who has been behind both John and Alice's deaths. Then we can make a solid plan to go back to the appropriate time, in order to prevent the crimes from happening at all. How, I still don't have a clue, but maybe something will come to me."

"I sure hope so because I don't want to be caught by surprise again."

"Oh, I forgot to tell you that I think we should put a leash on Buddy and take him with us. You remember how he protected you that time. Well, he may be able to warn us if something is going to happen, and he'll help defend us in case of trouble," he suggests quite confidently.

Elizabeth gives a big sigh of relief. "That's the best idea you've had so far. I do remember him defending me with that bully. This makes me feel a lot better already. I was thinking about the same thing a few days ago but I forgot to tell you."

"Let's go on the computer just to make sure nothing

has changed in relation to John's death. We don't want to go back to the wrong time again. Each time something like that happens we open ourselves up to more trouble."

Once the computer is up and running, they check the details of John's death and find that the date is still Wednesday, September 14 1927.

"Well, sis, nothing we've done so far has altered the past in the slightest. Which I guess is good, because that means we haven't disturbed the flow of time at all. I do wonder about one thing, though."

"What's that?"

"If we save Alice and John, will that change things for us too? Will the clock still be here? Will that also alter our timeline much? There are so many potential possibilities that it kind of boggles my mind."

"I see what you mean. It can change things for us and others too. But to tell you the truth, Matt, I think the clock was built for a reason and that we are meant to be a part of it."

"Yeah, I guess you're right. Let's figure out exactly when we want to go back to and make some preparations."

⋐⋑⋐⋑

Time is slowly running out as the end of the vacation comes closer each day. The two realize this, and Matthew makes a suggestion or at least runs a couple of ideas past his sister.

"What do you think of the idea of making more than one trip back on the same day here? We could always make a trip back to last Tuesday for instance and then make several trips back to John's murder from that day. We have less than two weeks of vacation left. Do you think that would work, or am I looking for trouble, trying to double up on trips to the past?" Matthew asks reflectively.

"There should be a plan in case we don't have enough time to fix things the way we've been doing things. I think more than one trip in a day is very feasible. Going back a few days or even a week and then using the clock to make another trip back from there seems risky to me. I don't know if it would even work. If it did work I think we might be in a real pickle if we didn't set the return times exactly right. Having Buddy come back with us is a good idea. This double trip thing scares the heck out of me. The only way I'd feel safe with it is if they're made on the same day, in the present time," Elizabeth confesses. She is more than a little nervous about the thought of what could potentially happen.

"I was wondering about that too, but thought that I'd run it by you anyway. We should prepare for the eventuality of being forced to make more than one trip in one day. It's entirely possible that we still may not be able to fix things in the time we have left. This at least gives us extra time back there," he tells Elizabeth with some of the optimism gone from his usually positive outlook on things.

She nods. "Let's see if we can't make the next trip soon. We don't need Mom and Dad to be gone long, but we do need them out of the way for an hour at least. This will give us time to get ourselves back together in case something occurs to either us."

The next morning Leonard and Kate have an appointment with Christine to see a home new on the market. This works out well for the two time travelers.

Chapter 37

The two make plans to go back to Monday September 12, 1927, two days before John's murder.

"Elizabeth, do you think we should warn John about what's about to happen? I'm sure he will remember us, don't you think?"

"I'm sure he'll remember us, and I feel we should warn him. Do we only mention his Uncle Robert or do we mention those horrible men from the Netherlands too. Then again, there is the possibility that there is someone entirely different in the picture that we don't know about."

"I think maybe we should ask John if he has seen them around at all or anyone else since he has returned. He has been back to his time for a few weeks and will probably know. There is one thing I think we really need to do, though," Matt says rather earnestly.

"What's that?"

"I think we need to disguise ourselves somewhat. If

that Uncle Robert recognizes us, he will know for sure that the clock functions as a time travel device. If he realizes that this is the case, John may be forced to disclose all he knows about it. He might be seriously hurt as well as being murdered. I'm sure the clock will be used by either Uncle Robert or someone else for illegal things. Maybe they already know it works, or maybe they don't. Who can tell for sure?" Matthew says to her.

"I'm sure that you're right about that."

"There's one other thing we need to prepare ourselves for and that's the fact that they will all be about twenty years older," he points out.

"I never really thought about that aspect of things. You're right, of course."

She's glad that he's here to think of these things. They make the preparations to go back in time to see John. Buddy has a long leash attached to his collar but not a modern one.

The three are in the clock room waiting for the clock to reach the top of the hour.

Buddy becomes slightly agitated as he feels something is about to happen. This is, of course, all new to him.

The time comes and, as Buddy whimpers, the room becomes cloudy. When the air clears, they realize that they are not in the same room as they were before. It becomes obvious that John has moved the clock to his own home. This makes sense, as John is now twenty years older than he was when the three first met each other.

To their astonishment, John is in the room with them, a much older version of him, of course. His eyes are wide open in surprise as he gazes at them.

Introductions are made and he soon knows that these are the two people who saved him from being trapped in his past. "I can't thank you enough for helping me. I was really worried that I was going to have to stay there the rest of my life. I stayed out of the way and had to get a job working on a farm in order to support myself. It's hard to believe you are the same Matthew and Elizabeth that Alice and I met so many years ago," John says with a sense of wonder clearly expressed on his face.

"We can understand that. We only have two hours here so we should fill you in on some of the things that we found out online," Matthew tells him.

"On what line, do you mean a clothes line?" John asks quizzically.

Matthew grimaces. "I'm sorry I forgot you wouldn't know what I'm talking about. We have ways of checking things in the future that you don't have now."

Elizabeth clears her throat. "What we want to say is that someone is going to kill you on Wednesday this week. We are here to try to prevent that from happening," she blurts out, regretting this almost immediately.

Buddy, up to now has been quiet, but can't sit still any longer. He walks up to John, wagging his tail and sniffing at John, as if he senses something is different about him.

John throws up his hands. "What do you mean going to kill me? Why would they do that to me? I haven't done anything in the time I've come back. Uncle Robert gave me the clock three years ago because he said it wasn't any good to him. He had it for many years and found it was just a funny old clock, not much good for anything. I only found out the true nature of it when I found the journal hidden in the secret compartment long after I got it."

"Did your uncle not know that his brother knew how to operate the clock?" Matthew inquires.

"He thought there was something odd about it but Alice's dad never told him anything about it."

"Those men from the Netherlands, have you seen them

since you returned to this time? Or have you seen anyone else suspicious?" Elizabeth asks.

"I haven't seen them in quite some time, nor anyone new. Why do you ask?"

"We have been wondering if they are still working with or for your uncle," she replies.

"We are trying to figure out who it is that kills you," Matthew says and immediately realizes that this has not been stated properly.

John's hands are trembling and his face goes pale, as he hears these words again. This is not something a person wants to know about their immediate future. As he appears to think about it more and more, it looks as if he's suffering from shortness of breath as well.

Elizabeth rushes to his side. "I'm sure we can help you with this, John, please try not to worry. We even brought Buddy with us to help. We'll make sure we're here with you during the critical time period," she tells him, trying to ease some of his fears.

John bends down and pats the dog who just loves the attention.

"Is there anyone else that's spending time with your uncle lately?" Matthew asks in a gentle voice, trying to make up for his earlier comment.

"Not anyone that I've noticed. He has been gone several hours at a time these last few days, but I haven't been watching him much. Other than that, I just don't know," John says with a frown, his eyebrows scrunched together.

"Do you know where your uncle is right now John?" Elizabeth asks.

"I think he is at his residence near the hotel."

"Why don't we go have a look and see what he's up to?" Elizabeth tells John, trying to take his mind off the situation.

With that, Matthew and Elizabeth don hats that will hide their identity somewhat. It is only a few hundred yards to the uncle's home and, when they get there, the three come up with a plan of action.

Matthew and Elizabeth walk to the side of the house and then to the window of the room where the clock used to be. John walks to the front door and asks the housekeeper if his uncle is available.

"I'm sorry, John, but your uncle is not in at the moment, and I don't know where he might be," the housekeeper says pleasantly.

"Thank you, Mrs. Bennett, I'll come back later in the day to see if he's back." John goes around the back of the house and signals his two friends, who come immediately. "He has gone out and the housekeeper doesn't know where. I have no idea how to go about locating him so we won't find out who he is with."

"We're only here for another hour so we better see if we can make plans to deal with your uncle on Wednesday," Elizabeth suggests.

The friends head back to John's house and sit in the clock room. A discussion takes place and the three make a desperate attempt to come up with something to thwart the events that are approaching.

"If you come up with some idea after we leave, we can discuss it when we return the day after tomorrow, all right, John?" Elizabeth says.

"I really wish you could stay longer," John pleads.

"Now that you mention it, I don't see why we can't come back tomorrow and stay here till after the incident is supposed to happen," Matt informs the two.

"That's a great idea, Matthew," John shouts excitedly, and the plans are made.

He lives alone so there will be no interference from anyone while they stay at his home. This will make things a lot easier. The two travelers can see the relief on his face. They are sure that the bad news they gave John has been weighing very heavily on him. The time slips by as they make as many plans as they can. Suddenly, the room clouds over and they are back in their own time.

Chapter 38

So what do you think we should do? Should we go back to stay with John today or should we wait till tomorrow to leave from here? I feel really bad for him, Matthew."

"I think we should get some things together and, if we have time before Mom and Dad come home, we'll go back today. If we aren't sure of how much time we have left till they return, we'll have to wait."

Matthew heads to his room with Buddy following him, tail wagging as usual. This adventure does not seem to have affected him at all. Matthew goes to his dresser, pulls out his slingshot, and locates his jack knife at the same time. He would like to take his baseball bat but, unfortunately, it's at home. Even so, he couldn't take it back to John's time with them anyways, as it is made of aluminum. He tries to remember when aluminum became a common material but comes up blank. He fetches his binoculars and heads back to Elizabeth's room with the items.

Elizabeth is on the computer checking to make sure nothing has changed.

"Let's go downstairs for some lunch, sis, I'm starving."

"Good idea, we can see what we can use to carry this stuff back with us at the same time."

Lunch is made and eaten, things are put away, and Matthew heads toward the storage shed. Once inside, he looks around to see what things may be of use in their travels. He spots a canvas bag that can be used to carry the things that will be taken with them. Upon further inspection, they find that there is little that they can use as defense against any attackers. John may have a gun but neither Matthew nor Elizabeth is keen on using this type of weapon to stop the deed that they are going back to prevent. Stopping someone from doing a bad thing is one thing, but killing them is quite another.

"Now that we have everything together, we can go back if we want to. We can set the stay for forty eight hours. That will be plenty of time to make sure the danger is past," Elizabeth suggests confidently.

"That sounds good to me. We can sleep at John's house and wait till the next day to try and find out who all is involved with the crime. Do you know what time on Wednesday John is supposed to die?"

"The body is found in the evening and the report in the paper, printed a few days later, says that he died in the late afternoon that same day. His body is discovered by his uncle in John's home in the room we were in. There were many bruises on the body," Elizabeth says with a tear in her eye.

They have grown very fond of John and Alice too. There is a somber atmosphere in the room while each sifts through their own thoughts.

"Matthew, should we give Mom a call to see how they

are making out. They'll let us know approximately when they'll be home, I'm sure."

"Okay, you want to call her? I'll go and start setting up the clock so were ready to go."

The call is made and, to her disappointment, Leonard and Kate are already on their way home. She goes quickly to the clock room and informs Matthew. They are eager to go back but now must wait for another opportunity. The room is closed up and the pair head downstairs and relax in the living room.

Mom shouts from the front door a short time later. "Hi, kids, we're home."

"Hi, Mom, we're in the living room, do you need any help with anything?" Elizabeth asks.

"Yes, maybe you can help your dad carry in the groceries we got, okay, Matthew?" she asks.

Matt goes out the back door and around the cottage to the driveway.

"Hey, Dad, Mom said you could use a hand, what would you like me to do?"

"Can you get the things out of the trunk and into the kitchen?"

This Matthew does and puts the bags on the kitchen table, looking inside and thinking that he might help himself to something sweet. His mother catches him and reprimands him with a smile on her face.

"So how was the home you looked at today, Mom?" he asks.

"To tell you the truth, it was disappointing. The home is in poor shape with a high price tag. It is nowhere near the ocean and the neighborhood leaves much to be desired. Christine has another one to show us tomorrow afternoon. She says it is a much better prospect for us."

They look at each other and a fleeting smile crosses Matthew's face. It disappears almost as fast as it came.

The last thing the two want to do is to arouse suspicions at this point. They both realize that their focus must be maintained on the problem at hand. Elizabeth signals Matthew that she wants to talk to him, and they go outside.

"This is a good break for us. We need to come up with an excuse for not going with them again tomorrow because, otherwise, it may look like we aren't interested," she tells her brother.

"We can tell them that we want to spend as much time here as possible, in case they don't find a home to buy while we're on vacation."

"Yeah, that could work. I'll see if I can't come up with something else too," Elizabeth tells him excitedly.

"We have to make sure that they don't take Buddy with them too. We need him with us for protection. He can be used as an early warning system."

"Good thinking, Matt, I almost forgot about that part of the plan. Why don't you think the plan through some more and see if there is anything else that may help us to save John?" she says.

Just then Leonard comes around the corner of the house.

"Who is it you are talking about? Did you say something about saving someone or something?"

"Oh, we were just saying that Matt might be able to get a good job when he finishes his education. Then save a lot of money if he is still living at home. Isn't that right, Matt?" Elizabeth says a little too quickly.

"Uh, yeah, that's right. What do you think about that, Dad?" he says a little sheepishly.

"Sounds good to me, as long as we can find a home here, which I'm sure will happen sooner or later," Leonard says as he walks away with a smile on his face.

He doesn't think that's what they were really talking

about but doesn't want to press the issue. He's sure the kids are up to something but feels he should allow them a little slack. If it's anything important, they'll come to him. This vacation has brought the two much closer together, so why interfere with it? This, he decides, is something he will keep to himself, no need to concern Kate with it. She likes to delve into things far deeper that he does.

"Wow, Matt that was close. We'll have to be a little more careful from now on."

"Boy, you sure can think quickly when you need too," he says admiringly.

The rest of the day goes by without incident and, as Matthew lies in bed, he thinks of what tomorrow will be like. He's concerned that they may not be able to save John either. So far, their attempts to change the past have come to naught. Both he and Elizabeth are very fond of John and desperately want to help him. He tries to think of anything that might be of use in this adventure. He drifts off, not really having any ideas to refine their present plans.

Elizabeth also is in bed, thinking of tomorrow. Her thoughts are more centered on whether or not they will survive this next trip into the past. Her hands are trembling as she imagines the worst case scenario.

She turns on the light and sits down on the chair in front of the desk. Taking a sheet of paper, she starts writing a letter to her parents. In the letter, she explains everything that has transpired so far. She informs them about the journal and how to operate the clock. The letter from John is with the journal, and she writes down all about their attempts to save both Alice and John.

Elizabeth knows that, after the initial shock of the situation, her father will know what to do. Like Matthew, he's extremely resourceful. He will figure out a way to help them should something go horribly wrong. At least she hopes this is the case. She offers a couple of solutions to problems that may arise, just in case.

Finishing the letter, she reads it over, correcting a few minor things. She puts the letter in the drawer till it is needed tomorrow. Getting into bed, she feels a little better but not sure all this will actually do any good. If the police are brought in because her parents don't believe the story, all will be lost and the two will die in the distant past. She knows this will be a traumatic experience for Mom and Dad and she's tempted to forget about trying to save John. Things are spiraling out of their control, and she suspects disaster is looming around the corner. Sleep comes slowly to Elizabeth this night, very slowly.

ᏚᏒᏚ

Morning comes with Elizabeth sleeping in later than usual.

"Are you feeling all right, dear?" Kate asks her daughter, concerned for her wellbeing.

"To tell you the truth, I'm a bit tired. I had a hard time sleeping last night. I think I'll have a nice hot shower later and lay down for a while this afternoon."

"I'm sorry to hear that, dear. Do you know why you couldn't sleep?"

"I'm not sure, maybe just too many things going through my head. I'm sure I'll be okay, so don't worry about me."

"All right, dear, but if you need to talk about anything just let me know, okay?"

"Okay, Mom."

Matthew spends the rest of the morning helping his dad tidy up the gardens. As was promised to the owner, they do a little work, repairing a loose board on the side of the cottage then drilling a couple of holes in a concrete pad. It is a good thing that quite a few tools were brought along, including a cordless drill and bits, as they find a few extra jobs that require doing. Matthew always makes sure the batteries for the drill stay charged. The two work together very well and enjoy their time together. Matthew and his father have always had a bond and, as Leonard looks at him, a feeling of pride wells up.

The time has come for Leonard and Kate to meet with Christine.

"Do you want to come with us Matthew, your sister is lying down so you might get bored here by yourself? We could leave Buddy in the house with her so she is safe," Kate says.

"Actually, I think I might go to the beach with Buddy, and I'll leave her a note telling her where I am."

"All right, Matt, just be careful okay?" Dad says.

"Oh, you don't have to worry about me. I've got Buddy to keep me safe, ha, ha," he says quite jovially.

With that, the parents are off to see another property. Matthew waits for them to drive away and, when he is sure they're gone, he goes to see Elizabeth. He finds that she is already awake and, maybe not actually eager, but at least ready to go.

"Are you sure that you're up to this, Elizabeth?" Matthew asks.

"Not really, but I don't think we have a choice. John is expecting us and I will always feel bad if we don't try to help him," she tells Matthew.

The two prepare themselves and head to the clock room with Buddy.

Chapter 39

As the cloud clears, the two find themselves back in John's home. John is not in the room so Elizabeth calls out. "John, we're back, where are you?"

"I'm downstairs. Come here, I have some news for you."

The two exit the clock room through an actual door rather than through the closet like they've been doing. They go down to a landing and then a set of stairs that are the same ones they have been going up and down all summer. This presents them with a slightly eerie feeling.

The two find John in the kitchen in front of an ice box. The two time travelers look at the antique refrigerator with a sense of awe.

"What's wrong, haven't you seen an ice box before?" John asks.

"The ones in our time run on electricity and don't require ice to keep things from spoiling," Matthew informs him.

"Really, how can this be? I don't have any idea as to how that would be possible. Maybe if I get through this, I might make a trip to your time. What do you think?" John asks enthusiastically.

"That certainly is a possibility," Matthews says with very little enthusiasm.

Inwardly, he doubts that this is a good idea. He is not all that familiar with this time travel business and isn't prepared to take undue risks for the sake of curiosity. Too many things could change if ideas are brought back to this time period.

"So what have you found out, that you wanted to tell us?" Elizabeth asks, bringing everyone back to the task at hand.

"Oh, I found out that my uncle went to see the Dutchmen that we saw when you went back to see Alice and me. Boy, it seems so long ago that you were here last. I miss Alice terribly," he says rather sadly.

"Where did he meet them and why didn't they just come to see your uncle?" Elizabeth asks.

"That part, I don't know. The only reason I can come up with is that they only came here to check up on the progress with the clock. I really don't think any of them has a real idea of what the clock can actually do. My uncle never did find the journal Uncle Ben left in the clock, and he also doesn't know about the panel that hides the dials to make the clock do what it does. The pins that release the little door are quite well concealed. He has come here a few times to see the clock, but I always make sure the panel is closed tight."

Matthew rubs his chin. "I wonder why the men from Holland have bothered with the clock all these years. They must really suspect the true nature of it, or they would have lost interest long ago. Maybe they're hoping you will find out how to operate it. That could be why it was given to you. Do you think it possible that they saw you when you were trapped in the past and put two and two together? If they did, they might have remembered you, and now your uncle would finally know for sure that you have been able to make the clock work."

"I don't think so but I can't be positive they didn't see me back then," John says thoughtfully.

Elizabeth steps forward with a raised hand. "At this point, we have no way of knowing. I wonder why they haven't just stolen the clock and taken it back to the Netherlands and then tried to figure it out themselves. That would seem to be the most likely course of action, at least to me. What about you?"

John shrugs. "I have asked myself that more than a few times. I spoke to a constable once long ago. The officer is related to a friend of mine, Gregory. That's the only reason he told me anything when I asked about the Dutchmen. He told me in strict confidence that the men have always been under loose surveillance. They aren't watched all the time but the police do keep tabs on them."

"Why are the police are watching them, did the constable say?" Elizabeth asks.

"All he could tell me was that they are part of a criminal organization. Although they haven't broken any laws here, the police are suspicious of them."

"How long have the police been watching them?" Matthew asks.

"As soon as they came to the United States, they were under the watch of the police, which has now been many years. I'm sure this is why they haven't just stolen the clock and taken it back to the Netherlands. They must suspect that they are being watched."

"At least they aren't nearby, right?" Elizabeth asks.

"As far as I know, this is the case. However, I don't think it will take them long to get here if they want to."

"That's too bad," Matthew says, shaking his head, "it would have been better if they were gone. It will be hard enough to deal with your uncle, let alone wondering if these other guys are around to complicate things. I still wonder if there's anyone else involved in all this."

All this time, Buddy has been sitting quietly, but apparently enough is enough. He barks for a little attention. John leans over and playfully pats the dog. Buddy licks his hand and rubs up against his leg in response.

"All right it's one o'clock, so why don't we take a look around, and see what your uncle is up to," Elizabeth suggests.

"Yes, let's do that. By the way, how long are you staying for? I know that the trouble happens tomorrow afternoon. Do you anticipate being here for a while after that?" John asks hopefully.

Mathew smiles. "We've decided to stay here for two days, if that is okay with you. Not that there is anything we can do about it now anyways, the clock has been set."

"That is wonderful news for me. I feel much safer now that I know that you will be here with me."

The three of them leave the house to go spy on the uncle, with Matthew and Elizabeth incognito. They round the corner of Uncle Robert's house to listen by the window as they have done before and almost run right into the man.

"What are you doing here? Who are these two with you? I don't recall ever seeing them before. Aren't they a little young for you to be loitering around with?" the uncle asks, looking suspiciously at Matthew and Elizabeth.

"They are new guests at the hotel and asked me for directions to the creek by the bridge at the edge of the property behind the hotel. I was just showing them the way, Uncle Robert," John says nervously.

"Have I seen you two before? Take off those hats and let me have a good look at you," he demands.

"I'm sorry, sir, but we have to get back to our parents," Elizabeth says. She turns to John. "Goodbye, sir, sorry to have troubled you."

They quickly walk toward the hotel, not knowing what else to do. Behind them they hear the uncle berating John for being so foolish as to be around children half his age and that he needs to be careful who he associates with. John tries to reason with him, saying he was only trying to be nice, but the uncle doesn't even listen to him. As the distance between them increases, the voices fade and, finally, John walks away too. The three get back together at the dock and discuss the meeting with John's uncle.

Elizabeth is concerned for John's welfare. "I would almost think your uncle doesn't like you or even hates you, despite the fact he is a relative. I guess I shouldn't be surprised at that because he is such a grumpy old man," she says with some disgust.

John sighs. "He has been this way ever since I have known him. Even my mother, who is his sister, has never gotten on with him since the inheritance dispute."

"You can pick your nose but you can't pick your relatives, like the old saying goes," Matthew tells John, at which he laughs.

"So now what do you think we should do, guys?" Elizabeth asks.

"Do you have any friends that work at the hotel, John?" Matthew inquires.

"I do know a girl who works as a chamber maid at the hotel. Why do you ask?"

"I was thinking that we could find out if the Dutchmen are scheduled to stay at the hotel soon, and what their names are. I think it is important to find out their identity.”

“I’ll ask the girl. I think she’s on duty so I’ll go see her now.” And he starts walking in the direction of the hotel.

Buddy, who has remained more quiet than normal, decides that it’s time for a swim. He pulls on the leash and, when Matthew releases him, he runs into the water and swims toward a gull that easily stays out of his reach.

“Why do you want to know about those men?” Elizabeth asks.

“I want to know if they’re going to be here or are already here. They’re dangerous men, and I don’t want to take chances with them.”

“Why do you want to know their names?”

“I have an idea in the back of my mind. I don’t even know what it is yet, but something is there, and I feel that I need to know who they are,” he says.

“Well, let’s hope he can find that out then.”

They go for a quick walk down to the end of the dock and look at the antique boats after putting Buddy on the leash again. Matthew appreciates the workmanship. There’s a real pride taken in the work done to build these beautiful boats. The wood used for their construction gleams in the sunlight. The boats are old to the pair, but, in reality, are new boats for this time in history. Being here is almost like being in a dream. This time period is way past and all the people they see are actually long dead. It takes a moment to wrap one’s head around the concept.

Buddy shakes the last of the water off his body, almost spraying a couple walking along the shore. The woman gives a shriek and steps quickly away.

Elizabeth apologizes for the incident and pulls Buddy closer. “Do you think that we can really change things here, Matthew?”

"I am still wondering about that. So far, we haven't been able to adjust history at all. Nothing so far has been changed in the slightest. Maybe, just maybe, things in the past are unable to be reworked to suit our way of thinking. I wonder if things can be changed and, if we can, how it will affect our time. If the Dutchmen get a hold of the clock and can make use of it, they will use it for their own illegal purposes."

"What do you think they would do with it?"

"I think if I was them, I would go into the past and pull off robberies. I would hide the loot where no one could possibly find it. I would then go back to my own time and retrieve the goods and be home free. They could become very wealthy that way. Imagine how history could be changed if a person used it to go back in time and assassinated someone like Hitler. It boggles the mind to think of the ramifications of such an event," Matthew explains, his mind is boggled by the endless possibilities.

"Do you actually think that would be possible, Matthew?" Elizabeth says.

"About the Hitler thing? I don't have the slightest idea. The changes that would be made might, in reality, be catastrophic. Who knows if it would be good or bad in the long run? But the robberies, I am sure, could be done quite easily."

The conversation stops as they see John walking back toward them.

"What did you find out John?" Elizabeth asks him as he gets closer.

"I found out that the men don't have any reservations at this time. This, of course, doesn't mean that they can't walk in and book a room whenever they feel the need. I got their names, though. Louise knows Andrew at the front desk quite well and he's familiar with those men. I guess they have made a rather poor impression on the staff with their rude behavior."

He hands Matthew a slip of paper with two names written on it. Elizabeth takes it and reads the names aloud.

"Johannus Van Aalten and Hendrick Rouhof, those are very Dutch names for sure," she says. "Which one is which?"

John repeats what Andrew told Louise, giving a description of each man.

"Let me have the paper for safe keeping, all right, Elizabeth?" Matthew asks, holding out his hand, receiving the paper, and putting it in his pocket.

"Why do you need those names Matthew?" John asks his new friend.

"He doesn't know yet, he just has an idea that it may come in handy," Elizabeth says for Matthew.

John nods. "I'm hungry, do you want to come back to my home and have something to eat?"

"Yes, please, that sounds wonderful," Elizabeth tells him.

The three enter John's house and sit on wooden chairs at a simple wooden table. John goes to the ice box and removes a small portion of butter and a block of cheese. There is a piece of cured meat brought out and a loaf of homemade bread. John proceeds to slice both the meat and cheese and brings everything to the table as well as plates and utensils.

A small bottle of milk is placed on the table and poured into glasses. The meal is a simple one, but the taste of the meat, cheese, bread, and butter is a real treat for the two from the future.

"This is absolutely wonderful," Elizabeth tells John with much enthusiasm.

"I think that in your time you must have much nicer

things than these meager foods," John replies with an air of disbelief.

"We do have a much larger variety of things but the things we have don't taste anywhere as nice as your food," Matthew informs John as he places a few more items on his plate.

"Really? This surprises me."

The meal is finished, and Elizabeth washes the dishes for John. The three retire to a simple living room that is sparsely furnished with things that are fairly old, even for this time.

"I'm at a loss as to how to proceed," John confesses.

Matthew leans forward, looking around the kitchen. "Things will come to a head tomorrow afternoon, and I think that, if possible, we should try to set up a means of defense. I brought a slingshot with me which might come in handy. Do you have anything that you can use to defend yourself with?"

"I don't have any firearms, if that is what you are asking. I could get a hold of an axe, but otherwise there is little that I have for that purpose. I have never been one for violence," John states, clearly worried.

"I think that as long as we're here and can catch him before he has a chance to really do anything, we may be able to stop him in his tracks. We'll then be witnesses that could have him put in prison. I'm sure this will be enough to deter him from any action in the future," Matthew says with more confidence than he actually feels.

"Yeah, he doesn't know that we're from the future and really can't testify against him," Elizabeth pipes in.

"I'm glad that you're here and feel so positive about the outcome," John replies, exhaling a sigh of relief.

The rest of the day is spent trying to watch Uncle Robert from a distance and also keeping an eye out for those dreadful Dutchmen. Fortunately, they are nowhere to be seen, and his uncle just stays put in his home. The evening arrives and, before they know it, it's time for bed. The house is locked up tight, just in case. This is the first time that the two have ever slept in the past. As they fall asleep, they try to prepare themselves for the upcoming day. Matthew furiously tries to anticipate what things may happen tomorrow. Elizabeth wishes that all this was over and they were back in their own time. She really wants this to turn out well, but deep down she thinks it will not, and she's frightened. Buddy sleeps on the floor, giving some comfort to those in the beds.

Despite everything, they all sleep reasonably well and are eager to get this whole fiasco over with.

"I wish we could let your uncle know that we're aware of his plans and that the authorities have been notified. To tell you the truth, I don't think it would affect the end result much, though. After all, we did leave that warning note before and it didn't help at all," Elizabeth says to no one in particular.

Matthew and John are both lost in their own thoughts as everyone is having breakfast.

℮℈℮℈

The morning drags by with little new information being made available by watching the uncle and the hotel. John decides to go over to the hotel to make sure the men didn't arrive during the time they were all sleeping. When he comes back, he shares the fact that the Dutchmen are not at the hotel. The three of them scout around the area and, after finding little to alarm them, they go back into John's house to wait.

The afternoon arrives and nerves are starting to become slightly frayed. John starts showing signs of irritation as the seriousness of the situation takes its toll. A few times he snaps at his guests and immediately apologizes for the outburst. He is, of course, forgiven as brother and sister realize that they are being affected the same way but not to the same extent.

As the afternoon slips by, Matthew and Elizabeth take up positions where they can keep watch and intervene if necessary. Matthew has his slingshot ready with a good supply of nearly perfectly round stones. These are more stable flying through the air than misshapen ones are. Elizabeth is armed with a three-foot-long piece of hardwood used in axe handles. This can be used to inflict quite a bit of pain if the need arises. She, of course, hopes desperately that this won't be necessary.

Elizabeth wishes they could have gone to the police. She knows that they would have no way of convincing the authorities of who they are without raising suspicions. How would they ever convince them that they belong in this time with absolutely no identification? John could vouch for them but, at some point, the police would check his story. Then John would be forced to explain his lies. No, they all feel this is their only option, slim as it might be. Given more time they could have some false identification obtained but there is no time for that.

The wait becomes almost unbearable as the time of the event approaches. Hands are shaking in anticipation of the worst. The time finally comes with nothing happening and then goes by. The scene is almost anticlimactic. One hour passes and then another and yet another. There is nothing happening out of the ordinary as the afternoon turns into evening.

"John, do you think that when your uncle caught us walking to the rear of his house he suspected that we are on to him?" Matthew asks.

"I think that is exactly what may have happened," he replies.

"Do you think this means that he will not pursue this matter anymore?" Elizabeth asks from her hiding place.

"I wish that I could say yes but I have no idea, "Matthew says.

"I think that because you two are with me, I suspect that he thinks he is being watched. I'm sure that he will give up the plans he has made." John says to his friends.

"If nothing happens between now and tomorrow when we leave, I think we may well have managed to avert this horrible event," Elizabeth says with a sigh of relief.

Matthew grins at the other two. "Let's stay indoors this evening and, if nothing happens, we can check things out tomorrow morning. Hopefully your Uncle Robert informs those dreadful men about our being involved and they just leave to go back to the Netherlands."

The evening passes and the morning arrives without incident. There is a feeling of relief in the home. Later in the morning, the two time travelers exit out through the back of the home and remain hidden from view. John goes out the front door and walks along the beach toward his uncle's home. Matthew and Elizabeth keep a wary eye out for anyone who may be lurking around spying on them. This whole misadventure may have been averted but it also may only have been delayed. There is no reason to suspect that all the danger is gone.

After John makes a complete circuit and is back at his home, all three meet indoors and discuss the present circumstances.

"Did you two see anything out of the ordinary while I was walking around?" John asks the two of them.

"We didn't see anything that raises any alarms for us," Elizabeth says.

"I sure hope it stays this way," John tells them.

Matthew runs over scenarios, trying to cover all the bases. "We have another four hours here. If nothing happens, I think we should be all right. Just to make sure it might be a good idea to open the front window. You sit on the front porch in the rocking chair, and we'll stay inside. This way it will look like you're alone and, if anyone is still thinking of harming you, they might try it while we are still inside."

"That sounds like a good idea, I'll go now. Maybe the two of you will see something that will help us"

John walks out the door, takes up his position in the chair, and starts to rock. He closes his eyes to make himself appear more vulnerable. Most of the time remaining for the two passes with no sign of trouble. When there is only half an hour left, John comes back into the house. Matthew and Elizabeth take one final look through each of the windows. There appears to be no one watching from anywhere that they can see. To all of them, it seems that there is nothing amiss. Even Buddy looks out the windows. Hopefully, no one has noticed them in the windows.

"It looks like I'm in the clear. Thank you so much for your help. You have been good friends, and I almost wish that I could go with you."

"We're just glad that we have been able to help you. We both wish we could have done something to help Alice too," Elizabeth tells him with a tear in her eye.

"Do you think you might come back to see me one day in the future?"

"That is entirely possible. The only thing to remember is that you will become older and we will be the same age," Matthew tells him, which none seem to have thought of.

"There is one other thing," Elizabeth says. "We're in the cottage where the clock is but not for much longer.

We're on a vacation and the clock is in a secret room there. So we can't be sure if we will have access to the clock much longer."

Matthew reaches out to shake John's hand. "I'm sorry, but it's time, Elizabeth. John, we wish you all the best and please be careful, all right?"

"Thank you and God bless you both and you too, Buddy. I'll miss you," John says as the room clouds over and they are gone.

Chapter 40

The cloud clears and the three of them are back in their own time. Buddy looks around as if amazed by the whole thing. Downstairs they look at the clock on the wall and see once again that hardly any time has passed.

"If you think about it, we actually gained two days in our lives. I'm pretty sure that we haven't aged the amount of time we've been gone," Matthew says to his sister.

"That's right, because when John was stuck in the past for several years, he hadn't aged at all when he finally returned. It really is an amazing occurrence."

"I guess we should check the computer to see if we finally managed to fix something," Matthew suggests.

⌘

Leonard and Kate have been gone for almost an hour and a half at this point, having met Christine at the home for a viewing. Things have gone very well this time.

"Do you want me to call the kids and let them know we are going to pick them up shortly, Leonard?"

"That's a good idea, that way we can get back to the home quickly and not have Christine wait too long for us."

The phone rings and Elizabeth answers. The two are just on their way up the stairs to check things online.

"Oh hi, Mom, what's up?"

"We just looked at a property and it looks pretty good to us. We're coming back to bring the two of you to see it. We don't want to make a decision without your input," Kate tells her daughter.

"How long before you are here?"

"We'll be there in ten minutes, can you be ready to go? We have Christine at the home waiting for us."

"Sure we'll be ready, Mom." Elizabeth turns to her brother. "Forget about the computer for now, Matt. We're going to see a house that may be right for us."

"Did Mom say where it is?"

"Nope, she just said to be ready to go in ten minutes."

"I guess we'll have to wait to see if things turned out the way we hope," he says, somewhat disappointed.

ↄ⊱ↄ⊱ↄ

Leonard beeps the horn. they run outside and hop into the car with Buddy's head hanging out the window again. The warm breeze blows through the back seat and the occasional sound of a bird chirping can be heard. The sun is high in the sky with a few large fluffy clouds drifting near the horizon.

Mom describes the home to her children, preparing them for what is coming. Leonard drives at a safe speed. He has learned long ago that if you rush, you really don't actually gain much. A few minutes later, they pull up in front of a pleasant looking cottage. The clapboard exterior is a pale blue with white shutters at the windows. The roof is a light green asphalt shingles that may need replacing, but not for a few years.

Christine is waiting on the front porch that spans most of the width of the home. There is a wooden railing completed with spindles to the porch floor, also in white.

"Hi, guys, how have you been? I hope that you like this property. I think it has much of what you're looking for," she says pleasantly.

"We're fine, thank you, how are you today?" Elizabeth says in return.

"I'm doing well but very busy lately. I'll wait out here and let you go through the house at your leisure," Christine says, moving to a chair farther down the porch.

The four go into the home with Buddy keeping the realtor company. She pats the dogs head and speaks to him like you would a child. Buddy appears to respond to the extra attention.

Kate leads the rest of her family through the various rooms of the home. The kitchen is located at the rear and on the left. The eating area and living room span the rest of the rear of the house. There is a den at the front left and the first of the three bedrooms is located on the right side at the front. There is a stairway in the center of the home in front of a small bathroom leading upward to a second story.

At the top of the stairs is a small landing with another bathroom. This one is larger and has a shower and bathtub in it as well as the toilet and sink.

On either side of the landing are the doors to two more bedrooms. One is considerably larger than the other, obviously the master.

"So what do you guys think of the place? If you look out the window, you can see the ocean a few hundred yards away. There is a nice size private backyard with another porch and a hot tub," Leonard says.

"It looks like a nice house with enough room for everyone. Do I get the upstairs bedroom?" Elizabeth asks quickly, hoping this gives her an edge.

"No, I get the upstairs bedroom. I'm older than you are so I should get first choice, right, Mom?" Matthew says, smiling at his mother.

"We'll have to decide that later. Does this mean you like the house enough to want to live here?" Leonard pipes in.

Both Matthew and Elizabeth nod their heads in agreement. The group goes into the back yard to look things over and they like what they see. There are two mature maple trees, one in each back corner, and a fire pit in the center of the grassy yard. There is even a detached oversized garage with a work area.

Leonard and Kate let Christine know they are interested in the property and discuss what the offer should be. The three arrive at a price they all feel is fair and the offer is written up.

Christine phones the listing agent and agrees to meet with him. She tells the family that this will take several hours and that it is best if they wait at home.

Back home, everyone is all excited as they talk about moving to a wonderful place where they can enjoy the beaches and the ocean. There is even talk of getting a boat so they can go fishing. The time drags by and even Matthew and Elizabeth forget about other matters that were so pressing only a few hours earlier.

At seven-fifteen, the phone rings and Kate answers putting it on speaker phone.

"Hello, Christine, have you heard back from the other realtor?"

"Yes, I have and I will drop by your cottage in half an

hour and show you the results, if that's all right with you?" she asks, without giving any information.

"Yes, certainly, we'll be waiting for you."

"So we don't know if we got the house," Leonard says quickly.

"Nope, as you heard, she'll be here in half an hour. I don't know what to make of it, at this point."

The time drifts by with various opinions being given by all. Finally, Christine arrives and is ushered into the living room.

"Well, I met with the other agent and he informs me that some people looked at the home right after you did and made an offer too," she informs the family.

"Do you know what the other offer is?" Leonard asks.

"No, they won't say, except that because the other party knew we put an offer in, their offer is much higher. So the question now is what do you want to do?"

Leonard frowns. "The offer we put in is close to what we think the home is worth. If we went much higher, we would always think that we paid too much for it. What do you think, Kate?"

"I agree with you. I think we have to let this one go. It is very disappointing but I, for one, would feel worse if we had to pay far more than we thought it was worth. Thank you for your help, Christine, maybe next time," Kate says, rather sad at this turn of events.

The rest of the evening is fairly quiet as the whole family is disappointed by this new turn of events. Even Buddy lies on the floor quietly. It's time for bed and everyone retires for the night.

The next morning brings a light rain which matches everyone's mood. It soon turns into a severe storm and, with it, come lots of thunder and lightning. The rain comes down in torrents and even manages to leak in through tiny openings in the window and door frames.

Everyone pitches in to help clean up the water. The rain comes down so hard that the ocean can't even be seen from the cottage. The scene is somewhat frightening for the family. This is not the kind of weather they are used to. The wind blows in fierce gusts with grains of wet sand striking the glass threateningly.

This continues for several hours then, as suddenly as it came, it is gone. The sun comes out and warmth comes in through the dirty windows. Some of the long grasses have been bent flat and there are small twigs on the path to the beach that were blown in from trees hundreds of yards away.

Everyone pitches in to clean up the mess. Leonard grabs a hose and sprays the sand off the windows. Matthew takes a garbage container and picks up the twigs and other debris in the vicinity of the cottage. After an hour's work, the cottage inside and out looks presentable again.

By this time, it's almost suppertime, and they're all a little weary. Instead of making supper, there's a unanimous agreement to go into town to a restaurant. The only decision to make is where. Matthew thinks fish and chips would really hit the spot. The rest of the family quickly agrees and they are off to the Shady Rest Restaurant.

The seafood restaurant is a warm and cozy place with fish nets hanging on the walls and a few prize fish mounted here and there. Dad has a nice cold corona and Kate enjoys a glass of deep rich colored Shiraz wine.

"Say, Matthew, you're eighteen now. Do you want to try a beer too?" Dad asks

"To tell you the truth, Dad, I tried it a few times, and I just don't like the taste much. Some of my buddies think it's great but it's not for me. I'd rather just have a root beer. Thanks anyway, though."

Everyone decides to have fish and chips with Leonard and Matthew having two pieces of fish and the girls having just one. The meal is so enjoyable that the melancholy mood of losing the bid on the home is vanquished from their minds. The rains have left a freshness in the air and life is good again.

At home, a fire is started up with Leonard and Kate sitting in front of it, warming up. Matt and Elizabeth are chomping at the bit to find out if things in the past have changed the way they hope. They excuse themselves and run up the stairs to fire up the computer.

Chapter 41

The information is on the screen and she reads it aloud.

"'The death of John Fielding Smith on September 21, 1927 was reported by the police. The body was discovered by the deceased's uncle who told the reporter it appeared his nephew was beaten. There are no suspects at the present time. The investigation is ongoing.'"

"Oh, my goodness, John died, anyway. Nothing we've done has changed anything. It only delayed John's death by a few days," Elizabeth says with tears in her eyes.

"I don't know what else to do. It seems that there is no way of changing the past. Maybe the past is the past, and no one can do anything to alter it. I so wish this wasn't the way it is," Matthew says, stricken.

"Uncle Robert discovered John's body," Elizabeth cries in rage. "Why was he at John's house, anyway? I'm sure he is the perpetrator of the crime. This must be his way of attempting to throw suspicion in another direction. He must think that the police won't think he had something to do with John's death because he is the one that notified them."

This has just turned into a bad day. They spend the rest of the evening staying upstairs away from their parents. From the landing, they say goodnight to their parents, telling them they're tired, and head to their beds, feeling quite defeated. Elizabeth and Matthew have both become quite fond of John and Alice. Despite all they have tried to do, they haven't been able to help them. They fall asleep and both dream about unpleasant things.

☙❧

In the morning, their moods are still not as jovial as they usually are. It's difficult for both to hide their feelings from their parents.

"What's up, guys? You seem completely out of sorts this morning. Is there something wrong?" Mom asks.

"I didn't sleep well last night and I'm really tired," Elizabeth tells her, wondering if it is wise to try explaining a little more fully.

Matthew informs everyone that he would like to go for a walk on the beach with Buddy, saying he's somewhat disappointed over the loss of the home. He heads to the water with Buddy bounding over the sand. They slowly disappear along the sandy beach.

His mind is trying to figure out what went wrong. Why did John have to die? It would appear that whoever killed him was after something, and it has to be how to make the clock work.

"It has to be the uncle. I wonder if John told him how the clock works. Darn it, Elizabeth and I forgot to see if John's uncle still dies by his own hand. We'll have to go online when I get back and see," he says to Buddy who isn't really paying attention.

Back at the cottage, Matthew talks to Elizabeth and asks her to go online and check about the uncle.

"Here is the story about the uncle, Matt. Robert Berger dies of what appears to be a self-inflicted gunshot wound. His body is found in a wooded area not far from a popular hotel by one of its guests."

"So he still does himself in. That means he probably couldn't live with what he did anymore. The clock is still in this room so it must be him. If the Dutchmen knew where it was they would have taken the clock to Holland with them. Do you think Robert figured out how to keep the clock hidden from them?"

"Yes, I think the uncle must have built the room to hide the clock from those men. I bet he took the clock to his house and showed the men from Holland it was no longer in John's house but in his own. Then I bet that he brought it back to John's house, when the sealing off of the room was almost completed and those men were away."

"He probably told them it was sold because the clock couldn't be made to work the way it was suspected and that he didn't remember who bought it," Matthew jumps in, very sure of his reasoning. "I'm sure his household staff would corroborate his story. That's why the clock was still in the hidden room where we found it."

"He could have destroyed it but must have thought that he might one day still try to make it work for himself. This way those awful men would have left him alone because the clock had disappeared and they no longer had any chance of retrieving it," Elizabeth says thoughtfully.

"I think you're right but I'm at a loss as to what to do now."

"Yeah, me too. I can't, for the life of me, figure out what we could have done differently. We don't have much time left here. If something doesn't happen in the next week, we'll be on our way home and then it will be too late," Elizabeth says dejectedly, thinking this may well be the way things turn out.

Matthew chuckles. "So far, things aren't going our way, but you have to admit, it certainly has been the most interesting vacation we have ever had."

With this, the two go downstairs in a surprisingly better mood. They should be upset but strangely they feel uplifted. The adventure has had its low points but, in reality, nothing has actually been lost. The past is still the past. Nothing has gotten worse. It just isn't any better than it was before this all started. Except for John that is, maybe it would have been better that he had been left stuck in the past.

Leonard and Kate notice the change and suggest a ride around the vacation paradise. It would be a waste not to take advantage of all the beauty. The family drives off with Buddy hanging his head out the window once again. They travel along roads that are new to them all. Jeremiah Way and Old Poocha Road provide interesting views. They park the car at Lelands Path and go for a nice little hike. By the time the hike is done, everyone is ready for lunch.

At an out of the way little bistro, they sit in the sunshine at a patio table. The meal is delicious, as all have been so far.

"I think we will need to call Mrs. Robinson soon to let her know Matthew will be staying there. That is, if you still want to, Matthew?" Kate asks her son.

"I think it will be great. I'm looking forward to being here. It would be nicer if we all lived here but all things in their own time, I guess."

"Atta boy, Matt, that's the way to look at things," his sister says as she playfully slaps him on the back.

"Your mother and I will miss you son, but I'm sure it won't be too long. It may even be good to be on your own for a while."

"Mrs. Robinson seems like a lovely lady. I doubt that you will be too lonely living in her house," Kate throws in.

The ride home is pleasant with the rain having washed the dust off everything. The trees seem greener and the sky appears even bluer than before. This is probably not the case but it sure looks like it is. The kids and Buddy decide it's time for some exercise along the beach. The Frisbee is picked up and a short time later they are playing on the beach.

Matthew and Elizabeth toss the toy to each other getting Buddy all excited running back and forth. The Frisbee ends up sailing into the water when Elizabeth throws it a little off target.

Buddy literally flies into the surf chasing it. He gets a mouth full of water and has to cough it out as he has gotten more than he bargained for. In the end, he retrieves the toy and bounds back onto the beach.

Matthew stops playing and turns to his sister. "I was just wondering, Elizabeth. Do you think that we should make another trip back just to clear some things up?"

"What is it that you want to find out?"

"I'm a bit suspicious of the way the uncle died. If he's responsible for all three deaths, what is it about John's dying that pushed him over the edge? Why did he not feel this way earlier? I may be all wrong, but this has been bothering me."

She purses her lips as she studies him. "I see your point. I hadn't thought about that. So what do you suggest we do?"

"I don't know I was hoping that you would have an idea."

She snorts. "Let me think about it and I'll try to figure this out, all right?"

"All right, but we don't have a lot of time left, you know?"

With this thought, the two head back to the cottage. They have been gone several hours, which is a real surprise to them. It seems as if they just left.

Scenarios are running through Matthew's head as he daydreams about possible strategies. He sits in his room, trying to ascertain the best way of getting any extra information about motives and details of all these crimes. How can he and Elizabeth make a difference is the question always in the back of his mind. Time slips by and, before he knows it, he hears his sister's voice from his doorway.

"Hey, Matt, what are you up to?"

"I'm just running through things in my head."

"Have you come up with anything?"

"As a matter of fact, I have. I think we should check online as to exactly when the uncle died and where. We should go back an hour or two before and wait for him. It might work if we could hide someplace close enough to hear him and see exactly what is happening. How does that sound?"

"What do you hope to learn from that?"

"I really don't know yet, but I'm confident that what we read online isn't all there is to this situation," he says, shaking his head.

"I'm not keen on seeing someone blow his brains out, to tell you the truth," Elizabeth says in disgust. "Neither am I, but I'm not totally certain that everything is as it appears. I think that it's possible there may be more to it than we know. We can always interrupt him by making a noise that may distract him. Who knows? Maybe he'll change his mind."

"I guess, maybe. Who knows?" she says doubtfully.

"Hey, guys, it's time for supper. Get washed up, all right?" Mom calls from downstairs.

"All right, Mom, we're on our way," Elizabeth shouts back.

Supper consists of hamburgers and corn on the cob. Everyone enjoys this immensely.

Matthew gets up and hugs his mother and father. "Hey, Mom, this is really great. I just want you to know that, no matter how it turns out, this is the best vacation we have ever had. Thanks so much, both of you."

Mom gets a tear in her eye as she thinks of how wonderful her children have turned out. Leonard is of the same opinion and expresses his sentiments with a smile. The supper is done and cleaned up when the phone rings again. Christine is on the other end and she expresses her regrets about the home offer falling through. She promises to keep looking but says that she thinks there is a lull in the market at the moment. This means that it is entirely possible that no new homes will be coming up soon.

"This is a situation that comes up quite often at this time of year. With school starting up, most people are more concerned with that then selling their homes," she informs her potential buyers.

It's not what the family wants to hear but is a fact of life. This is also creating a problem for the two travelers. It means that they may not have the opportunity to make a trip back as easily as they have been. With only one week left, time is rapidly running out. Matthew and Elizabeth start trying to think of ways to have the parents go out somewhere by themselves. Elizabeth finally has a bright idea which she mentions to Matthew.

"What do you think would be Mom and Dad's response if we suggested them looking for some for sale by owner homes again, Matthew? I don't think most agents will show these because there's less commission for them. There must be at least a few being sold that way."

"I think you have a pretty good idea there. Have you thought of how you'll present it to them, sis?"

"Not at the moment, but I'm sure it will come to me," she says.

⁌⁌⁌

In the morning after breakfast, she mentions the idea to her parents, casually dropping it in their laps very nonchalantly. You would hardly know that it was totally planned by the young girl. Leonard and Kate talk about it for a few minutes and come to the conclusion that this may be worth a shot. They have nothing to lose, so what the heck? After a couple of preparations and a bit of viewing online, they find a few that interest them. With addresses in hand, they drive away in search of a new home.

Chapter 42

They have checked online for all the information available. While they're looking for what they need, they run across a story about a robbery at one of the museums that happens shortly before the two go into the past for the first time. An exhibit of fine jewelry on loan from the Darmstadt Artists Collection worth almost half a million dollars is stolen. A guard is killed and the perpetrators are never apprehended.

The information they need is found, and the clock is set for their next journey. The layover time is set at three hours, and Matthew sets the timer on his watch to coincide with the return time minus five minutes.

The room clouds over and, when it clears again, they're in the clock room in John's house but the changes have been made. This is the room from where the two started the adventure from. The only difference is that the room has no dust and is clean and newly built. This makes sense to them as they figured that it would be this way before they left their own time.

Matthew opens the trick door and reseals it after they leave. The two head to Robert's house and listen by the same window as before. Then they go to several other spots around the house to see if they can hear anything.

"I don't hear any sounds coming from anywhere in the house," Elizabeth whispers.

"I think he might be making up his mind about his course of action."

"The time of death for him is coming up so we should get there well ahead of time. That way, we can find a suitable hiding spot. What do you think, Matt?"

"Right you are, sis."

They make their way to the woods where Uncle Robert's body is going to be discovered. They're careful to check that there is no one about to see them. Matthew has his slingshot and a few stones with him, just in case an emergency arises.

Slowly they make their way to where the uncle is reported to do himself in. They arrive there well before the man does. They are sure they are fairly close to where they need to be, but make a very careful search of the area to be certain.

Being careful to remain hidden, Matthew makes a circuit of the scene. He finds nothing and makes his way back to Elizabeth. The two pick a place to hide that will give them the opportunity to move away unnoticed if need be.

They wait for almost an hour before they finally see some movement in the trees not far from where they are. What they see is a bit of a shock for them. Uncle Robert, who is supposed to have taken his own life, is not alone. There are two men with him who are forcing him to a spot within thirty yards of where the travelers are hidden.

"All right, that's far enough," Johannus says in a very heavily accented voice.

"Now we will have a talk where we will not be disturbed," Hendrick says.

"Where have you hidden the clock? We know you have put it somewhere. We will find it anyways, no matter where you have left it," Johannus tells Robert.

"I don't know where it is. It was stolen from my house during the night when I was in Edgartown for a few days," Robert lies. "You can ask my housekeeper."

"We have already done this. We think she would lie for you, so we do not rely on her statements," Hendrick says.

"We know that you are responsible for your brother's death and that is how you got the clock in the first place. So, in actuality, the clock does not belong to you anyways," Johannus shouts.

"I have told you before that Benjamin's death was an accident. I had nothing to do with it," Robert says, desperately trying to convince the men.

"You have said this many times and yet we do not believe you. Is that not right, Johannus?" Hendrick asks.

"I have killed no one, this is the truth," Robert cries.

"Do you think that we won't kill you? We had no trouble killing that nosey girl called Alice, even when you chased her, trying to warn her about us. We still don't know who the boy and girl are, the ones that we hit on the head. Tell us who they were and where they went," Hendrick demands.

"I don't know anything about them," Robert insists.

"When we interrogated your nephew John about how to work that infernal clock, he died too. It was unfortunate that occurred when Hendrick hit him too hard. We were not finished with him at that point. So do you really think that we will hesitate to kill you too? Is that what you think, Mister Berger," Johannus asks.

Elizabeth is sobbing quietly with her hand over her

mouth as she hears of her friends and how these murdering brutes killed them. Matthew almost jumps up to fire the slingshot at the men but manages to control himself. He knows that one way or another these men must be brought to justice.

"Why did you have to kill my niece and nephew? There was no need for it," Robert sobs loudly.

"It is time for answers, or time to die, the choice is yours," Johannus says.

There is no answer and Hendrick takes the pistol, making Bob hold it in his unwilling hand. The hand is forced to bring the gun to his temple.

"One last chance, tell us what we want to know," Hendrick shouts.

Robert just sobs and says nothing. The trigger is pulled and Robert collapses to the ground with the sound of the shot, echoing through the woods.

Elizabeth gasps at the sight and Johannus looks around quickly. "I think there is someone here. I'm sure I heard a sound nearby. Hendrick, you look over that way, and I will search in that place with all the shrubs," he shouts, pulling out a pistol of his own.

The siblings in the bushes are almost in a panic. This is surely the end if they are found. Elizabeth starts to shake and gets ready to run but Matthew grabs her arm, forcing her to stay. "Shhhh, I have an idea, sit still, please Elizabeth," he pleads. He takes hold of the slingshot and places a small stone in the pouch.

The two men are searching for the intruders and talking back and forth. As they search, there is the sound of breaking twigs under their feet. Matthew times his shot with their talking and as Hendrick's foot comes down, and there's the snap of a twig, he lets the stone fly.

The sound of the slingshot is masked by the sound of the breaking twig and the stone flies far away from where the two are hiding. It bounces off a tree and lands in some bushes making enough noise to draw the attention of the men. The men shout to each other and run toward the place the stone landed. This gives Matthew and Elizabeth the time they need to make their escape in the opposite direction.

When they are safely away from the two men, it hits them just how close they were to getting caught too. Matthew and Elizabeth are in shock as the enormity of the situation hits home. Their hands are trembling, and Elizabeth cries as Matthew tries to comfort her.

This has not turned out at all as they thought it would. All along they thought that Uncle Robert was the guilty person. The people actually responsible for the murder of their friends just killed an innocent man.

"How could this have turned out so badly? The uncle has been innocent all along. How can this be? Why did we not see this earlier?" Matthew cries in dismay.

"I feel so badly for him now. We were totally wrong about the man. It was those evil Dutchmen the whole time," she sobs, unable to stop.

Another hour passes before the clock does its job once again. This gives the two a little time to settle their nerves and collect their thoughts before the journey home. It has been a rather frightening and traumatic trip. The air clouds once more and, when it clears, they are home once again and safe from the evils of the past.

Chapter 43

Home, and the security it brings, allows the two to finally relax enough to discuss what has happened. The last hour in the past was filled with the fear that they might be discovered by the murderers. Neither have any doubts that they too would have been dispensed with if they were found. Now back home Buddy runs into the room adding to the feeling of safety.

Elizabeth hugs Buddy, still shook up. "My goodness, I have never been so scared in all my life. Seeing those men murder Robert the way they did was just awful. I almost screamed."

"I just about let loose with the slingshot as I saw what was going to happen. I had no idea that John's uncle was an innocent man." Matthew says incredulously.

"I know how you feel. It was a shock to find out that he hasn't been guilty of anything except being a miserable man. I thought for sure that he killed Benjamin

Berger but now it seems that his death really was an accident."

"So how do we deal with this new information? Three people have been murdered and so far there is nothing that we have been able to do about it," Matthew exclaims, having no more optimism at this point.

"I have no idea what to do. This is so frustrating, knowing what has really been going on, trying to change things, and not helping in any of them."

Matthew nods and drapes and arm around her shoulders. "What makes this even worse is that we only have six days to fix things. After that, we'll be back home, and I'll start college near here. I'll be so close but still won't have access to the clock. There'll be new owners in the cottage, and surely someone else will discover this room. I'm sure eventually Alice will be seen running down the beach and start someone else thinking about the connection with this cottage." he says, sighing despondently.

"Maybe Mom and Dad will find another house and we might one day get the clock out of here."

"I really have grave doubts about that happening. It would be breaking and entering, and if we are caught we will be in big trouble. No, I think this is probably it for us. Once this vacation is over, our access to the clock will be gone. I don't see any way out of this. Just for the heck of it, I think that we should keep all the journals and letters. I'll close the panel on the clock and we'll seal the room up as tightly as we can. I'll use Dad's drill to screw the door shut and maybe that will keep everyone out," Matthew tells Elizabeth sadly.

"I guess there's no use going back, anymore, if we don't have a plan to help any of them, is there?"

"I can't think of anything to help that we haven't already done. I'm starting to think this is a lost cause.

Maybe we just aren't the right people for the job. Maybe this requires someone who can actually kill those men before they have a chance to murder Alice," Matthew explains.

"I think that you may be right. We cannot possibly do that to anyone. Those men are a totally different breed than we are. The average person doesn't have it in them to kill another human being. I guess this is the end of this adventure."

"Well, I think I'm going for a walk on the beach," Matthew tells her. "Come on, Buddy, let's go."

With Matthew gone, Elizabeth is left alone with her thoughts. This day is unlike any other she has ever had. She has, in the past many weeks, seen and done things she's not sure she would do again if she had the choice. She and her brother were given a chance to right a wrong and failed miserably. Maybe if they had left John in the past, instead of restarting the clock, he might not be dead. He would still be stuck living in a time not his own but at least he would be alive.

Lying on her bed, she softly weeps. After a time, she falls to sleep, releasing her from the anguish she feels.

❧❦❧

Matthew heads down to the water's edge with Buddy at his side. He also feels like a failure. No matter how he and his sister tried to help their friends, nothing they did helped to change what has already happened. Maybe the past is something unalterable, no matter what tools you are given. The clock seemed like it was the perfect device for the job at hand. How wrong that thought has turned out to be.

True, this has been the wildest vacation ever, but it has also been the most horrific. Traveling into the past and meeting lovely Alice and her cousin John has been the experience of a lifetime. There will undoubtedly be nothing in the future that will ever compare to this. They will soon lose access to the clock, and life will return to a predictable routine. If only things were different.

At least there is one consolation to this entire episode. The awful Dutchmen won't be able to use the clock to perform the robberies they most certainly had hoped to.

"Boy, it's hard to keep the tenses straight. I'm having a hard time thinking of things now that are in the past and being there and thinking of them as now—it gets so confusing," Matthew mutters to himself.

Buddy barks in agreement, or so it seems. This line of thought has triggered a thought in the back of his mind but it's too elusive to bring to the forefront. There's a nagging feeling that he's missing something very important. No matter how hard he tries, the thought remains hidden.

The walk along the beach becomes less enjoyable as time slips by. Matthew, in frustration, goes back to the cottage. He makes himself a sandwich and lets his mind go blank for a while.

Chapter 44

Driving from one address to the next, Leonard and Kate look at the homes listed for sale by owner. With most of the list crossed off, they have seen nothing that piques their interest. So far, it has been a disappointing morning. The choices offered are either too pricey for what is being sold or too run down to consider.

Kate sighs. "I wonder what those two are up to. I hope they're not getting bored with us being gone so much looking at houses."

"I doubt that they've been sitting around doing nothing this whole vacation," Leonard replies.

So, as they pull up in front of the second-to-last house on the list, they have a pleasant surprise. The home is well within their budget and appears to be the right size and in good repair. There's a phone number on the sign, and Leonard proceeds to dial it on his cell phone. After a moment, someone answers and Leonard asks when they can see the home. Unfortunately, there's no one home at the present time and a viewing will have to be done after the owner comes home from work. An appointment is made for five o'clock today.

"Okay, Kate, let's go look at the last house on the list just to make sure."

They drive for twenty minutes and end up in front of a nice home. Unfortunately, the property is in a subdivision that is far away from the water. This fact takes the home off the list and so with only one contender, the two decide to go for a late lunch in town to discuss their options.

"Boy, this is turning out to be a difficult procedure," Kate says, sighing at her husband. "I would have thought it would be easier than this to find a suitable home. I guess if we had one of the ideal homes we wouldn't want to sell either."

"I hope this one we're looking at later today is as nice inside as it is on the outside. It's in a nice area and its close enough to the beach to make the walk in five minutes."

"Yes, I like this one too. It's not as nice as the cottage we're in but it does come close. Do you want to take the kids with us to see it, dear?" she asks.

"I think we should because, if we like it, we'll be moving on it quite quickly. Why don't you call and let them know what our plans are?"

Matthew's jolted back to reality as the phone chimes and vibrates in his pocket.

"Hey, Mom what's up?" he asks.

"We've found an interesting prospect and we'll be picking you and Elizabeth up. Be ready to go at around four-thirty so we can have a look at it. Is that all right?"

"Yeah, that'll be great. I'll let Elizabeth know. See you when you get here," he says with more enthusiasm than he feels.

He walks up the stairs to Elizabeth's room. The door's open so he walks in and, when he sees that she's awake, he starts talking to her, first letting her know about the viewing. But she's pale and withdrawn, not her usual self.

"Hey, Elizabeth, are you all right?" Matthew asks, genuinely concerned for her welfare.

"I guess seeing a man die has shaken me up. How are you doing?" she asks in return.

"I'm okay, but I have this feeling that I'm missing something real important. The thing is that I can't quite figure out what it is," he says, quite perplexed by it all.

"Well, you'd better figure it out soon because our vacation's almost over."

"I think that's part of the reason that I can't get a hold of the idea. Time is running out and it's putting more pressure on me. I'm having a hard time relaxing enough to let the thought surface naturally. I know it may be the solution we're looking for. It's so aggravating. I'm so close and still it's not coming," he says, frustrated by this lack of progress.

"Well, try to let it go. You always manage to come through. I have faith in you. Let's go outside and rummage through the shed. We might find something interesting," she suggests, knowing that getting Matthew sidetracked has helped him figure things out in the past.

In the shed, they look at items from the past. The workmanship impresses Matthew more than Elizabeth. He knows quality when he sees it. Some of the furniture has been made by skilled hands. The joints are perfect, even now. It's a good thing these items have been stored in a dry, protected environment.

The floor is made of old wooden planks that were rough milled many years ago. The walls have held up amazingly well too. In the corner of the building, a section of the floor is loose and, when he lifts the short planks up, he notices something. The soil, although fairly settled, shows signs of having been disturbed in the past.

"Did you see a shovel anywhere in here?" Matthew asks.

"There's one by the door. Do you want me to get it?"

"Please do, I want to see if there is something buried in the dirt," he tells her excitedly.

With shovel in hand, she returns, giving it to her brother. Matthew starts to carefully dig into the slightly compacted earth. As he digs deeper, there's the sound of an automobile coming into the driveway.

"Darn it, why now? I wish we had another fifteen minutes to find out if there's something here," he says disappointedly.

"Later, Matt, you can do it later because it's best if Mom and Dad don't know what we're doing. Smooth out the dirt and let's get out of here," Elizabeth tells him sternly.

The two come out of the shed and head to the car.

"What were you guys doing in the shed?" Leonard asks.

"There's some interesting stuff in there. We thought it might tell us more about who once lived here. It's neat but we didn't learn much," Elizabeth informs them.

The drive takes about twenty minutes. Once they're parked in front of the house, everyone gets out and does a quick walk around the property. When they get back to the front, the door opens and the owner welcomes the family.

The tour starts at the foyer and into the kitchen, which is in the front of the home. To the right is the living room and a small dining area is between them. At the rear on the left is the master bedroom. Next to it is a large bathroom and to the right side of the home there are two more small bedrooms.

There is a crawl space under the home, which no one wants to see. As soon as the door to it is opened, it becomes evident that it's also the residence of many spiders. The inside of the home, overall, is not as well maintained as the exterior and is a little disappointing to the viewers.

"How flexible are you on the price?" Leonard asks kindly.

"We need to get close to asking price because of the bills we owe and the mortgage still on the property."

"Thank you for your time. I don't think this home is what we're looking for," Leonard tells the man.

On the way home Mom apologizes.

"We're sorry we wasted your time. The house looked so much better on the outside. It really is a mess on the inside, isn't it? I'm glad your father didn't want us to go into the crawl space," Mom says, laughing.

Everyone giggles over that and the mood is lightened somewhat. The rest of the ride back to the cottage is fairly subdued. With supper out of the way, the two head upstairs for a quick chat.

"Have you come up with any ideas, Matt?"

"No, not yet but that nagging thought is still back there and it won't come out," he replies, running his hands through his hair in frustration.

"Gosh, what are we going to do? We only have five days left," Elizabeth whines.

"I don't know. I have no idea how to fix this mess of a situation. I almost feel responsible for all of them being dead. I mean all of them having died prematurely. This gets so confusing for me."

"Hey, kids, do you want to play some scrabble with us?" Mom shouts from downstairs.

"Sure, we'll be right down," Elizabeth calls out.

"I don't want to play."

"I don't either but we should so they don't start asking questions and, besides, are we just going to mope around up here the rest of the evening?" Elizabeth asks her brother.

So, like it or not, the two put on a happy face and head downstairs. During the course of the evening, they actually end up enjoying themselves. Matthew ends up being the winner of the scrabble game, despite the fact that he has so much on his mind.

"How did he win the game? He can't even spell his own name. I think the game was rigged," Elizabeth declares loudly.

"I don't need to be able to spell my name to be able to beat you, ha, ha, haaaa," Matthew laughs and everyone joins in.

"Good one, bro," she confesses.

"Well, this wasn't the greatest day but it turned out all right," Kate says, feeling somewhat better.

"I think I'm going to head for bed," Leonard says to the family.

Lying in bed, Elizabeth mulls over the events of the day. This only lasts for a minute and she's asleep. The day has been longer than normal because of the extra hours spent in the past, and it has finally caught up with her.

Matthew is tired too but manages to stay awake considerably longer. There is a thought somewhere in his head that keeps evading capture. He drifts off, wondering if it will ever come to the forefront. This night, he dreams of the uncle being shot and then being chased himself as the men realize that he's in the bushes. He runs and runs but can't lose the pair pursuing him.

∽∾∽

The morning comes with Matthew feeling drained. He has his shower, which partially makes him feel better.

After a decent breakfast, he is almost back to normal. He thinks about getting back in the shed to dig up whatever is in the soil, wondering what it could be.

"Your Dad and I are going for a stroll on the beach. Anyone want to go with us?"

"I think I'm going to do some reading, but thanks, have a nice walk," Elizabeth replies.

Matthews shakes his head too. "I'm going online to check out the college. I might as well familiarize myself with it, seeing as how I'll soon be there."

With the parents gone for their walk, the two head for the shed. Matthew starts to dig carefully, not wanting to damage anything, in case it has some value. Little by little the dirt is removed and then there is a sound of the shovel scraping an object. Putting the shovel aside, he gets on his knees and brushes the soil away with his hands. In the corner of the hole, a slightly shiny metal object is exposed. The digging continues and little by little a small box is uncovered. Finally, enough dirt is removed to free the metal container. The box is brought out of the hole and, with a flair for the dramatic, Matthew asks for a drum roll.

"Oh, Matthew just open the box," Elizabeth says, giggling.

The lid to the box is opened, revealing a number of letters. The paper is very old and, when he opens it, there's a handwritten note. The note turns out to be correspondence between a young man and a young lady he is obviously infatuated with. The rest of the dozen letters are all by the same young man. This all becomes another disappointment to Matthew and his sister.

"Gee, I was hoping to find something of value or at least something relating to Alice and John. All this is nothing but love letters some guy wrote to a girl he was crazy about," Matthew confides.

"I was hoping for the same thing, or at least some buried treasure someone was hiding," Elizabeth agrees.

Chapter 45

Matthew gasps in shock. It has finally dawned on him, the idea rolling around in his mind but never being clear enough to grasp.

"I've got it, I've got it!" he shouts joyfully. "I finally figured out what has been eluding me for these last few days."

Elizabeth sits up quickly. "What, Matthew, what is the idea?"

"Those awful men wanted the clock for a purpose, you remember that, right?"

"Yes, I remember that. That's why they ended up murdering Alice, John, and their uncle," she says excitedly.

"We assumed they wanted to use the clock to pull off robberies in their past. Then they would bury the loot and dig it up later. They wouldn't get caught because they could go to some other town. They could go as far away as they could get in the time allotted them and pull off the theft. They would probably already have the hole dug, put the stuff in it, and fill in the hole. It wouldn't matter where they were when the clock did its thing. The clock always brings the people back to the same spot where the clock is. They would be able to rob a whole lot of places in their past and be home free. They would have four days to get where they want to be and pull off the heist. All they have to do is dig up the things later."

Elizabeth nods, excited. "They could do any number of things to hide the loot. The authorities couldn't catch them because they would never be there long enough to be apprehended."

"That's right, they would never get caught. Not unless they made some errors, at least. That story about the jewelry robbery must have put the thought in the back of my mind. I couldn't think of what it was till now," he concludes.

"Okay, so how does this help us? That's the part I don't understand."

"I think that we can use this to our advantage, even though the Dutchmen never do get to use the clock," Matthew tells her, all excited again.

He goes on to explain what he has in mind, going into great detail so that, when the time comes, there won't be any mistakes made.

When he's finished, Elizabeth marvels at the ingenuity her brother is capable of.

"Wow, I would never have thought of that. I see why you had to go into so much detail. This is going to have to be done right because if we get caught we could end up getting hurt or dead," Elizabeth says with a bit of apprehension.

"Let's get everything we need together and then go online to find the information that we need. When the time is right, and Mom and Dad are gone for a few hours, we'll make our move. We'll have to make several trips, one after the other. That is going to be a crucial part too, because the timing has to be absolutely perfect."

"Why don't you start getting the things we need to take with us, and I'll start finding some of the information we need online," she says to her brother.

With this, the two go about their respective duties. They're close to getting most of what they need when Leonard and Kate arrive home from their walk.

"Are you two ready for lunch," Mom asks.

"Yes, that would be great. I didn't realize I was this hungry until you mentioned it," Matthew says enthusiastically.

When they are all sitting at the table eating lunch, Kate turns to the kids. "We were wondering if you two want to go for tour around the island this afternoon. We won't be here that much longer, so we thought that you might enjoy it. You don't have to go but we thought you might enjoy it."

Elizabeth shakes her head. "Why don't the two of you go off by yourselves? Matthew and I would like to go explore the beach a little more. Like you said, we won't be here much longer, and we'd like to make the most of it while we're here," she says, acting like she thinks this is a good idea and hoping her parents don't want to come along.

"I guess that would be all right, dear. What do you think Leonard?"

"Oh, that's fine with me. I'm sure we'll have a nice time by ourselves. Maybe we'll go out for supper at the same time. Is that okay with you guys?"

"I think that's a great idea, Dad," Matthew says fairly convincingly. "You have been at work in the oil fields for so long, this will be a nice time for the two of you."

"You're not trying to get rid of us are you, Matt?" Leonard asks, breaking out into a laugh.

"No, no, Dad, we just want you to have some extra fun," he says a little more sincerely.

"That's right, Dad, go have fun," Elizabeth joins in.

℘℘

Being alone again, the two make the final preparations for the rest of this adventure. Matthew writes down the sequence of times the clock needs to be set at. Elizabeth double checks everything, making sure there are no overlaps or misprinted times. Matthew has all the items he feels are necessary ready to go in the canvas bag they found in the shed. Luckily, he managed to get into the trunk of the car to retrieve a crucial tool. Elizabeth finishes handwriting a letter, explaining a detailed set of instructions.

Buddy unfortunately will have to be left behind. If he should run off at the wrong time, things could go sour very quickly. There's no use in taking chances at this stage of the game.

The clock is set and the time is here. The room once more clouds over and the game is a foot.

Chapter 46

Once more, the air clears, and the two find themselves in Uncle Robert's home. Knowing the layout of the room allows the two to position themselves in a corner. This way, there will be little chance of being found out as they appear suddenly in the past. For a moment, Matthew wonders what would happen if they were to position themselves wrong. Could they end up inside a wall or is this not possible?

The two quickly climb out the window, making sure the way is clear first. They now have one hour to contact John. They've arrived at a time after their first meeting with him. It takes approximately fifteen minutes to locate John, so time will be of the essence. Matthew takes the lead and attempts to fill John in on what will happen in the future. He tells John about their attempts to change events and what for John and Alice will be the future. He explains what it is they're attempting to achieve and how they plan to do it.

John understands almost immediately what is required

of him. He's given the letter, which he must not allow to fall into the wrong hands, no matter what. He's warned not to inform Alice of what is about to transpire. One mistake could very well spell catastrophe for all. John swears he will follow the directions to the letter and supply the two with exactly what they need, when they need it.

With this portion of the preparations taken care of, the two travelers wait for the clock to bring them home. Matthew allows John to see them disappear, in order to reinforce the fact that what they told him is real. The wait until they vanish is short, very short. It leaves an amazed boy in the past.

Chapter 47

The air clears and a second time is set on the clock. The return time is lengthened and, after quickly having a bite to eat and checking on Buddy, they are off once more. Thankfully, they arrive without incident once more.

As promised, John has ready the things required to fulfill this part of their plans. Tickets for the local train have been obtained, and John gets them a ride to the station. John wants to come along with them, but this is totally out of the question. Matthew explains why and John understands. Still, he'd like to participate but he is needed where he is.

The train ride starts at Barnstable after a ferry ride to the main land and takes the two on to Providence. Once in Providence, the two find their way to an address where they are going to make an unauthorized withdrawal that they need to make their plan work.

Matthew has brought tools with him that he thinks should do the job. It's essential that these tools are not lost or fall into the wrong hands, as they are an invention of the future. He has studied photos online, detailing the obstacles he needs to overcome. The apprehension builds as things are about to happen.

As night falls, the building is vacated by the public and, because of the fortified aspects of the building, there are no security guards. Matthew and Elizabeth have managed to hide in a spot that Matthew noticed when he was studying the pictures online earlier. An hour after the building is empty, they make their move. Good fortune is with them once more as the pair makes their way using a flashlight to locate the item of their search.

The piece of Egyptian history is locked in a glass front cabinet. It's by far the most valuable piece in the museum. The sides and back of the exhibit are made of a top quality metal. That is, it is top quality for this period in time. Matthew has borrowed his father's high end cordless drill and both his carbide drill bits, several high speed steel and ceramic bits. These are far superior to anything available at the turn of the century.

Matthew picks his spots to drill and proceeds to work. The holes are slowly made in the cabinet. It's good that he brought an extra charged battery for the drill. It takes less than a quarter hour to get the cabinet open and they remove the object from the case, wrapping the item carefully so as not to mark it in any way. They have to wait for another hour for the clock to bring them back home.

ﬠﬨﬠﬨ

As the air clears, they find themselves back in their own time, sitting in front of the clock.

"Well, that is the first part of the plan done. I'm a little tired, what about you, Matt?" Elizabeth asks.

"Yes, I am too but we have to go back for the next segment of the plan. We're staying longer this time, so we'll sleep there. John will have made all the arrangements," Matthew tells her.

The clock is set, after they have eaten and gotten themselves ready once more. The air clears, and they have returned once again, this time a day after the one where they got on the train. John is there, waiting, and has things prepared once again. This time, they are going to a town not as far away as Providence and not quite as large.

They make it three hours later, again by themselves. This time, there's a piece of artwork that has great value being stored in a warehouse temporarily. Thank goodness for the internet, otherwise, the two would never know the item is here at this particular time. Unfortunately, this time there is a guard standing watch. The man is placed at the front entrance and the only other way in is a window at the back of the building that is about ten feet up. There's a bolted metal screen covering the glass window. The heads of the bolts are smooth so there is little danger of entry being gained this way.

Fortunately, Matthew has an attachment for the drill. With this he is able to sand a flat spot on the head. This will allow him to have a place to start the high speed drill bit. He will then just drill out the bolts, and then remove the screen. A grapple hook has been provided by John. He tosses it up to the roof and then climbs the rope up to the window. A harness also courtesy of their friend holds him in place leaving his hands free.

Elizabeth stands guard while Matthew gets into position and starts work. The noise is kept to a minimum, thus not alerting the guard on the other side of the large building. The occasional carriage going down the street helps keep the guard's attention. It takes almost ten minutes to gain entry. The screen is lowered by a light rope as well as the tools and harness. Elizabeth packs up the few tools and moves the other things out of the way to be left behind.

Sliding down their rope, Matthew maneuvers inside. Now comes the hard part. He has to locate the painting. He uses his flashlight to find his way around the interior. He looks everywhere, taking more time than he wants to but can't find it. There's a small office with a locked door. This must be where it's being kept.

Elizabeth waits outside, counting off the minutes as they go by. This is taking far longer than it should. Matthew should already be out by this time. She's getting nervous. She peaks around the corner to make sure the guard isn't making a circuit around the building. So far nothing is happening but this can't last forever.

Matthew is stuck. He can't gain entry into the room without making considerable noise. There's a window in the door that has wire mesh embedded in it. Through the window he can see the box where the painting has to be. The hinges on the door are unfortunately on the inside so he can't pull the pins to remove the door. He is at a loss as to what to do. He decides to walk around the room to see if there are any weak points.

There are no places he can use to gain entry. Fortunately, he does find a small crow bar that is used to open boxes. He picks it up and goes back to the door. He has to push quite hard to get the flat sharp end into the tiny space between the door and the doorjamb beside the lock. He uses the bar to put more and more pressure on the lock. There is a creaking sound and a snap. The noise he is sure has alerted the guard. He grabs the box and runs back to the window. Luckily, he has moved a few light crates closer and gets up to the window quickly. Dropping the box to the ground as gently as he can,

Matthew slides down the rope with the grapple hook on the end of it. He grabs the box tightly as Elizabeth informs him of new developments.

"Hurry, Matthew the guard is running down this side of the building toward us. We have to go this other way," she tells him anxiously, pointing to the direction she wants him to go.

"You there, stop," the guard shouts as he rounds the corner. However, the two are already well under way.

The teenagers run as fast as they can. They keep ahead of the guard but are not outpacing him. The package with the painting is slowing Matthew down. The bag of tools hinders Elizabeth but not as much, as they are much lighter and not as awkward to carry. There are few places where they can ditch the guard around this area.

"Stop you, thieves. I order you to stop immediately," the guard continues to shout.

It's a good thing they familiarized themselves with the area before getting to the warehouse. They make their way to a narrow street. There are a number of apartment houses at the end of this road, a hundred yards away. If they can make it into one of them, they may be able to lose the guard. Elizabeth takes a quick look behind to see where the guard is. Not paying close enough attention to the irregular surface causes her to trip. She falls on the cobblestone road, screaming in pain. Matthew turns back and helps her up picking up the dropped bag of tools handing it to her and the two are on the run again. Elizabeth has a slight limp from a banged up knee, but, luckily, it's nothing too serious.

It seems to take forever to get to one of the buildings. Finally, they get to the entrance, quite out of breath and perspiring. The front door is open and, as they go through, Matthew stops and turns around. There's a deadbolt as well as a key operated lock on the heavy door. He slides the dead bolt into the locked position and places a chair under the door knob. Turning toward his sister, he gestures. "This way, to the end of the hall. I think I see an exit down there."

They start running again in the direction he has indicated. Just then, the guard starts banging on the locked door. They run down a long hallway to what appears to be a rear entrance. Matthew opens the door and takes a quick look, making sure the guard hasn't thought of this exit too. No one is visible and, once more, they are on the run. Ten minutes later they make it to a hiding place and wait to make sure they are safe. When there is no sign of the guard, they move to an address that John has written down for them.

John comes an hour later and picks them up. "Are you all right? Is that blood on your knee, Elizabeth?"

"Yes, I tripped on a rough spot on the road while we were being chased by the guard at the warehouse."

"I see you got the painting and still have your tools," John comments. "The two of you have a lot of nerve."

"To tell you the truth, it was all quite scary for a while there," Matthew says. "At least most the horrible things are over. Now we just have one more difficult thing to do."

It feels strange being in a horse drawn carriage but the two are grateful for it. John says that he borrowed it from a friend's father. By the time they get to John's home, they are both dreadfully tired. The ride has been far too bumpy to even attempt taking a nap. It has been a very long day, and the adrenalin rushes have taken their toll.

John has found them a place to sleep and the pair is dead to the world very quickly after lying down. John takes the painting and places it in a secure spot. The Egyptian artifact is still in the present time and will have to be retrieved. Right now though, it's time to rest.

The morning comes, and John brings them to his own home for breakfast. His mother is out on an errand and won't be back for some time. Everyone thought it best to have her completely unaware of the visitors. The Dutchmen are not booked into the hotel at the moment so Matthew and Elizabeth wait for the clock to bring them back home. This will happen in less than two hours.

The painting is moved to a spot under lock and key that will be easily accessible to the travelers. The final preparations are made and John understands exactly what he needs to do. The three run into Alice who is eager to hear what has been going on. She, of course, knows nothing of what has transpired in the last few days. Elizabeth and Matthew excuse themselves for a moment and discuss if it is wise to bring her up to speed or not. The two cannot decide so John is asked for his opinion.

"I think that Alice can be trusted with the details of what is going on. However, I'm not sure she needs to know yet. You say she will soon die. But if your plan works, this will all be averted, her death and mine too. If this is so, why should she be told all this? The future will be changed and she will remain alive, according to what you have told me. No, I don't think we should inform her. I'll just tell her that I'll reveal everything to her later," John finally decides.

He walks back to Alice and an animated conversation takes place. When they are finished, she doesn't look happy, but nods her head and walks away.

The three go to a quiet area and wait for the return time to approach. When they disappear, John is left there marveling at the process.

Chapter 48

The air clears yet again as the two are brought back to their own time. Looking at the clock in Elizabeth's room, they see that almost no time has gone by. It's two in the afternoon and the parents won't be home for at least four or five hours.

This should give them lots of time to finish the last part of their plan.

Matthew replaces the tools he borrowed from his dad. It's really a good thing that his dad is one of these people who come to a place prepared for anything. Buddy greets them enthusiastically and wants to go out to play. Unfortunately, there's no time for this. Elizabeth's knee needs some attention. In the bathroom, the first aid kit makes short work of the injury, as it is certainly non-life-threatening.

The enormity of the chase and thefts they have committed hits home as they talk about what could have happened.

"I think you might have missed your calling in life,

Matthew. You could easily become a thief you know. You're really good at it," she says jokingly.

"Not a chance. I was never as scared as when that guard was after us. The whole time we were running, I was expecting to hear him fire a pistol at us," he replies nervously.

"That's a good thing because sooner or later they all get caught, and I wouldn't want to see you in prison. Remember what happened to that older boy named Bobby? He ended up in prison and he was almost killed after he received a horrible beating in there," she reminds her brother.

"Yeah, I remember that. It was really hard on the family as I recall," he answers thoughtfully.

After the scrape is taken care of, the two make the final preparations. They check the times and also go online just to verify that no surprises are awaiting them. It would not do to have history changed without them knowing about it. They check all the dates and events once more very thoroughly and find that all is as it should be.

There are the two stories in a newspaper printed long ago, displayed on the computer screen. It tells of the theft of the artifact and the painting. The items have disappeared and there are few clues as to what happened to them.

Buddy is taken care of and the clock is reset yet again.

Chapter 49

The air clears in the uncle's home and the two realize that they are not alone. They stay low and out of sight as the uncle attempts to discover the secrets that are hidden within the clock. He mutters to himself as he studies the device. During the other trips, their feelings toward the man were unpleasant to say the least. They now see him in a different light. He is grumpy, yes, but not the horrible man they thought he was. In exasperation, he leaves the room grumbling. The two use this opportunity to make their escape out the window.

"Whoa, that was close. I almost got up before I realized that he was in the room," Matthew confesses to her.

"To tell you the truth, so did I."

It takes very little time to find John as he is expecting them. The three go to where the painting is hidden and the artifact is placed in there with it.

"Have you checked to see if Gregory's friend the

police constable is in the vicinity?" Elizabeth asks John hopefully.

"Yes, he's on duty and will be for the next six hours."

"How long do you think it will take for him to get on the scene?" Matthew asks.

"He should be able to be here in about an hour, from the time we get in touch with him."

"Good, that should be fine," Matthew says, thinking that it's a long time compared to response times in his own time.

"Can you go see your friend that works in the hotel and find out if the Dutchmen are in their room or not, we already know they checked in today. If they aren't, we'll have to try to find out where they are so we'll know if we have the time to do what we're planning," he asks John, hoping he finds out quickly.

"All right, I'll go and see."

John hurries toward the hotel. The two wait for fifteen minutes, keeping an eye on the people coming and going. They would not want to miss the men if they were to either go in or come out.

When John comes back, he informs the two that the men are indeed in their room.

"I hope they come out and go somewhere in the next hour or so. If not, we may have to give them a reason to go someplace," Matthew says.

"We can write a note, asking them to see Uncle Robert and sign his name. That will get them out of the room," John suggests to them.

"It will get them out but they'd soon find out that your uncle hasn't sent for them and this will raise their suspicions," Elizabeth tells him, squashing that idea.

"Yes and once their suspicions are aroused, they might find out what we are up to and spoil our plans," Matthew adds for good measure. "We have to come up with something else, all right, John?"

"Yes, I see what you mean."

"I guess we'll have to wait and see if they leave. It's about an hour before lunch. Do you know if they eat at the hotel, John?" Elizabeth asks.

"I believe they usually go to the restaurant at the edge of town not far away. They go by carriage and are gone for about two hours. I haven't really paid a lot of attention to them concerning this, but this should be fairly accurate."

"One of us should stay here and keep an eye out, while John and I get the stolen things ready," Matthew says, looking at Elizabeth.

"Gee, I wonder who he thinks should stay here," Elizabeth says with a smile on her face while looking at John.

Matthew hugs her. "Good girl. We'll get back here as soon as we can and, if by chance those men do leave, you know where to find us, sis. Just make sure you know if they're going in a carriage so they don't surprise us by coming back early."

John and Matthew go to the stored items and prepare them for transport to a new hiding spot. They are back beside Elizabeth shortly after.

"They just came out and are getting in the carriage," she informs the two as they kneel down.

"Have you spoken with your friend that works in the hotel John?" Matthew asks.

"Yes, I have and, by this time, she should be on the second floor near the room those men are in."

"Let's wait for fifteen minutes to make sure they really are away," Matthew suggests, although he is eager to proceed.

The time goes by ever so slowly because everyone

wants this part to be over with. If they are caught, it will be very dangerous for them. Finally, the moment arrives, and John walks to the hotel to find out if his friend is ready. John says he will signal from a window on the second floor landing if the way is clear. Five more long minutes go by, and there's the signal.

Matthew gathers together the things he requires for the next phase of the plan and heads for the door of the hotel. Elizabeth waits outside in case of trouble. They have arranged for her to blow a shrill whistle if the men return prematurely.

John is waiting in the hallway outside the Dutchmen's room as Matthew comes up the stairs. He is about to enter the room with John when the whistle blows long and hard.

"Damn, they must have returned. Do you have the key to lock the room, John," Matthew asks.

"Yes, I do. You head away from here while I lock it and then I'll follow you."

He just finishes and is walking away when Hendrick comes around the corner from the stairway. Fortunately, John is wearing a hat and the Dutchman pays no attention to him. From around the corner at the other end of the hallway, they keep watch from a distance as Hendrick unlocks and enters the room. He's in there for a very short time and comes out carrying a small suitcase. Locking the door he races down the stairs and is out of sight. John runs down the hallway too and, at the landing, looks out the window as the two men leave in the carriage once more.

Elizabeth comes out of hiding and looks up as John gives her the all clear sign. Matthew takes a deep breath as the two enter the room. "We have to make sure we leave the room exactly as it is."

John looks in the closet to see what's in there and

notices that if anything is changed in the closet, it will be very obvious. Matthew decides that the rope they brought with them can be used to do the job at hand. He completes his task in short order with John's help. A quick look around to make certain nothing is left behind or visible and the two vacate the room, locking it as they go.

The key is given back to the chambermaid with a big thank you from John. He explained earlier why it has been necessary to enter the room. Because the men have been quite rude to her, she had no problem loaning John the key. Especially when he explained that he would take nothing. Luckily, she didn't see them carry the items into the room.

John's given a hand written note by Elizabeth. This has been put together by her with Matthew helping with the wording. If by chance the handwriting is compared with either John's or Alice's at a later date, there will be no similarities.

The three take the carriage once again and head to the police station three quarters of an hour away. The air is pleasant, although there's a feeling of nervousness present. There's also a good chance that this whole adventure may still turn out unfavorably. So far everything the pair has done has had no real impact. At this point, the imminent deaths of three people have not changed. Both are wary but extremely hopeful that this final effort will finally be successful.

If, for some reason, this only ends in failure again, they both realize that there will be no more chances to correct these terrible wrongs.

The ride takes more time than the three would like, but is finally over. The horse needs to be given a drink of water which is taken care of by Matthew. John walks into the small station and inquires into the whereabouts of

Gregory's police friend. He's directed to a back room where the officer's doing some paperwork.

"Good morning, Officer, I have been asked to give you this letter by an acquaintance. He has had to leave town and could not deliver it himself. He asked that you open it and read the letter immediately, please," John requests.

The officer opens the letter and reads the contents. His eyes open wide, and he jumps up, rushing to the officer in charge. He shows the sergeant the letter and there's a quick discussion as John slips out the door. He does not want to answer any questions about how the information in the letter has been obtained.

John quickly heads back to the carriage, and the three are on their way back to the hotel. On the way, they are passed by a number of police vehicles. John hides his face as the police rush past, heading to the same destination as the three.

When John brings the horse and carriage back to the owners, he quickly unhitches the horse and brings it to an open field, after giving it a fast rubdown.

Matthew and Elizabeth are already stationed out of sight in a place where they can observe the hotel. Looking about carefully, they notice officers in various hiding places. It appears that they're waiting for the return of Dutchmen. The two men must still be away, otherwise, there would be no need for officers to hide. The group chatters nervously as to whether or not this gambit will be successful. There's always the chance that the men may spot the police or become suspicious. All kinds of adverse scenarios are discussed by the three.

Finally, Alice comes up to the group from behind. "What are you up to, why are you watching the hotel so intently?"

The three, startled by the sudden presence of Alice, jump up turning around.

"Gosh, I wish you wouldn't do things like that, Alice," John scolds her, trying to catch his breath.

"What are you all looking at?" she insists.

As there is no longer a need for secrecy, the three decide to tell her what has been going on for the last while. When she hears about what happens in their futures, she finds that she needs to sit down. This is a shocking revelation to her and her hands tremble as she attempts to take stock of the situation.

"Sorry to interrupt, but I think the enemy is returning," John says with a bit of theatrics in his demeanor.

The four watch as the scene unfolds before them. The Dutchmen seem unaware of anything being amiss as they pay the driver of the carriage and walk into the hotel. The police remain hidden, for the time being, clearly waiting for orders to spring into action.

The time slips by ever so slowly as nothing seems to happen. John's group is impatient for this to be over with. Suddenly, there's is faint shouting coming from inside the hotel. There's a crash from the second story that sounds as if glass is being shattered. Johannus jumps out the broken window. He hits the ground rolling and jumps up, running as best he can to the rear of the building. He has a slight limp but this only slows him down a little.

The police spring into action, giving chase.

Johannus disappears into the woods with the officers commanding him to stop. The chase is on, as a desperate man attempts to flee justice. The pursuit takes most of the officers into an unfamiliar forest.

Johannus has been exploring the area for a considerable time and knows where he might have the best chance of escape.

The police fire a warning shot into the air to no avail.

This man is intent on remaining free and will do whatever is necessary. There's a second and third shot fired, then one more shot followed by a scream of pain. Johannus is apprehended and brought back to the hotel. All the fight has gone out of him, at this point. He's placed in handcuffs alongside Hedrick and his wound is tended to.

Coming out of the door of the hotel are two police officers, carrying both the stolen painting and the artifact. Johannus shouts at the officers. "We know nothing of these items. We didn't did not steal them. They must have been placed in our room by someone else in order to frame us."

"You are guilty, so don't bother denying it. We know that you have been up to something for a long time. What I want to know is what you have done with the jewelry collection you stole from the museum. Where is it?" the sergeant shouts at him.

"I have no idea what you are talking about," Johannus shouts back.

When the incident is over and the police are gone, there's a collective sigh of relief.

"Did you know about the stolen things in the room," Alice asks.

"Yes, because Matthew and Elizabeth have made many trips into our future and their past. During those trips, they found that they were unable to make any changes at all to save us. They then came up with a plan. Matthew and Elizabeth stole the painting and Egyptian Artifact for the purpose of framing the Dutchmen. I don't know why the police man was asking him about the jewelry theft? Do you think the Dutchmen were actually involved with that?" John asks.

"I have no idea about that. I'm just glad they are being taken to jail," Matthew tells him, sighing with relief.

"Didn't all this put you at risk too? Why would you do

this for us?" Alice asks them with affection.

Matthew tells her about seeing her running down the beach in the middle of the night and how they felt the need to help her.

"Everything we tried to do failed up to now. We just hope that this will finally change your futures. We won't know this for sure until we get back to our time, though. It was John who helped us get to the places we had to go. He also helped put the stolen items in their room," Matthew informs her.

"My friend in the hotel gave me the key to the Dutchmen's room, and we planted the evidence. I'll explain to her why all this has been necessary, otherwise she may have doubts and talk to the police. I'll tell her that we had to make certain that these men had actually stolen the items by inspecting their quarters. When we went into the room with her help, we saw what we needed and went to the police," John tells his cousin.

"Good idea, not the whole truth, but at least she won't have doubts about you," Matthew says.

"We all three went to the police station and I gave Gregory's friend Allan a letter. Elizabeth wrote it, informing the police that those men had stolen the painting and artifact. The note said that the items were in the men's room, and that they were planning to take them out of the country shortly. The rest you know already," John tells Alice.

"It's getting close to departure time so we'll have to find a secluded spot soon Matthew."

"I don't know how to thank you enough. It has been wonderful getting to know you. Will we ever see you two again?" Alice asks.

"We couldn't stand by and do nothing, so you're welcome," Matthew says, looking into Alice's eyes. "But it's unlikely that we'll ever see you again."

"Maybe we can use the clock to come and see you," John says.

"Unfortunately, I don't think that can happen. We only have access to the clock because we found it during our vacation. Our parents tried to buy the cottage but it has already been sold. Once the vacation is over, we don't know if we can get into the room again. When you get the clock from your uncle, make sure that the clock remains in the cottage in the same room we showed you. Keep the room hidden the way we told you that your Uncle Robert did. I have drawn the plans for the room on this sheet of paper. I also have drawn the locking mechanism so you will be able to secure it properly. This way it will be there in case we somehow still rent the cottage sometime in the future," Matthew tells John earnestly.

"By the way, I don't think your uncle is as mean and grumpy as he lets on," Elizabeth tells Alice who, at hearing this, gets a tear in her eye. "We found out during one of our trips that he had nothing to do with your father's death, it really was an accident."

"Thank you for telling me this."

"We have to go now. I doubt that we will meet again. Good luck and we hope that this has finally done the trick," Matthew says to their friends.

There are hugs and handshakes and then the two time travelers are on their way to a secluded spot for the trip back home. The air clouds over one last time.

Chapter 50

Back home, there's a feeling of apprehension as they two head to the computer. The device warms up and, as the information comes on the screen, Elizabeth reads what is written there about the past. She breaks out in a laugh.

"Matthew, we did it, we did it. They are no longer murdered, any of them. It says here that Alice and John live long and what appears to be productive lives. There is a story back farther here about the apprehension of two criminals from the Netherlands. They were sent to prison. There's another story about the hotel years later burning to the ground and never being rebuilt," Elizabeth informs him.

"I wondered about that because there's no hotel in our time. At least there wasn't since we've been on vacation here. We may have to have a look around later to make sure. I wonder what other changes there are that we may never know about."

"I'm so happy that we were able to help John and

Alice. It makes this whole trip worthwhile. This really has been the best vacation ever, hasn't it?" she asks him with a grin from ear to ear.

"That's for sure. I'll tell you one thing, though; I'm not going to stay up very late tonight. Boy, am I ever tired. How about you?"

"I sure am. Maybe we should have a short nap."

"No, I'm too wound up to lie down right now. Besides, Mom and Dad will ask us why we're having so many naps during the day," he says and heads down to the kitchen for a bite to eat.

This has been a good day. Things have turned out the way they should and the two feel they have made the world a little better place.

Chapter 51

ate and Leonard sit at a table in a lovely little restaurant in town.

She sighs. "This vacation has been a bit of a rollercoaster ride. But, overall, it's been nice getting away with the kids. I hope they haven't been bored too much. We've left them alone for quite a bit of the time."

"I'm sure that they don't mind. They keep themselves entertained and probably enjoyed exploring the area. I know I sure have."

"We haven't found a home to our liking, but Matthew has a nice place to stay. I'm sure he'll get along just fine on his own. Mrs. Robinson seems pleasant and will look after him."

"I think he'll do well in the auto technician course too. He has a real aptitude for that kind of thing," Leonard tells his wife.

They enjoy a glass of wine while they wait for the steak and lobster dinner to be prepared.

"Boy, this is the life. I could get used to this quite

easily. I wonder how much a boat would cost here. It sure would be nice to go out fishing now and then," he says, his mind filled with dreams.

"I think you can forget about that for the time being. We can't seem to find a decent place so far. I think it may take a while for the right one to come along. I do think it will happen, but not for a while though," Kate says.

"Yeah, you're right as usual. We'll have to wait for a bit, but it will happen, I just feel it," he replies with an air of confidence.

"We have two more days left here. Do you have any ideas as to what you'd like to do?" she asks.

"I think we should ask Matt and Elizabeth if there is anything that they would like to do."

The rest of the meal is done and the two head back to the cottage, taking a nice route they haven't gone on before. There's a scenic lookout, and they stop to gaze out across an inlet. There are a few sailboats out on the water, drifting with a gentle breeze. They tack back and forth across their view, making their way to destinations unknown. The whole scene is almost surreal. It leaves them with a feeling of peace as they get back into the car and head for home.

"Hi, kids, were home," Mom says.

"Hey, Mom, we're in the back yard," Matthew calls out and Buddy lets out a bark, letting her know he is happy to see her too.

"Did you kids have supper," she asks.

"Yes, we did. We had grilled cheese and wieners," Elizabeth answers for the both of them.

After a few more minutes of conversation, Kate asks if they want to do anything in particular tomorrow.

"How about spending the day on the beach? I'd really like that," Matthew expresses with enthusiasm.

"I think that would be nice too," Elizabeth agrees.

"All right, a day on the beach is what we'll do," Leonard says.

The rest of the evening is spent relaxing and, later, both Elizabeth and Matthew excuse themselves and go upstairs. They go to the clock room for what they know will be one of the last times.

Looking at the clock, Matthew notices an envelope inside the front door behind the glass. He opens the clock and picks it up. It is addressed to Mathew and Elizabeth. They go back to her room closing up the clock room securely. Opening the envelope, Elizabeth reads the letter inside.

"'Dear friends, enough time has passed for us to know that what the two of you have done has actually saved us. We cannot express our gratitude enough for the unselfish act of courage the two of you displayed. We would not be here if it was not for you. We owe you our lives.'"

"'Our uncle has done a complete turnaround. All it took was a little kindness on our part, and he is now Alice's guardian. The Dutchmen have gone to prison and will not be bothering anyone again. Allan the police officer says that if they are released in the future, they will be deported with no chance of returning.'"

"'Life is good for both of us, and I have done as you asked with the clock and the room it is in. But then again you already know this as the clock is still where you first found it, or you wouldn't be reading this letter. We both send our best wishes to you and maybe one day you will have access to the clock and will come to visit us. God bless you both.'"

"'Your friends, John and Alice.'"

Matthew grins at the letter with a feeling of euphoria. "Boy, do I feel good. I'm so glad this all worked out the way it did. I was sure that we failed them, but I guess you should never stop trying, right?"

"I know exactly what you mean. I feel the same way too. I can hardly believe that we, of all people, had a chance to do what we did."

He nods. "My only regret is that this is probably the end of this adventure. I doubt very much that we will ever be able to use the clock again."

"Oh, well, better this, than never having had the opportunity at all," she says.

"You're right, I should be happy we got this chance at all. Soon, I'll be in college and our whole lives will change," he says, as he realizes that they will soon be separated. She too will be headed off for college in one more year.

Matthew goes to his own room to ponder his future. He's soon asleep and does not wake up till the following morning as does Elizabeth. It has been an exhausting few days.

∽∾∽

The next day is spent frolicking on the beach. Buddy is having a great time again and the family plays various games. Everyone is generally enjoying this second last day here. With their parents needing some rest, the two go for a walk along the water. Occasionally, they go in for a swim and watch the waves roll onto shore. They collect a few shells as reminders of their holiday. The homes they see on the beach are not all the same as when they walked here before.

"I think that with us changing the past, it has made a few things different than they were when we first got here. That house over here wasn't there when we walked this way last week," Matthew says, pointing to a pleasant looking home.

"Now that you mention it, you're right. That one over there and those two are new ones too."

The main thing both agree is the fact that Alice, John, and Robert didn't die needlessly. Matthew and Elizabeth spend another hour roaming here and there before heading back to the cottage.

After supper, Kate suggests that it will be a good idea to start packing a few of their things.

"We will still be here tomorrow but we'll leave early the next morning," Kate says to her children.

"What are we doing tomorrow?" Elizabeth asks her parents.

"We thought we would maybe go to town for a last stroll as a family there. Your mom thinks it might be a good idea to drop by Mrs. Robinson's and make sure everything is all set for Matthew to live there while he is going to school," Leonard says.

The pair runs upstairs to pack some of their clothes so there won't be much to do the next day. It doesn't take long for most of the work to be done. Matthew comes into Elizabeth's room and sits on her bed.

"I'm sure going to miss this place. We've had more adventure these last few weeks than we have our entire lives. Wouldn't it be nice to go back one more time?" Matthew says to his sister.

"It would be nice, but I don't think that it's practical. I think we might be pushing our luck a bit if we did go back again. I don't know why I think this but I really feel strongly about it. I have the feeling that if we go back, something else will come up and we'll be compelled to solve another mystery," Elizabeth tells him, fighting that feeling of dread again.

"You're usually right when it comes to things like this, so no more trips it is," Matthew agrees.

With this, they call it a night. On his way out of the

room, he glances at the painting of Alice running down the beach with the look of fear on her face. Only thing is, there isn't that look of fear anymore. She is looking at the artist with a smile on her face. There is no longer a ghostly look about her either. The scene is a happy one and it almost seems as if she is smiling at him.

"Elizabeth, look at this." When she walks over and sees that the whole thing has changed, she breaks out in a laugh.

"This is wonderful. It reinforces the letter that the two sent us. I'm so glad this has changed too. I'm going to take a picture of the new painting as a souvenir. I have one from before, and now I'll have one of after," she says, smiling ear to ear.

Just to make sure, she scrolls back in her camera to double check that the previous photo is still the same and is happy when she sees it's still there. Matthew continues to his room, thinking about how happy he has been on this vacation…well, at least most of the time. Both are asleep in short order.

Chapter 52

The family is up nice and early and, after breakfast, gets ready for a last day in town. It's a pleasant drive down the country roads while enjoying the warm sea air and the sunshine. They take their time going anywhere. This is going to be a leisurely day spent together. By mid-afternoon, everyone is in a good mood and ready to finish packing.

Kate's phone rings. "Hello, Christine, how are you?" she asks and then listens to what the agent has to say. "Actually, we don't have much time today as we're leaving to go home early tomorrow morning." She continues to listen to the voice on the phone for a moment. "I don't understand….Okay…Goodbye." She hangs up. "Christine wants us to drop by her office at three o'clock. She won't say why but is quite insistent. I said we'd come by."

Leonard frowns. "I don't think we have time to be looking at any more homes. It takes way too long to look at them and hammer out a deal."

"We could do the finalizing from home when we get back if it comes to that," Kate says.

"Yeah, I guess so, but it is a little short notice. Oh, well, I guess it can't hurt to look."

Kate turns to Matthew. "I think you and Elizabeth will have to come with us. We don't have the time to drop you off at the cottage. You don't have to come into the office but you probably should come to see the home. Wouldn't it be nice if it turned out to be something we could enjoy, Leonard?"

"It would, but I doubt very much that this place will be any better than the ones we've already looked at," he says.

The family has already had a nice little tour around the island and eaten lunch. Everyone is curious as to what Christine is so eager to tell them about. The hour goes by slowly, taking away from the enjoyment of the last day here. They all expect that this will probably not be what they want. *Nevertheless, you never know*, Leonard thinks. He is still the eternal optimist of the group.

Three o'clock finally arrives with Leonard and Kate going into the real estate office without the kids.

"I'm sorry to have been so vague on the phone. I had to check a few details first," Christine says apologetically.

"That's all right," Kate says expectantly. "That's what we came to see you for in the first place. What is it that you wanted to see us about?"

"When you first got to the island you asked about purchasing Lilac Cottage. The owners had already sold it at that point," she says to the eagerly listening couple.

"Yes we remember that, it was very disappointing at the time," Leonard says.

"Things have changed since that time. It appears that the buyers have run into some problems and have had to back out of the deal. When you made the offer a number of weeks ago I let the owners know that you were interested in case something went wrong. I spoke to the owners when they phoned me this morning. They're very disappointed, but I told them you might still be interested in purchasing the cottage."

"What did they say to that?" Kate asks eagerly, almost bouncing out of her seat.

"They told me that they would accept an offer of the same price that it was sold for, plus you would have to pay my fees. They didn't use an agent when they sold the first time and think that if they did use an agent they would be able to sell it for more. I have written out the offer, including my fee, for you to consider," Christine says as she passes them the papers.

The two read the papers over, going quickly to the numbers referring to the price. Leonard looks at Kate and smiles.

"Can we have a moment to discuss this, Christine," Kate asks.

"Certainly, I'll step out of the office for a minute. Just call me when you're ready," she tells them as she gets out of her chair.

"So what do you think, dear?" Kate asks when she and Leonard are alone.

"The offer is only two thousand higher than we were going to pay in the first place. Since then, every place we looked at has been higher and not as nice. I think we should jump on it, how about you?"

"I think this is the best news we have had since we started looking. Without a doubt, I want to sign this. The kids will be so happy. I can't wait to tell them," Kate tells her husband joyfully.

Leonard goes to the door and signals Christine.

"So what do you think?"

"We want to buy the cottage," Kate informs the agent. "The price is very reasonable and we're so pleased that you stayed on top of this for us. Another bonus is that everything in the house and on the property is included."

"That is great, isn't it? I love it when things turn out for my clients. Just sign your names to the contract, write a check for the deposit, and I will present the offer. Remember at this point, it is still only an offer. The owners still have the right to refuse it. I doubt that they will, but in this business you never know until it's over. I will present it immediately and get back to you shortly," Christine informs them and gets ready to go when everything is signed.

Kate and Leonard go out to the street in search of their children. They walk down the road and find them in the park across the street from the office.

"Hey, guys, we have some really good news," Kate calls out to them.

"What is it?" Elizabeth asks as the two come running.

"The original buyers of Lilac Cottage had to back out and we just made an offer to purchase it. It's not a done deal yet but we should know in a few hours," Leonard cries out in excitement.

The youngsters are almost speechless, thrilled at the news. Everyone is ecstatic as this just turned into an absolutely wonderful day. The family is now too excited to do anymore sightseeing so they drive back to the cottage to wait. Even Buddy seems happier as the siblings discuss this turn of events.

Two and a half hours later, the phone rings and Leonard quickly answers it.

"Hello, Christine, so what's the verdict?" he asks and then listens to her reply.

There's a moment of apprehension as everyone in the room waits to hear the answer.

"That's wonderful news, thank you so much. You have our email address so we can finalize everything from home as we put our house up for sale too. The deposit on the cottage has been accepted and everything can be handled easily from our end?…That's just great, you don't know how happy you've made us. We'll be in touch soon," Leonard tells her as he ends the call.

There is a sigh of relief as the pent up nervousness is released.

"My word, this has been quite a holiday, hasn't it," Kate says.

The two teenagers jump up and hug their parents. This means that Matthew won't have to move out into someone else's home.

"Should we let Mrs. Robinson know what is going on, Dad?" Matthew asks.

"Good idea. I'll call her right now and explain." He does this as he has the phone in his hand anyway.

The lady is pleased at the turn of events, congratulating the Janssen's. She informs them that she has another student who wants to move in, so all is well. She will send them back the check in the mail.

"We'll have supper and then I think we should pack the rest of our things," Leonard says to the family. "We want to get an early start in the morning. I think I'll give Gerry a call letting him know that he can list our house as soon as we get back."

That evening after the packing is done, Matthew and Elizabeth take one last venture into the secret room. Both feel the need to have another look at the clock and to reminisce about their fantastic experience. The two don't know what may be coming into their future but they do know that it won't be boring. Hopefully, Mom and Dad won't ever find out about this room. It would probably spoil things, so they will have to be careful.

☙❧

The ride home is pleasant and the feeling of anxiety that Elizabeth had on the trip to the cottage has been replaced by one of excitement. The home goes up for sale and is sold in less than a week. The family will be on the island and living in Lilac Cottage before Matthew starts college. They all say goodbye to their friends, promising to keep in touch. The truck is loaded and the family is on its way to a new life. Who knows what adventures are in store for the two time travelers? Life is good.

The End…For Now!

About the Author

Born in the Netherlands, Leonardus G. Rougoor moved to southern Ontario at the age of four and grew up in the Niagara Peninsula. As an adult, he worked in various fields, until settling down in the tool and die industry. Moving to Kelowna in his mid-forties, he started working in the steel fabrication industry. Quality control, safety rep, machining, and training other employees in various areas of the industry led to a fulfilling career.

One week after retiring, Rougoor started writing his first novel. He has a heart for the underdog and dislikes injustice intensely, so this was the driving force in his first mystery/thriller series. Now, having six novels in several genres contracted with a publisher and more on the way, this is turning out to be a wonderful and satisfying new career.

Rougoor is married with two children and several grandchildren. Living on Vancouver Island in the Maple Bay region allows him and his family to enjoy boating on the sheltered portions of the ocean. His philosophy is: If something isn't going to affect your life much a year from now, why let it overly concern you today?

www.ingramcontent.com/pod-product-compliance
Lightning Source LLC
Chambersburg PA
CBHW061016120726

47910CB00006B/1977